DANGEROUS INTERFERENCE

BJ WANE

Copyright © 2017 by BJ Wane

Published by Stormy Night Publications and Design, LLC.
www.StormyNightPublications.com

Cover design by Korey Mae Johnson
www.koreymaejohnson.com

Images by The Killion Group and 123RF/Tommaso Nuti

All rights reserved.

1st Print Edition. January 2017

ISBN-13: 978-1542468855

ISBN-10: 154246885X

FOR AUDIENCES 18+ ONLY

This book is intended for adults only. Spanking and other sexual activities represented in this book are fantasies only, intended for adults.

PROLOGUE

Sheriff Randy Janzen pulled his official Ford Explorer into the circular driveway of his longtime friend, Bryan Hirst. Cutting the engine, he took a moment to savor the scenic view of Blue Springs Lake out his windshield, recalling lazy summer days he spent swimming and fishing the six hundred plus acre waters set amidst the temperate broadleaf and mixed forest trees indigenous to southern Maine. Dark green towering pines and spruces surrounded the lake, the inland landscape opposite the craggy cliffs along the Atlantic shore just a few short miles away. Spring in his state welcomed moderate temperatures in the mid-fifties, but he felt anything but warm today.

Opening his door, he slid out of his vehicle with a sigh, reaching for the picture of the young, blond-haired, green-eyed coed off his seat. There had been more than one time in the last twelve years he'd been with the county sheriff's department that he'd had to drag those pristine waters for a missing body or lead a group of volunteers through the woods searching for a lost hiker. Climbing the steps leading to the wraparound porch of Bryan's Cape Cod, two-story lakefront home, he worried the impish grin and devil-may-care look on young Ashley Malloy's face had landed her in unforeseen trouble and it was his duty to check it out. He hated that his investigation had sent him here for clues about the missing college student and prayed Bryan could give him something that would lead to a positive outcome for the young girl.

Lifting his arm to rap on the door, he paused when he heard the distinct sound of leather snapping against bare skin followed by a high-pitched cry. A wry grin teased the corners of his mouth as he pictured the scene he would be interrupting. He was well acquainted with Bryan's home, and the pleasures he had it equipped for. Beyond the foyer he would be able to see into the great room that looked like any ordinary main living area in an upscale home. But Randy had intimate knowledge of the tucked away restraints attached to most of the furniture as well as the upstairs rooms designed for different proclivities of Bryan's guests, such as spanking benches, dangling chains for bondage, and closets filled with toys for any kink one could imagine. In the kitchen, Bryan had cleverly placed a convenient drawer of utensils handy for spanking next to the high padded stools at the long granite-topped counter. Randy had availed himself of the assortment of bamboo spoons and rubber spatulas on more than one occasion.

With another sigh of regret, he gave the door a sharp rap then waited for the telltale sound of footsteps. Bryan's irritated scowl changed to a smile of welcome when he opened the door and saw who had the piss-poor timing.

"Sheriff," he drawled with a twinkle in his blue eyes, opening the door wider in invitation. "What brings you out here this afternoon?"

Stepping inside, Randy's gaze snagged on the plump, bright red ass bent over the arm of a suede sofa, a pair of hands secured with a scarf behind the woman's back. He recognized those soft, round thighs and brassy blond hair, not surprised to find Carlee and his friend were enjoying one of their on-again phases of their decade-long relationship. The diner owner possessed a fiery temperament Bryan had failed to tame over the years, no matter how hard he'd tried.

Turning her flushed face and dark eyes around, Carlee gave him an unabashed grin and wiggled her ass. "Hello, Sheriff."

"Knock it off, Carlee," Bryan snapped, but his eyes gleamed with humor.

"Sorry, both of you, but I need to ask you about this girl, Bry. Her family's filed a missing person report with Portland PD and they contacted me this morning stating she was last seen with Kevin leaving The Well last week to presumably come up here." He handed him the picture and watched recognition replace his frown.

"Yeah, yeah, she came out with Kev, they were on spring break." Handing the picture back, he added, "I checked hers and several other kids' IDs carefully, Randy. They were of age and I didn't allow them to leave the great room. You know how strict I am when my brother brings guests to play. I'm sorry she's gone missing, she was a sweet kid; I walked her out to her car myself and made sure she was good to drive. They didn't have any liquor while here, but I can't vouch for the time they spent at the bar."

"Thanks and yes, I know how careful you are, but I had to check. Neither she nor her car has been seen since leaving here last week. She sent her friends a text first saying she'd be at their cabin in fifteen minutes, then another text a few minutes later stating she was heading back to Portland instead. There were five of them, so she had her own car and they had an extra one for her four friends to get home in the next day. Which means she disappeared somewhere along the way back to Portland. Her friends were pissed at her until she didn't show up for class last Monday."

Carlee struggled to stand, turn, and plop her butt down on the arm of the sofa, her eyes wide with worry when she gazed at the picture clutched in Randy's hand. "I was here that night. God, what a shame. She was having a good time."

Randy watched her closely when he asked, "And did you

see her leave or notice anyone leave right after her?"

"No, I went to the restroom and when I returned she had already left." Shrugging, she sent Bryan a wicked grin, unconcerned with her nudity in front of Randy. "I'm afraid I became rather involved after that."

"Bend back over, sub," Bryan growled even though a small grin turned up one corner of his mouth. Swiveling back to Randy, his grin disappeared as he too shrugged. "I'm sorry, and really hope she turns up okay, but I'm afraid that's all I know about the girl. Kevin hasn't heard anything from her, or maybe his friends?"

"Not a word, according to Portland PD who spoke with all of them. Well, thanks, both of you. Sorry for the unannounced visit."

"Shit, buddy, you know you can pop in anytime. Give me a call on your next day off and we'll dip our poles in and spend a lazy afternoon drinking beer and complaining about uncooperative women."

A rude snort came from Carlee where she managed to get herself turned back over. Smiling, Randy tipped his hat, saying, "I'll see myself out."

Anger and denial churned in his gut as he buckled himself back in his seat and took another moment to gaze out his windshield. This time he wasn't enjoying the view but recalling the look on Bryan's face when he had first laid eyes on Ashley Malloy's picture. The jolt of surprise and underlying tension couldn't be disguised, even though Bryan had tried.

They'd been friends since they met at a club in Portland over ten years ago, and Randy knew Bryan well. He'd been twenty-seven when they first met and Randy had already been introduced to and indulged in alternative sex. When Bryan had informed him he owned a second home on Blue Springs Lake, so close to his small home town and the county sheriff's department he worked for, the two of them had become close.

Which was why he suspected Bryan had lied or knew

more than he had let on. Turning the key, he drove away, glancing once in his rearview mirror, hoping he was wrong. He took his job as sheriff as seriously as he valued his friendship. He hadn't cut Bryan any slack when dealing with his much younger brother's rebellious teenage troubles and he wouldn't now. Subterfuge didn't settle well with him, especially when it involved a close friend.

CHAPTER ONE

Two months later

Flipping on her blinker, Alena Malloy took a left off U.S Coastal Route 1 at the exit for Blue Springs, leaving behind the steep border of jagged rocks and cliffs along the Atlantic coast she had been traveling for a good portion of her seven-hour trek from New York. *Damn Ashley for putting me through this.* The eleven-year age gap between her and her younger sister had kept them from bonding as children. Their mother's slow decline into alcoholism starting with the death of their father ten years ago had had Alena, at the age of twenty-one, reluctantly picking up the reins of her ten-year-old rebellious sister's upbringing.

And the past ten years had been fraught with pulling her sister out of one scrape after another. There had been the drug-and-alcohol stage in her teens as well as the promiscuous stage that landed a twenty-four-year-old computer hookup in jail when Ashley had been but fifteen. Between working two jobs and attending college part-time, Alena had done her best but had had to rely on her alcohol-soaked mother when she absolutely couldn't be there. She had hoped once Ashley had been accepted into the

University of Southern Maine in Portland that she would buckle down and work at making something of herself. Gifted with a beautiful voice, Ashley had surprised Alena when she'd announced that she had earned a full scholarship to the out-of-state school, the only way she would have been able to attend.

The first year things had looked up and the two of them had grown closer as sisters for the first time. That short-lived reprieve had ended this past year when Ashley had taken up with yet another wild group of kids and lost her scholarship but had refused to return to New York. Instead, she had taken out student loans and continued her irresponsible, self-destructive behavior. The final straw had been when she'd called Alena to bail her out of jail after getting caught with a one-pound stash of pot in her car. As hard as it had been, Alena had finally resorted to tough love and had told her sister she would just have to get herself out of her current bind.

That had been right before spring break, two months ago, and the last time she'd spoken with Ashley. Her curses still rang in her ears from her shocking decision. But in the past ten years, she had never gone this long without talking to Ash, either to fight, lecture, or try to coax her into better behavior.

Gripping her steering wheel, Alena's tension over the possibilities of her sister's disappearance kept her body taut as a bow. She could no longer sit back and wait for the authorities to find some clue as to her whereabouts. Which was what had led her to take a leave of absence from her job as a forensics photographer with the NYPD and why she was traveling almost four hundred miles to the last place her sister had been seen.

"Oh, good Lord," she muttered, looking at the towering forested pines the now two-lane road wound through. "Where did they all come from?"

As a city girl through and through, she'd grown up amid skyscraper buildings, bustling activity, and shoulder-to-shoulder people around every corner. This vast nothingness of Mother Nature was as foreign to her as any overseas country. Just as she despaired of ever getting to civilization again, she came around a bend and spotted the 'Welcome to Blue Springs' sign with relief, then read the population count with disbelief. *Twenty-two hundred?* "Are you frigging kidding me?"

Her GPS guided her to the main hubbub within a few minutes, the street sign, Main Street, drawing a reluctant smile from her, the single traffic light a sigh of incredulity. Keeping to the twenty-five MPH speed limit with gritted teeth, she found the county sheriff's office at the end of the street right where her instructions had said it would be. She tried to quell the panic threatening her composure when she imagined spending more than a few days in this secluded town and swore when she located her kid sister she would find a way to get through to her or wash her hands of her for good.

Parking in front of the two-story brick building, she got out, stretched, and took a deep breath, her nose twitching at the fresh woodsy scent along with the sweet aroma she assumed emitted from the large barreled pots of brightly colored flowers lining the sidewalk. The Portland detective in charge of Ashley's case informed her he had already spoken with the Blue Springs sheriff, who had done a follow-up on their report stating this was the last place Ashley was seen. According to her group of friends who also took Kevin Hirst and his two buddies up on their suggestion to spend spring break at Blue Springs Lake, Ash had last been seen by them leaving the local bar with the three guys, promising to meet them back at the cabin they had rented later that night. She hadn't been seen since, and, as stated by the police, had left the Hirsts' lake home alone in her car then just disappeared after telling her friends she decided to head back home without waiting for the next morning, or them. Now, *that* sounded like Ash, inconsiderate and irresponsible. On more than one occasion she had up and taken off for days without a word as to where she'd gone or when she'd return. Usually her short disappearances meant she'd gotten involved with a new guy and when things went sour, usually in a matter of days, she would return and pick up as if she'd never caused anyone grief.

But she had never disappeared for so long, always managing to return in time to make up her grades, sometimes barely passing, but passing nonetheless. It had been almost impossible at first to get anyone to listen to Alena after two weeks had passed due to Ash's past, but after another week went by without word, they finally assigned her case to missing persons where it had been stalled now for the last five weeks.

Tired of getting no answers, of sleepless nights and stress-filled days wondering and waiting for news, Alena had decided to take matters into her own hands. The answers were here, somewhere in this backwoods town, with someone in this vicinity and she intended to find them, with or without help from the good ol' boys in charge.

Entering the cool interior of the sheriff's office, she would start here and try to play nice by letting the sheriff know her relationship with Ashley and why she was here, but she wasn't a patient person by nature and wouldn't be thwarted in her need to uncover the truth about her sister's whereabouts.

"Can I help you?" the bubble-gum popping receptionist asked as Alena let her eyes adjust to the dim interior after coming in from the bright June sun.

She knew nothing about small communities, but suspected the gossip grapevine would be short and fast. Making a quick decision, she opted to keep her identity between her and the sheriff for now. "I'd like to speak to the sheriff, please. It's a personal matter."

"Go straight back. Sheriff Janzen's in his office." After pointing down the hall with a smile, the unconcerned girl went back to filing her nails.

The fact the girl didn't announce her visit worked in Alena's favor. Taking the sheriff by surprise would give her the upper hand, at least starting out.

Rapping on the closed door, she waited for his call to enter before stepping inside, announcing, "Sheriff Janzen, I'm Alena Malloy, Ashley's..." then coming to an abrupt halt when she saw not one man behind the large, window-backed desk, but also another perched on the corner. "Excuse me," she faltered, wondering if she just blew her chance to remain anonymous to everyone but the sheriff. "I assumed you were unoccupied since I was directed to come straight back here."

"Come in, Ms. Malloy and tell me how I can help you."

Both men unfolded their tall frames with unhurried grace at the sight of her. The slow, deep drawl from the man behind the desk looking at her out of piercing black eyes sent a frisson of combined unease and pure, unadulterated lust zinging through her bloodstream. Or was the interested light of speculation in the cobalt blue eyes from the other man responsible for her warm, uncharacteristic response? So much for having the upper hand, she mused with rueful acceptance of her body's unusual reaction to a pair of really, *really* hot guys. Squelching that reaction, she strode forward with her hand outstretched. "Sheriff, I want to know what you've done to find my sister, Ashley."

She found her hand engulfed by his larger, callused palm, his grip just shy of too tight. Not liking the tingles shooting up her arm, she pulled back, but kept her eyes on his, refusing to back down under his close scrutiny and raised, inquiring black brow.

"Randy Janzen, and this is Nash Osborne. You should've called, Ms. Malloy. I could have saved you a trip. Have a seat."

Alena returned the nod from the other man, struggling to figure out why his intense gaze had her tightening her thighs together against the startling pulse between them. *I must be tired*, she thought as she followed their lead and sank into the chair facing the desk, mustered up her composure, and then said, "I'm tired of the evasive non-answers I've been getting for two months now, Sheriff. Ashley was last seen here, in your town and here is where the answer to her disappearance lies. If I can't rely on law enforcement to find it, then I'll damn well find it on my own."

She caught the conspiratorial look that passed between the two men before Nash surprised her with his British accent when he replied, "Not wise, luv. You need to trust everything is being done that can be to find Ashley."

"I don't mean to be rude, but who are you and what do you know about my sister's case?" She sensed English wasn't just an acquaintance of the sheriff, then became sure of it when another telltale look passed between the two men. "I don't like being kept in the dark, gentlemen. I want answers."

With a deep sigh that could have been regret or irritation, the sheriff rose again, saying, "Why don't you let us treat you to a nice dinner, you can stay the night at our bed and breakfast before returning home. I promise I'll get to the bottom of your sister's disappearance."

Trying to keep her cool as well as fight against her strong, annoying reaction to that deep, gravelly voice, she looked at him with a raised brow of her own, refusing to be intimidated or coddled. "Do you have anything more to go on besides her last two messages to her friends?"

"There are a few things we're looking into." He held up his hand, forestalling her demand to know what with that commanding gesture and the tightening of his sculpted, five o'clock-shadowed jaw. "I can't disclose the facts of my investigation, especially those that have not been substantiated. Please. Take us up on our offer of dinner and a night in Blue Springs B & B before you return home. Even though Portland is only a few hours' drive, you'll enjoy a brief respite in our town despite the tragic circumstances that have brought you here."

Alena slowly came to her feet, vibrating with conflicting

emotions of anger and heightened awareness pulsing through her body. She had no clue which man had set off her sexual radar, and right now, she didn't care. All she cared about was finding Ashley.

Leveling a frigid glare at both, she sugarcoated her tone as she answered. "FYI, Sheriff, I hail from New York and have taken an extended, much needed leave from my job as a forensic photographer with the NYPD to find my sister. I'm not leaving until I get the answers I came for."

Pivoting, she walked out, feeling two pairs of eyes boring holes in her back.

"Oh, good Lord," she groaned as she settled in her car and leaned her head back. How could she be so angry she could spit when all her happy places were humming to life? An even harder dilemma for her to find an answer to was which man stirred up her interest and her juices more—the buttoned-up Brit with the sexy accent or the rugged, dark sheriff—and which was responsible for her body taking over her rigid control and common sense?

She wasn't a prude, but she also wasn't ruled by basic urges. She didn't need much more than just the desire for an orgasm to go to all the work of hooking up with a friend for a night or two to scratch an itch. If someone wasn't available, nine times out of ten she could rid herself of the pesky sensation better and with more efficiency than any of her fuck buddies.

Starting her car, she forced her mind on to more pressing matters than her libido, such as finding a place to stay for the next few weeks if necessary. She may not know which man ticked off all her boxes, but she knew she wasn't leaving without learning the whereabouts of her sister.

• • • • • • •

"Pretty woman," Randy said, leaning his head back and popping a few sugar-coated almonds Nash had him addicted to in his mouth.

"Could put a kink in our plans."

Looking at his temporary partner, houseguest, and new friend, he still found it surprising they got on so well given they were complete opposites in looks, dress, and nationality. It helped that the Scotland Yard detective enjoyed dominant sex and movie trivia, the only two things that made them compatible when Nash arrived in his town after following a lead in a murder case in London.

"I think we can ward off any potential problems."

Heaving a sigh, Nash pondered a moment before shaking his head. "My brain's been turned to mush over a red-headed, green-eyed spitfire who's round and soft in all the right places. We're going to have to keep an eye on her. She could jeopardize everything."

"Then the best way to do that is to fuck her." And Randy wouldn't find that a hardship in the least. The twitch of Alena's enticing ass drew both their eyes as she stomped out, her attitude akin to waving a red flag in front of not one, but two angry bulls.

"A woman like her, especially one with an agenda, wouldn't be easy to tame."

Rising, Randy slapped him on the back. "No, but if she pushes us we both know how to push back. She doesn't look a thing like her sister, which works in our favor if she does make a pest of herself. Come on, let's hit the diner, I'm starving."

"Sex'll do that to you."

"I didn't have sex."

"Thinking about sex'll do that to you."

Laughing, Randy returned, "Who am I to argue with such logic?" Passing the front desk, he glared at his receptionist. "Daisy Mae, next time I have a visitor, page me before sending her back. And lose the gum," he instructed on their way out, doubting if either order would be met. The granddaughter of his mother's best friend, he had done the girl, her mother, and his own a favor by hiring her for the summer, something he'd regretted for the past month since she'd graduated from high school. Luckily, Daisy Mae would be heading off to college in two months, so he'd just suck it up until then to keep the peace. After all, that was his job, keeping the peace.

"We haven't gotten far," he said, thinking of his job as he and Nash strolled down the wood-planked sidewalk. "The only thing we have going for us in our favor is Bryan thinks I've told Portland PD we're a dead end here." Deceiving his friend didn't sit well with him, but it just might be the only way to prove Bryan was innocent of any wrongdoing involving Ashley Malloy's disappearance.

"Yeah, I know, mate," Nash answered with the release of a frustrated, pent-up breath. "And while the two gatherings we've attended at his place since I've been here were fun, they didn't turn up anything new."

"No, but his place is where we'll find something, if there's something to find. Neither Bryan nor Kevin have shed any light on her disappearance, nor are they likely to. Hell, Nash, you know I don't think either of them knows anything else."

The unexpected arrival of Ashley's sister added to Randy's frustration over the stalled case and was a complication they didn't need. When Nash had contacted him about a cold case from last summer involving a dead college girl in London about the time Kevin and his two constant friends, Brad and Joel, had been on a European tour, he'd wanted to discount the coincidence to his case, but he wouldn't be doing his job if he didn't check out every angle.

"Maybe they don't, but I'm not a fan of coincidence even if stranger shit has happened."

"Afternoon, Mavis," Randy called out to the mercantile owner as they passed her filling bins with fresh produce.

"Sheriff, Nash. Off to the diner, are you?"

"Of course. Have you ever known me to miss the chicken fried steak Sunday special?" Randy returned with a rueful smile.

"Can't say that I have, Sheriff. You two stop in for a sundae afterwards, my treat," the plump older woman offered, her ice cream counter a popular draw in the summer months.

"It's a date, ma'am." After they were out of her earshot, Nash added under his breath, "I've gotten downright country since landing in this place."

Slapping him on the back again, Randy laughed outright at his disgruntled tone. "I told you we'd grow on you."

After comparing their two cases and not liking the similarities or who those comparisons suggested they focus their attention on, they both agreed to keep Nash's Scotland Yard employment a secret along with their dual investigation into Ashley's disappearance. Randy had attended Bryan's parties on occasion over the years so his continued acceptance of the invitations seemed natural. Thus far, Bryan and the rest of the townsfolk believed his introduction of Nash as an old college buddy.

An hour later Carlee had just taken their empty plates away and left them with a beer and the tab when Alena Malloy entered. As luck would have it, the only available seat was the small booth next to theirs and Randy couldn't help but grin at her obvious ploy to pretend she didn't see them. Settling back, they exchanged a silent look of communication and kept quiet. Carlee, bless her heart, could pull a secret from a priest if she was curious enough, which she usually was.

• • • • • • •

"Welcome," Carlee greeted Alena, setting a plastic menu down in front of her with a beaming smile Alena found hard pressed to ignore. Amusement over the restaurant's simple name, Diner, still tickled her as she noted the classic throwback fifties décor of checkered tablecloths and Elvis paraphernalia adorning the walls. Thinking of her favorite sushi bar and its posh, upscale atmosphere, she knew she would have passed this place by without a blink if there had been any other option.

"Thank you. I'm in a hurry, so would you mind just recommending something?"

"Can't go wrong with the special, hon; then again, I own the place so I'm honor bound to say things like that. You visiting, vacationing, or just passing through?"

Alena couldn't prevent the grin tugging at her lips. "Vacationing, and I'll take the special."

"You got it. Staying at the B & B or rentin' a cabin? Got some pretty nice places along the lake."

Now she was tempted to ask the woman with the friendly brown eyes to mind her own business, but if she intended to get answers without revealing who she was or the real reason for her stay, she knew she'd have to play nice. Conscious of the sheriff and his friend seated behind her, she wished she could see their faces when she replied, "Neither, I rented a boat. I thought it'd be fun to stay on the lake, right in the middle of everything." *That is if I don't go stark, raving mad first*, she thought as she imagined trying to sleep with all that quiet going on around her. She missed her apartment and the constant noise and activity of the city already.

"Just mind where you moor or you'll get a hefty fine. Be right out with your salad and tea."

Alena waited a moment, then breathed a sigh of relief when the men spoke quietly behind her but remained in their booth, tempering her irritation at seeing them. Carlee seemed like the perfect person to glean information from, but not with *those* two sitting so close.

Thankful the two men remained seated, she wondered just how close their relationship was and hoped they weren't a couple. That would be a crime against all heterosexual women and if her desperation to find her sister became too intense, she knew she wouldn't be above using sex to find the answers she'd been looking for.

She had just taken the last bite of her salad when Carlee

returned with a plate full of chicken fried steak and mashed potatoes and gravy that surprised her with the mouthwatering aroma, the steaming meal looking as good as it smelled. "Thank you. This looks delicious."

"It is," Carlee returned with confidence. "Save room for pie and let me know if you need anything else. I've lived here all my life, if you want some activity tips."

"I might once I'm settled. Thanks."

She almost groaned aloud at the first bite, closing her eyes to savor the taste before her enjoyment took a nosedive at hearing a now familiar deep voice that sent her pulse to racing.

"I think she likes it, Nash," Randy drawled as he slid into her booth opposite her, Nash joining him.

"Either that or she's aroused. Do you look like that when you're aroused, luv?"

Snapping her eyes open, this time she did groan aloud when her body responded to one or both of them again with the same fervor as a few hours ago, proving her initial reaction wasn't a fluke. *Damn it.* "This could be construed as harassment, guys," she told them before ignoring their smirks and going back to her dinner.

"So, a boat, huh? Wonder why a city girl would want to rough it on a boat when she could have the comforts of a first-class B & B?" Randy mused aloud.

"From what I've seen, there's nothing first class in this hick town," she retorted before ignoring them and returning her attention to her meal. She didn't like the way their identical, probing looks sent a wave of heat through her any more than she liked them interrupting her dinner. She took her food seriously, as her rounded hips and thighs attested to.

"Then you should go back home," the friendly Brit said, his tone cooler than she had heard from him before.

Her annoyance escalating to anger, she attempted for payback by giving them a bone to chew on using her sweetest tone. "Didn't I say? I've decided to spend my extended leave expanding my photography skills to include pretty, scenic views." Releasing an exaggerated sigh, she added, "Photographing nothing but dead bodies and bloody crime scenes tends to wear a person down, you know?"

The sheriff accepted her new reason for hanging around with a skeptical lift of one coal black brow, his obsidian eyes cool and mocking. English's blue eyes were just as mocking, only warmer.

"Tread carefully, Ms. Malloy," Randy warned, his voice laced with warning that sent a shiver up her spine. "I won't tolerate you interfering with my investigation even if I sympathize with your impatience for answers and your worry over your sister."

As the sheriff nudged Nash, the two slid out of the booth, the sheriff walking away without another word, Nash standing there a moment looking down at her from his six foot plus height before stating with quiet emphasis, "There are things in play here you don't know about, Alena. Be good and don't make waves in waters you're not familiar with. We'll find your sister."

"We? Are you a cop, English? I thought you were just a visiting friend."

When he braced his hands flat on the table and leaned down into her face, Alena resisted the urge to cringe back in her seat, not out of fear, but straightforward lust that shot directly to her core from his heated gaze. *Oh, good Lord.*

"I *am* just a visiting friend. Remember that and don't hint otherwise or the sheriff won't be the only one meting out repercussions if you step over the line."

Oh, God, Alena moaned to herself, fisting her shaking hands under the table as she watched their loose-limbed stroll out the door. As a pair, they were lethal to both her libido and her plans. There had to be something seriously wrong with her. Finding both men equally attractive, their tall, well-built bodies lust inspiring, wasn't anything to be concerned about, it just proved she was a healthy, red-blooded woman. But the rapid thumping of her heart, her sweaty palms, and the spasm she experienced between her legs when both men had threatened consequences if she didn't stand down wasn't normal, was it? She'd never been into dominating men, preferring to call the shots when it came to sex. Being in control made it much easier when she was ready to walk away without entanglements.

She didn't like her attraction to them, and certainly didn't care for the flare of excitement their threats sent prickling along her skin. But if she needed to, she'd use sex and any other means at her disposal to find her sister. Then she'd wring Ashley's neck herself for the trouble and worry this latest stunt had caused her.

CHAPTER TWO

Standing at the rail of her boat, Alena tried bracing against the slow roll beneath her while keeping a tight grip on her camera as a wave rocked her small temporary home. In the past two days of acquainting herself with the area, she had spent most of her time on the lake, only returning to the marina to drive into town for food, making herself known as a friendly tourist and photographer. The first night she spent below on the small bunk she had almost gone bat-shit crazy. The constant hoot from owls kept her awake; the other sounds she couldn't name emitting from the surrounding woods gave her a queasy stomach. She hailed from New York, for pity's sake. Murders and muggings were a daily occurrence, her job put her smack in the middle of some horrendous crime scenes, and she had cowered below deck, quivering under her thin blanket like a rabbit hiding from a swooping eagle. The periodic lulls of quiet grated on her nerves as much as the wildlife night noises.

Raising her camera, she focused in on the stately, two-story lake home peeking out among the surrounding trees and caught a glimpse of a large man enjoying the summer afternoon with a beer as he lounged on his wide front porch.

He had to be Bryan Hirst, she thought, older brother of Kevin Hirst, whom Ashley had last been seen with. Like Carlee at the diner, but unlike the sheriff and English, Bill at the marina had been a font of information and only too happy to point out the wealthiest homes around Blue Springs Lake and name those fortunate enough to own them. Not wanting to draw too much attention, she didn't press for more.

Being able to keep an eye on the lake house from this close was why she opted to spend uncomfortable nights and most of her days on the small rental cruiser. She had no idea what she hoped to find by spying on the place her sister was last seen, but she had to start somewhere. She could hear the whir of motorboats out on the lake as they pulled skiers behind them and wondered at the patience some people exhibited sitting on the shore with a pole in hand, biding their time waiting for a nibble. She failed to grasp why having a picnic at a wood table with insects vying for food would be enjoyable. Going through some of her snapshots last night, she did have to admit photographing beautiful scenery and catching a gorgeous doe with her two adorable fawns on film was much more relaxing than snapping shots of blood-soaked corpses or torn-apart crime scenes.

While trying not to be too conspicuous, she shifted her focus away from the house and caught sight of an official vehicle pulling up to the dock where she had been sitting illegally moored since last night. Lowering her camera, she exhaled a sigh of frustration and studiously ignored the leap in her pulse as she watched the sheriff get out and amble up the wood-planked pier toward her. *Oh, good Lord*, she bemoaned in silence when the scowl he gave her did nothing to cool the heat pooling between her legs at that black-eyed, intense look.

"Ms. Malloy," Randy greeted her as he hopped aboard without waiting for her invitation. "Weren't you informed you can only dock at the marina if you own your own pier? You are moored at a private dock, which is clearly posted."

At five foot six, she wasn't short, but she had to tilt her head back to look up at his rugged, tanned face. "Gee, Sheriff, I just stopped for a minute to take a few pictures. What's the big deal?" Sheesh, why did he have to be such a tight ass as well as hot?

"I'm duty bound to enforce the law, which you should know since you claim you work for the police. Move the boat, Alena, or you'll incur consequences you may not like or be ready for."

There went that annoying shiver down her spine at the veiled sexual threat in his tone and heated look, which made Alena desperate to be rid of him. "Fine," she snapped, not bothering to hide her irritation. "I'll move on. Now, go away and leave me in peace. You're ruining my vacation."

More like ruining her spying, Randy judged, both aroused and frustrated with her obstinance. "Behave, Alena."

She watched him stroll back to his vehicle, eyeing the way his jeans hugged his taut buttocks and wishing she didn't find him so appealing. Whipping up the small motorboat, she coasted around the bend and idled until she saw the last of the taillights of the sheriff's cruiser then bided her time for another five minutes before returning to her spot. The man she assumed was Bryan Hirst no longer sat on his porch, but she didn't let that or Randy's threats deter her. Who she most needed to find was Kevin, the one who had invited Ashley and her friends to the lake for spring break, the one Ashley had been hanging out with lately at college, and the one with whom she'd been seen leaving the local bar before disappearing later that night.

Alena believed the police had questioned each of the college kids in detail and she didn't suspect them of anything, but they *had* to know something or maybe they had omitted something out of fear of getting blamed. In all honesty, she didn't care if a party got out of hand, maybe they had all indulged in too much alcohol or drugs then let Ash go off by herself, she just wanted answers. She wanted to find her sister.

An hour later, she didn't have time to do anything except lower her bare feet from where she had them propped on the rail and rise from her deck chair when she spotted the sheriff returning to the scene of her crime. *Damn it.*

This time he approached the boat in an angry stride, the look on his face one of irritation with an underlying expectancy that had all her happy places sitting up and taking notice.

Double damn.

• • • • • • •

Just because Bryan no longer hung around outside didn't mean Randy could let this infraction slide, nor did he want to. His palm had itched to connect with Alena Malloy's ass since she'd stormed out of his office two days ago. Coupled with her insistence on jeopardizing his and Nash's plans to keep attending Bryan's parties as guests in the hopes of uncovering something that would give them a new lead, she had just forced him to act on his threats.

Leaping aboard, he stalked right up to her and glared down into her wary but defiant green eyes. "You deliberately defied my order, Alena. As I don't think just issuing you another warning will do any good, you've left me with no choice but to act."

He surprised her with a yank that brought her into full frontal contact with his rock-hard body, then shocked her when he made good on his threat as he twisted and bent her over one muscle-bulging arm. But it was her body's response to the painful smacks he leveled on her upturned butt that astounded her, the unmistakable arousal simmering beneath the heat building across her buttocks impossible to ignore or deny.

Her surprise changed to indignation and set her to struggling, but whether she fought against the gall of his chastisement or her response to it she wasn't sure. "Damn it, let me go!"

Randy tightened his arm under her then pinned her flailing legs with his left leg, all the while smacking those soft, round globes over and over. "I warned you in my office and again today to back off. You should've listened."

She cried out as he put more weight behind the next volley of swats, the strength of his hold unbreakable, leaving her no choice but to suck it up and bear it. Her thin shorts were no barrier against his hard hand, or her escalating arousal as the burn slid downward to fill her sheath with pulsating need. Never in her life had she imagined she would get turned on from a humiliating spanking. Never could she have envisioned her nipples peaking from the sting, her core throbbing with unfulfilled lust.

He caught her bare thigh with a sharp whack, eliciting a startled, pain-filled cry from her at the blistering difference between smacking her bare skin and the flesh that was covered with light cotton.

Twisting her head, she glared up at him through the tangled curtain of her hair. "Damn it, *that* hurt!"

"They're all supposed to hurt," he returned without remorse, giving her other thigh an identical smack that had her cursing and him smiling. He could feel her pebbled nipples against his arm, a response he tested by cupping his palm between her legs. "I don't think you're all that upset over this."

She had no time to respond to that astute observation as he resumed swatting her butt, over and over until she hung like a limp noodle over his arm and her gasps of outrage were reduced to mortifying whimpers of humiliating need.

"Sheriff, please."

She cringed at the soft plea in her voice, but if he didn't let up soon, she'd humiliate herself even more by giving in to her body's demand for release from both the painful swats and her throbbing arousal. When he stopped as fast as he had begun then lifted her with a much gentler hand, her head swam in dizzying circles that forced her to lean against him. The comfort of his arms wrapping around her brought tears to her eyes, which pissed her off as much as his high-handed behavior had.

Breaking away from his embrace that felt too good, she shoved her unruly hair back and set her hands on her hips. The little knowing smirk playing around his mouth poured fuel onto the angry fire stewing inside her. "You've had your fun, now leave and I'll do the same."

Reaching into his back pocket, he withdrew a small pad, flipped it open, wrote something, then ripped the top sheet off and handed it to her.

"Spanking you was fun, but this is my responsibility. It's just a written warning. Next time there'll be a fine." He pivoted and hopped down to the short slip before swiveling and tossing out one more warning. "You also won't get to keep the comfort of your shorts, Red. Then we'll really give the lakers something to gawk at."

Flipping her a mocking two-finger salute, he sauntered back to his Explorer, leaving Alena gasping in utter discomposure at the sight of a boat idling about a quarter of a mile down the lake, the wide grins splitting the four passengers' faces too easy to see.

"Oh, good Lord," she muttered in exasperation as she worked through the completely irrational, annoying thrill his parting words and their unknown audience set off. Her body had no business tingling in response to that humiliating, painful spanking or her exhibitionism. She would just ignore it, she vowed, reaching down into her small ice chest next to her chair and plucking out a cold wine cooler. Popping the cap, she took a long pull, determined to disregard the ache between her legs as well as the lingering, warm throb of her buttocks that seemed to egg that ache on. She refused to be a slave to her body's demands even if she wondered what her response would be to a bare, harder spanking.

By the time she finished her cooler, her chaotic thoughts had settled down but not so her body. Determined to get the upper hand, at least with her hormones, she made a quick decision and dove off the side of the boat into the frigid lake. An accomplished swimmer, she glided with swift strokes in a back and forth pattern for ten minutes before giving in to the inevitable. Setting her feet down on the sandy bottom, she shivered as the chest-deep water lapped around her but did nothing to ease the heated, pulsing need still clamoring for relief.

With one hand snaking up under her shirt to flip open the front catch on her bra and knead the soft fullness of her breast and one sliding down her loose shorts to palm the denuded, sensitive flesh of her pussy, she caved to her body's demands. Leaning her head back, she closed her eyes and let the sun's warm rays heat her face and shoulders as she worked her fingers to heat the rest of her body.

She loved to touch herself, so this bore no hardship. What galled her was giving in when she'd sworn she didn't want to, just needed to for comfort's sake. Yeah, that really went against the grain, but it didn't keep her from rolling her nipple into an even tighter nub or from delving inside her sheath with two fingers to root out her clit. The slickness of her channel had nothing to do with the water she soaked in and everything to do with an arousal that wouldn't be denied.

Her soft cry as she thrust her fingers over and over her clit echoed in the small cove. With her back to the rest of the lake, she couldn't hear any boats zipping by or know if there was anyone else idling or sitting on the opposite shore, but her need had risen to such a state, she flat out didn't care at this point. Switching to torment her other nipple, she put more pressure on her thrusts then slowed as she rasped back and forth over her swollen bundle of nerves until she shook more from the building pressure of release than from the cold.

Succumbing to the spiraling fall her touch led her to, she pinched her nipple and clit at the same time, milking the two pleasure points until the blinding pleasure of her climax exploded throughout her jerking body.

· · · · · · ·

Randy took care lowering his zipper over his straining erection, cursing his weakness and lack of control concerning one Alena Malloy. He'd pulled back onto the road then parked where he had a view of her boat through a break in the trees, unable to resist seeing what she'd do now. Not only did it make him a pathetic bastard to be sitting in his car, spying on her as she got herself off in the lake while mulling over how nice it had felt to cuddle her against him, but to get so turned on without catching even a glimpse of nakedness was downright pitiful. He should be worried about her causing waves over that spanking and hindering his investigation rather than enjoying the unbelievably erotic picture she presented standing in the lake with her hair slicked back to reveal the stark pleasure on her face. The movement of one hand under her shirt and the disappearance of the other down her shorts left him in no doubt about what she was doing.

Wrapping his hand around his cock, he squeezed his aching flesh as he recalled the plushness of her lush ass under his hand, her thin cotton shorts no barrier between his palm and her soft buttocks. She had taken her spanking better than he anticipated; in fact, he'd bet the reason for her jump into the cold lake had more to do with cooling down her libido than an effort to relieve her anger with him. He admired her spirit, spunk, and independence, even if he feared those traits would lead her down a path he suspected she'd never traversed before.

Stroking up and down his rigid length, he imagined what her bare ass would feel like, look like. The way her wet tee shirt clung to her breasts outlined their soft fullness, the nipple not covered by her hand a prominent pinpoint he would love to wrap his lips around. Cupping his smooth mushroom cap with his palm, he glided his thumb underneath the rim to tease along the ultrasensitive skin there. Gritting his teeth, he fought back the urge to let go, wanting to draw out the pleasure as he watched her.

Shifting his pre-cum dampened palm back down his cock, he smiled when she laid her head back and closed her eyes, her hands getting busier under her clothes. Pondering the look on her face when he pointed out the audience neither of them knew about until he released her from his hold earlier, he figured she had fought against not only the pain-induced arousal he'd brought on, but the thrill she'd experienced learning they had been watched. He doubted either reaction would sit well with her, but they did bode positive for both him and Nash if she continued with her obstinance and insisted on getting in their way.

Alena's soft cry of release catapulted his own urgent need into crawling up the root of his shaft and spewing from his cockhead. Leaning back against the headrest, he shut his eyes and basked in his own pleasure as he pictured her sandwiched between him and his new friend. He took his time savoring his ball-busting climax and enjoying the small contractions of lingering pleasure as it eased before rousing himself to look back down at the lake.

Grabbing a tissue from the glove box, he cleaned up as he watched her swim back to her boat and climb aboard, her wet thin clothes clinging to her abundant curves, leaving little to the imagination. When she whipped her bra off without removing her shirt and tossed it on the deck chair, he groaned at the best view of a wet tee shirt plastered over braless breasts he had ever been privileged to observe. She started her motor, and he waited until she pulled away before doing the same, wondering if she had more success in exorcising him from her thoughts than he had of her.

Ten minutes later, Randy pulled up to his rustic cabin home located on the outskirts of Blue Springs but close enough he could get to the office in under ten minutes. The Jeep Wrangler Nash had rented sat in the gravel drive and it still surprised him how easy the two of them had found living together the past month. Of course, they had law enforcement in common along with a penchant for spanking and kinky sex that included voyeurism, exhibitionism, and threesomes. And then there were the coincidences in their two cases that they were both determined to solve.

As usual, guilt nipped at his conscience every time he thought about his case and his suspicion Bryan knew more than he had let on. The man he'd known for over ten years would never hurt a woman and Randy didn't suspect him of having anything nefarious to do with young Ashley's disappearance. He may like his sex rough and preferred partners who got off on harsher pain than Randy liked to dish out, but he had never crossed consensual or safety lines. However, Bryan was very protective of his younger brother, Kevin, who'd gotten into trouble more than once sowing his wild oats, trouble Bryan had always bailed him out of because of misplaced guilt over Kevin's father, Bryan's stepfather, walking out on him when he was eight. But to Randy's knowledge, the kid, now twenty-two, had kept his wild ways to excessive drinking along with the occasional drug use, irresponsible drunk driving, and overly loud parties that always ended with fist scuffles. Most of Kevin's shenanigans had taken place in Portland in his high school years with Randy having to interfere a handful of times during the summer months and since he started partying at Bryan's lake home during college breaks.

But even with his penchant for troublemaking, Randy didn't think Kevin or his friends were criminally responsible for whatever befell Ashley. He'd believed Bryan when he'd said that he'd walked Ashley to her car and she hadn't been impaired to drive. But when Bryan had told him a few weeks after he'd questioned him that he planned on spending most of his time at the lake, working from home and only returning to Portland periodically when necessary, his suspicions over something being amiss with his friend had grabbed hold and had refused to let go. He would know more when Kevin arrived to spend a few weeks of his summer break with his brother and he could see them together.

Stepping out of his vehicle, Randy stretched then winced when his back popped. Damn, he was getting too old to be jacking off in the cramped quarters of his SUV. He now preferred to stretch out someplace comfortable, or better yet, he thought as he trotted up the steps to his front porch, stretch out with one lushly curved redhead.

"You look pleased with yourself," Nash greeted him at the door, holding the screen open for him.

"Had to take our girl in hand this afternoon. It wasn't too much of a hardship."

"I'll bet. Give."

They strolled into the spacious, ten-foot-ceiling great room where Randy moved straight across to his liquor cabinet and poured each of them a whiskey, a habit they had started on Nash's first night as his guest. Settling in his ancient, worn, but comfortable recliner, he sipped his drink, savoring the warm burn as it slid smoothly down his throat.

"Caught her spying on the Hirst house, illegally moored at Bryan's dock. She ignored my first warning, returning after I left, so I gave her something else to think about before defying me again. Clothes on," he finished on an exaggerated, long-suffering sigh.

"And you didn't call me?" *Bugger*, Nash swore, he would've loved to seen that. "You think that'll sink in? From the few minutes we spent with her in your office, I wouldn't have thought she'd back off even after suffering some embarrassing swats."

"It wasn't planned, so I didn't have time to let you know, you voyeuristic pervert. She managed a little payback without knowing I was watching when she jumped into the friggin' lake and masturbated when the cold water didn't do the trick."

Nash's grin widened and Randy couldn't help but smirk in return. "Well, we thought she was going to be a handful."

"Yeah." Randy sipped his drink again then sighed, saying, "And what a handful. It may just take the two of us to keep her out of trouble and from blowing your cover as a friend of mine visiting here for a few weeks of vacation."

"Well, mate, I can think of worse ways to amuse myself in this backwater town of yours while we sit around with our thumbs up our arses waiting for something to go on."

Randy understood and sympathized with his frustration. "She'll at least liven things up, that is if one or both of us doesn't arrest her and lock her up for her own good and that of our investigation."

As if the thought of Alena behind bars amused him, Nash quirked an eyebrow and drawled, "I have a feeling that would only compound our situation."

"Yeah, you're right. Let's hope it doesn't come to that. I'll grill, you put together a salad."

CHAPTER THREE

From Alena's few trips into town, it hadn't taken her long to discover the sum total of Blue Springs business district and shopping mecca could be found along Main Street. As she drove from the marina into town one week after arriving, she tried to rein in her frustration over the dead end results of her constant surveillance of the Hirst lake house. Taking a wild guess, she assumed the town's beauty shop would be as much of a gathering place for local gossip as her own upscale New York salon and headed that way this morning. If all else failed, she could always use a trim.

She found it near the end of Main Street, aptly named Beauty Shop, located across from the town library, its catchy name—Blue Springs Library—drawing a reluctant grin from her. Shaking her head, she mumbled, "What the heck am I doing here?" If she weren't so riddled with both worry and anger over Ashley's latest stunt, she'd hightail it back to her beloved big city in a heartbeat.

Finding the library helped ease her frustration though. Whenever the stress of her job got to be too much, she would hole up in the library and bury herself in ridiculous romance novels. She preferred the quiet ambience of the old building to her boring apartment when she took a much needed break from the blood and gore of her job and photographing the terrible things people were capable of doing to each other. Although, she mused, stepping out of her car, if the boredom of photographing trees and deer started to get to her, she might have to check out a good murder mystery.

Oh, good Lord, she groaned in silence as she entered the beauty shop and found herself smack dab in the middle of the movie *Grease*. Pink hair dryers along with pink-draped stylists damn near blinded her, but the small shop was almost full, so she had to count that as a plus.

"I'm Cora Sue. What can I do for you, sweetie?"

The woman behind the counter looked to be her age, her smile as warm and friendly as everyone else's in this town.

"I just need a trim, but I don't have an appointment."

Waving her arm, Cora Sue indicated an empty *pink* seat in front of a bank of mirrors. "Oh, walk-ins are most of my business. Have a seat." Whipping a drape over Alena's shoulders, she asked, "You on vacation with family?"

Alena didn't even question how the woman knew she wasn't a resident. From the quick research she had done on this area, the lake provided vacation homes for a lot of people but the lack of any other activities kept a steady flow of nonresident vacationers to a minimum. "No, it's just me getting away from the big city and work to get a little R & R." Taking a chance Cora Sue wouldn't ask for specifics, she tacked on, "A coworker recommended your lake and I'm pleased she steered me here, at least so far."

Twisting Alena's top layer on top of her head, the stylist picked up a pair of scissors without asking Alena her preferences. Before she could stop her, Cora Sue nudged her head down and started snipping. God, she really missed Rico, who knew exactly what she wanted, and his classy, modern salon. "Huh, just a trim, not too short."

"No problem, sweetie. Now, me, I've vacationed in

some of our country's finest cities, but lord, can all that hustle and bustle tire a body out. Always a pleasure to arrive in someplace new and different, but I'm usually ready to hightail it home before too long. You into lake sports, camping, fishing, or just hanging out?"

Alena knew she'd be ready to hightail it home before long. "Mostly hanging out, hiking a few trails and doing some sightseeing." Sucking in a breath, she ventured tentatively, "But I have to admit I'm now a bit leery about staying on. I just heard about a girl who went missing from around here." She gave a fake, delicate shudder before continuing. "My friend never said anything about the crime rate in these parts."

"Crime rate!" the older woman seated next to her exclaimed in a huff. "Why, I've lived here all my life and can vouch for our peaceful community. It's just those kids getting themselves into trouble is all."

"Well, the young girl was seen with the Hirst boy and his friends, and we all know how wild that trio used to be." This tidbit came from a woman who popped her head out from under her dryer, obviously having heard the exchange.

"Kevin's not near as bad as his brother, probably because of the seventeen year gap in their ages. Why, I just happened to be walking by his place late one afternoon and, well," the woman getting her nails done fanned her face with her free hand, "let's just say the rumors about the goings-on at that lake house are true!"

Cora Sue chuckled and rolled her eyes as she loosened Alena's top hair then leaned down to whisper, "One of our part-time residents likes to come up here to indulge in some, well, let's say, extracurricular activities of a different nature." Rising, she sent an admonishing look around the room. "Come on, ladies, you know our sheriff not only goes to those private parties, but he makes sure anything that might offend some of you or a visitor is kept under wraps."

Alena liked the amusement she heard in Cora Sue's tone, and she wondered if perhaps she had firsthand knowledge of what went on at those parties, but she kept quiet, hoping something would be said that she could look into.

When the conversations started to turn to other topics, she spoke up again. "Maybe this girl went to one of those parties and things got out of hand." A sex party would be right up Ashley's alley, and she had to admit she was now even more curious about what went on at that lake house, as well as the sheriff who apparently had a 'do as I say, not as I do' attitude.

"That's doubtful, hon. I've known Bryan Hirst since he bought that place, and while it's true he's a tad overprotective of his brother, he wouldn't condone or cover up any mischief of that nature. Just ask Carlee down at the diner. Those two have been on and off again for years."

"So there's no truth to the rumor this girl is missing?" she hinted, gleaning as much as she could.

"Oh, she's missing, but Sheriff Janzen's on the case. As soon as the Hirst boy returns to town for his summer visit, he'll pin him, Joel, and Brad down for more details. I heard Carlee say Bryan left for Portland the other day and will most likely return in about a week along with Kevin."

"Well, I hope it'll be soon and he can shed some light on the girl's whereabouts," Alena said as Cora Sue removed the drape and fluffed up her hair. Eyes widening, she gave her head a shake, liking the bouncy sway of her now shoulder-length hair. "Thank you, Cora. I really like this," she commented, surprised at how much she liked what the stylist had done.

"Next time I'll treat you to a nice scalp massage, but I don't have time today."

She followed her to the register and paid her with a fervent, "Thank you," leaving the shop with the tidbit about Hirst being gone giving her ideas. If her snooping still didn't turn up anything, once Kevin Hirst returned, she'd do whatever she had to pull answers from him.

• • • • • • •

"That can't be good."

Nash and Randy stepped out of the sheriff's office and they both spotted Alena's bright red hair as she emerged from the beauty shop. Seeing Randy's frown, Nash asked, "Why?" as he watched her fold that round, lush body into her car, his cock twitching as he imagined the feel of her underneath him.

"Because Cora Sue, along with half the women in this town, is the biggest gossip within a twenty-mile radius. I made the mistake of playing with her one night at Hirst's and damned if we weren't labeled a couple by noon the next day. That was the first and last time I fucked anyone who lives in my county."

"I do love your small town antics. What do you think our girl was up to?"

"Ten to one, she's been prying again."

As they strode down the boardwalk, Cora came out of her shop with a broom. Nash liked the way the shop owners along Main Street kept their places neat as a pin, making sure the large barrels filled with colorful flowers were kept watered and the walk swept clean. "Shall we find out?"

The sheriff heaved a sigh, replying, "Yeah, I guess we better."

Randy's disgruntled tone amused Nash. He continued to be surprised by how much he enjoyed his temporary partner and new friend's company despite their differences. He was more laid back, tended to be easygoing over small matters, such as interfering redheads, whereas Randy had been as tense as a cat in a room full of rocking chairs since she'd walked into his office. On the other hand, Nash had little control over his temper over the big things, usually exploding first and asking questions afterward. The sheriff, on the other hand, always maintained a tight rein on his anger, but he'd seen kids and adults alike cringe from just a cold look and a few softly spoken words from the man.

"Come on, how bad can it be?" Slapping Randy on the

back, he grinned and picked up their pace until they approached Cora.

"Afternoon, Cora Sue. That one of our visitors I've seen around?" Randy asked her by way of a lead-in.

"Sure was, Sheriff. Alena, I think she said her name was. Full of questions about that missing college girl, but otherwise seemed to be enjoying her stay. Liked the cut I gave her. How're you, Nash?"

Enjoying the flirtation from the other woman as much as the scowl from his partner, he replied, "I'm good, how about you, luv?" He almost laughed outright when Randy rolled his eyes.

"Can't complain. I…."

"Cora, what did Alena want to know? I can't have tourists poking their noses into my investigation or worrying about their safety," Randy interrupted, wanting to move along.

"Oh, she just heard about what happened is all. I let her know you were on top of it and would question both Bryan and Kevin together when they returned. Really, Randy," she said, frowning at him. "I do know how to keep our visitors both happy and wanting to come back."

"Sorry, I'm just edgy because that girl's case has been stagnant for so long. Have a nice day."

Nash waited until they had walked down to the end of the street before admitting, "Okay, Ms. Malloy might get up to mischief knowing Bryan isn't in the vicinity right now."

Randy sent him a rueful grin. "Your turn to keep tabs on her and put the fear of us in her if need be. I'm going to do something easier, like check for signs of poachers in the south woods."

"Very funny, chap. I'll be happy to take prickly, interfering woman duty. And if I catch her snooping where she doesn't belong, I won't be as nice as you were."

Nash spun back around, Randy's rude snort following him as he returned to the sheriff's office where he'd left his Jeep. A mile out of town, he took the turnoff that put him on the narrow, two-lane road that wrapped around the lake, elevated above the water just enough to afford motorists glimpses of the crystal clear expanse between the tall pines. No one had been more surprised than he at how much he had come to like the area, the town, and the people. A far cry from foggy, damp London with its crowded streets, he discovered the dense forests, sometimes too friendly residents, and sunny days were a pleasant change and diversion. If he hadn't been so obsessed with solving the case of the twenty-year-old girl pulled out of the Thames last summer, he would have missed the opportunity to visit this state and get to know Sheriff Randy Janzen.

Randy's tenacity and determination to find his missing victim matched that of Nash's to track down his perpetrator, both of them agreeing it was too much of a coincidence Kevin Hirst and his friends were among the last people to have been seen with both college girls. Having been a member of a private sex club back home for several years, Nash knew right away what had caused the ligature marks around his victim's wrists and ankles. Restraints applied with too much pressure, or left on too long were signs of a sadist or a completely incompetent newbie to BDSM, either one unacceptable to him. Bruises had covered the girl's back, buttocks, and thighs, the beating she had endured resulting in several welts deep enough to break the skin. Unforgivable. Add to all of that torment, when the coroner's report stated Lisa Ames had suffered through several episodes of autoerotic asphyxiation and died from the final strangulation, he knew he wouldn't rest until her killer was caught and punished.

Having dual citizenship, Nash subscribed to several online periodicals and had just happened to come across the article detailing Ashley Malloy's disappearance, which included a list of people questioned. Randy hadn't welcomed him with open arms or embraced his theory the three boys connected their cases with enthusiasm. But, being the thorough lawman he now knew the sheriff to be,

Randy wouldn't out and out dismiss the possibility.

As much as he had enjoyed his stay this past month, bunking with Randy and the two get-togethers they had attended and indulged in at the Hirst lake house, he wouldn't let anything get in his way of getting justice for both these girls, especially if his and Randy's cases proved to be linked. And that meant finding and dealing with Alena if he caught her where she didn't belong, possibly putting their case at risk. Which would be a nice perk of this otherwise tedious, slow investigation.

It didn't take him long to spot her boat rental moored in an alcove around the bend from Bryan's private dock. Shaking his head, he counted himself lucky she didn't realize she wasn't as hidden as she thought. Pulling into the entrance to the Hirst property, clearly marked with a sign and double iron gates barring entry down the long graveled drive, he hopped out of his Jeep and bypassed the gate on foot through the woods. A few minutes later, he found her crouched at the back door, using a nail file as she attempted to jimmy the lock, curses flying right and left as she met with failure at each small twist.

Bent over, he took a moment to admire her lush ass nicely displayed in loose, thin shorts, her long legs conjuring up fantasies of the feel of those soft thighs clutching his waist as he rode her hard. He took another moment to indulge in a few more scenarios before he forced them to the back of his mind in order to focus on the problem at hand.

He grinned, anticipation zinging through his veins as he stepped forward and took her by surprise. "Problem, luv?"

With a squeal that made her blanch in mortification, Alena whirled around and found Nash Osborne not two feet from her. How the hell had he snuck up on her? Those cobalt blue eyes held amusement, but the stern set of his very enticing mouth told her she was in trouble. Again.

Taking heart he wasn't the law, just a friend of the law, she bent to retrieve her purse and dropped her nail file in it, trying to act as if she hadn't been caught doing anything illegal. "No, English, no problem. Just out for a stroll, thought I'd ask for a glass of water, but it appears no one's home, so I'll be on my way."

She moved to walk around him when he wrapped his large hand around her upper arm, stopping her with his gentle, but firm grip. Glancing up, his look confirmed she was in trouble before he spoke.

"Had a nice chat with the beauty shop owner, Cora Sue, I believe her name is. You've been prying again."

She refused to give him the satisfaction of trying to pull her arm free and failing to break his hold, so she stood her ground and pasted on a cool look of unconcern, she hoped. "I told both you and the sheriff I was going to find my sister, or a lead to her whereabouts. I'm not leaving until I get something I can give to the Portland PD."

The smile that creased his lean, tanned face sent a shiver of warning down her spine and a warm gush of heat between her legs. *Oh, good Lord*, she almost groaned aloud. This couldn't be happening again, not with the same reaction to a different man.

"You have two choices. I can haul you into town and to the sheriff and let him know I caught you attempting a break-in of one of Blue Springs' finest residents in another attempt to hinder his investigation, or you can suffer the consequences of your actions the old-fashioned way again." Nash almost made the mistake of chuckling aloud when he dropped that hint he knew of Randy's discipline and her eyes widened in shock, and just a touch of arousal.

Heat curled low in her abdomen from the look in his eyes, his suggestion responsible for the warm pulse flooding her sheath with moisture. Was she turning into a spanking slut or was it just these two men whom her radar had zeroed in on and refused to let go?

"Randy already tried that," she responded, attempting to defuse his intentions and regain her sanity.

"An introductory lesson, from what he relayed to me. I

won't be as nice." Turning, he sat on the small glider, keeping hold of her arm as he looked up at her. "What'll it be? Bend over my lap or a trip to see the sheriff?"

She really didn't want another confrontation with Randy, he just might toss her in jail for the night and she certainly couldn't afford an attempted break-in charge on her record. That could cost her her job. With a sigh of resignation, she ignored the leap of her pulse and the light in his eyes as she replied with a terse, "Fine. I'll take the spanking."

Before she lost her nerve, she followed his slight tug and lay across his thick, hard thighs. But when he yanked her shorts down, along with her panties, she twisted around to glare up at him. "Hey! I didn't agree... *ow*!" The crack of his hand on her right buttock startled her, but not nearly as much as her response to the sharp sting that left her skin throbbing with heat.

"Do I continue or do we go have a nice chat with Sheriff Janzen?"

Oh, she honestly did not care for his cool, amused tone or the knowing look in his eyes, but, God help her, she did like the soft stroke of his broad palm over the tender skin he'd just abused. Determined to win this battle, she huffed out an annoyed breath then flipped back around, making a desperate attempt to ignore the way the warm breeze caressed her bare buttocks, the outdoor exposure adding to the arousal his slap had initiated.

"That's a girl, luv." Nash smacked her other cheek, enjoying her reluctant capitulation.

She groaned as that accent curled her toes and the next swat landed with blistering heat on her other buttock. Biting her lip, she concentrated on stifling her escalating arousal as he rained a litany of steady, hard smacks across her butt. Each one burned hotter, stung harder, and worked to increase her arousal. By the sixth stroke, her buttocks throbbed with heat and pain she felt reciprocated in her sheath.

A moan slipped past her compressed lips as he moved

down to land a well-aimed smack on the sensitive skin of the under curve of each buttock before continuing down to smack her thighs. "*Shit!*" Swiveling her head, she leveled another icy glare at him. "That, that's... uncalled for!" His low chuckle grated on her as much as his soothing caresses calmed her ire. God, was she confused!

"I don't think so. You keep poking your nose where it doesn't belong." He liked the feel of her warm skin under his hand as much as he liked the fire in her green eyes.

"She's my sister," she snapped in her defense, the urge to shift under his now still hand difficult to ignore. She didn't know whether she ached for more swats or for more caresses, which only added to her frustration.

Nash slapped her ass again. "She's Randy's responsibility now, not yours." *Smack! Smack! Smack!* "You need to trust him to find the truth and quit getting in his way."

She suffered through three more sharp, quick slaps that rendered her incapable of speech, then those oh so soft, so tantalizing caresses that fueled the fire raging between her legs. Her buttocks throbbed with discomfited, heated pleasure he interrupted when he started kneading her cheeks, the tight squeezes reigniting the sharper pain. Her instant struggles to escape his hands were halted by his leg pinning hers in place and a shocking, eye-opening coast of his fingers down her crack to her seam.

Alena's glistening slit, confirmation of her arousal, proved too tempting to ignore and instead of helping her up, Nash kept her lush body over his lap for a few minutes of sensual torture sure to torment him as much as her. When his fingers encountered the bare flesh of her labia, he stroked the baby-soft skin. "You're full of surprises, luv." She rewarded his comment with another green-eyed glare that couldn't disguise the lust lurking behind the frustration.

Keeping his eyes on hers, he glided his hand between her soft, round thighs, biting back a grin when they fell open without hesitation as she turned her face away from him again. "You can't hide from this truth, Alena," he told her as he cupped her damp crotch.

"I can try."

Criminy, but she was a delight, he thought, her low, muttered reply wringing a wide grin from him. "Okay, go ahead and try." He teased her slick entrance, slipping his single digit between her folds with buttery ease to encounter wet heat. His grin widened even further when those slick walls closed around him in a tight-fisted clasp followed by a telltale shudder of her entire body.

"You have a body that speaks loud and clear, luv, a paradise of delight for a man to indulge in."

Alena turned a disbelieving look up to him, refusing to fall for such polished words, even if they were uttered in a sexy accent. "Let me up, you moron."

"I'd believe you meant that insult if you weren't soaking my finger." A deep push had him embedded up to his knuckle and, from the sudden jerk of her body and the lust shining in her eyes, he knew he found her g-spot. She turned her head, but he still heard her soft cry, still felt the warm gush of pleasure as he pulled back and teased her swollen clit until she squirmed those lovely red buttocks in a way that had his cock swelling with painful insistence against his zipper.

A few more finger thrusts followed by teasing glides over her protruding bundle of nerves and he felt the small clutches heralding her orgasm. Satisfied, he pulled away from her snug heat and lifted her to her feet, keeping hold of her arms to steady her as he looked up into her 'red as her ass' face. Placing the same finger he'd had inside her over her mouth, he shut off her complaint before she could voice it.

"Remember this, all of this, the next time you go snooping or you may not be lucky enough to have just one of us take you in hand. Randy and I have discovered we like sharing."

Alena watched him stroll off without a backward glance, her arms tingling where he had clasped them, her nose still twitching from the scent of her own arousal on his finger and her body raging in protest of its orgasm denial. Yanking up her shorts, she swore she would get back at both of them if it was the last thing she did in this godforsaken town.

With her butt still throbbing and sore and her pussy reduced to an aching pulse, she stomped back through the woods to her boat thinking there must be something seriously wrong with her. It just wasn't normal to respond with such overwhelming lust to two such different men, the height of her response to each of their handling exceeding anything she had felt when having sex with any of her lovers. If they could reduce her to near uncontrollable combustion with a spanking and a few light touches, what would sex be like with either of them? Or both?

That last thought plagued her as she maneuvered her small, floating hotel room out of the cove she thought had hidden it, as did the arousal Nash had reawakened with his hard hand and probing fingers. The late afternoon sun added heat to her already warm body, the slight breeze coming off the lake doing little to cool her.

She waved to the elderly gentlemen parked on camp chairs on the shore, fishing rods in hand as they called out together, "How ya doing, missy?" like they did every time she cruised by them.

Smiling, she tossed them her standard reply of, "Just fine. You?" Their same answer, "Can't complain," drew a smile from her as she coasted by, wondering how they couldn't be bored to tears spending hours every afternoon just sitting there waiting for a nibble.

That minor distraction didn't last and as she turned off the small motor and let the boat drift on the calm water, she grabbed a wine cooler from her stocked little ice chest, hoping the fizzy alcohol would cool her enough that she could ignore the way her body continued to demand relief. Leaning against the rail, she tried tuning in to nature, having read somewhere that was the purpose of spending so much time in the supposedly great outdoors.

Nope, she conceded fifteen minutes later with the last swallow of her drink. Standing there, listening to birds twittering, and other unknown critter noises coming from the surrounding woods as she swayed with the slow rocking of the boat did absolutely nothing to ease the lust still tormenting her.

"The heck with it," she griped aloud, giving in to the inevitable and skipping down to her small bunk. Snatching her favorite toy, a simple, eight-inch ridged phallus, she stripped, lay down, and got to work relieving the ache that sadistic bastard had left her with.

She didn't waste time with teasing foreplay; Nash had already taken care of that. One simple shift of her hips getting situated reignited the soreness of her buttocks, which sent a lightning bolt of sizzling pleasure straight to her core. Her little buddy slid with lubricated ease inside her as she gripped a nipple and rolled the tender bud to the point of discomfort. "God, what have they done to me?" she questioned aloud when that slight sting released added moisture to flow over the dildo. With her knees bent and spread, she thrust in and out with hard strokes, trying to picture one of her past lovers in its place when she closed her eyes. When the sheriff's hard, dark face surrounded by his mane of ebony hair popped up right alongside English's face with his tied back, rich mahogany hair and cobalt blue eyes, she swore a blue streak and pumped harder, sliding over to her other nipple to give it equal attention.

With her hips jerking up with each downward plunge as she rasped the thick, fake cock over and over her clit while she worked her nipples, she drove herself straight to the brink. Within seconds, her climax exploded with all the fanfare of shooting stars and perspiration-inducing ardor, the strong tremors encompassing her from head to toe rivaling, if not exceeding anything her previous lovers had driven her to with their naked bodies.

With her breath still coming in fast pants, she lay trembling in the aftermath of pleasure so intense it scared her. Taking a moment to soothe her still spasming pussy with much slower, softer strokes, she worked to calm both her body and her rioting emotions. She was here to find her sister, or at least unearth a clue or evidence about where she'd gone or what had happened to her so that she could take the information back to the Portland police, or if necessary, ask a favor of one of her NYPD friends to do some digging. She didn't have the time to indulge in an affair, or even a few bouts of sex, but wondered if that would eventually be her only option if she was going to find any answers.

And if her responses to masturbating after both Randy and Nash took her to task were anything to go by, sex with either of them, or, God help her, both of them, might damn well kill her.

CHAPTER FOUR

The next day, Alena set aside the erotic dreams that had plagued her sleep, fantasies centered around two men with hard hands that drew responses from her she had never felt before, and set her mind back on task. Finding Ashley, or some clue to her whereabouts, had to take precedence. She couldn't let her body's demands derail her from her goal, or from getting back to New York where she belonged.

She used to think sexy was as easy as a man with neatly styled hair and a loosened tie, not as complicated as being equally attracted to two opposite men, one in tight, butt-hugging jeans sporting a perpetual five-o'clock shadow, the other with wavy mahogany hair and a toe-curling British accent. When she returned home, she'd look up one of her fuck buddies and scratch the itch she couldn't seem to rid herself of since coming here, or, if one of them wasn't available, she'd scratch it herself. She ignored the inner taunting voice reminding her of her recent masturbation sessions, which had left her anything but completely sated.

Satisfied with both her plan and with lying to herself, she returned to the marina, waved to the owner, Bill, then slid into her car. The loud grumble from her stomach reminded her she hadn't eaten, which gave her a great excuse for stopping in at the diner. She could appease her hunger and hopefully coax a few answers from Carlee about Bryan.

The lake and small town catered mostly to both the full- and part-time residents of Blue Springs and a handful of summer tourists, and Alena suspected the popularity of the throwback eating establishment came from long-time patrons. But luck was with her and the diner didn't look too crowded by the time she parked out front a few minutes later. Stepping inside, she inhaled a deep, appreciative whiff and damn near slid into a puddle of salivating hunger pangs at the smell of freshly made cinnamon rolls. If she had one weakness, it was anything warm, yeasty, and calorie laden.

"Tell me that's homemade cinnamon rolls I smell," she practically demanded when she slid into a booth and Carlee handed her a menu.

"Fresh out of the oven five minutes ago. Good to see you back, Alena."

"If I can have two of them with a large cup of coffee, it'll be more than good to be back, it'll be…" She really had no comparison she could find apt until Carlee provided one for her with a teasing grin.

"Orgasmic?"

"Oh, God, you nailed it. I'm a slut for donuts, bread, anything with wheat, yeast, and sugar, preferably served warmed."

"Got it. You might want to check out our bakery down the street while you're here. Wilma Davies has been baking for this town for forty years and has no plans to stop anytime soon. I'll be back with your order."

A bakery just might be worth the hassle of this trip and the trouble her sister had caused her, she thought with longing. She didn't let her round figure keep her from indulging in her fetish for yeasty baked goods. Even though her body was a far cry from most men's preferences of short and petite or tall and willowy, she never had trouble finding a willing partner when the need for one came calling. If one wasn't available, she had a nice stash of toys next to her bed she was quite fond of and very good at applying.

"Oh, please forgive me if I drool." Alena released an exaggerated sigh when Carlee set a plate in front of her, the scent of cinnamon wafting up from the warm rolls teasing her senses and fueling her hunger. "Can you keep me company a minute in case I make a complete idiot of myself as I devour these?"

"Sure, hon. We usually stay slow in between breakfast and lunch." Sliding in across from her, Carlee smiled when Alena put a bite in her mouth and moaned in enjoyment as she chewed. "I guess you like them."

"Oh, I do, I most definitely do. Here comes another pound or two." She pulled off another piece and plopped it in her mouth before asking with what she hoped sounded like innocent inquisitiveness, "So, what do you do for fun around here? I was talking to Cora Sue down at the beauty shop about that missing girl, and she happened to mention one of the people to have seen her last is your boyfriend. I imagine you're pretty limited on places he can take you for a night out."

"It never takes newcomers long to hear more than I imagine they want to about the townsfolk here once they step foot inside Cora Sue's." Carlee's rueful grin indicated she didn't mind being on the gossip vine. "Bryan and I have a great time without having to spend an arm and a leg on fancy amusements like the big cities offer. We both enjoy the outdoors, and my guy is quite inventive when it comes to finding ways to keep us both... satisfied."

Alena returned her wicked grin, grateful for the opening. "Yes, I heard about some wild parties at his place. Seems like it was at one of them that girl was last seen."

"Yeah, I was there that night. She was a pretty thing, hanging all over Bryan's brother, Kevin. Of course, girls usually do. That one's a looker, and he knows it. Sure hope they find her."

"Well, maybe when Kevin comes back this way he'll be able to tell the sheriff something they can go on. Hopefully it won't be too much longer." She sipped her piping hot coffee to help swallow the piece of roll that had lodged in her throat when Ashley's face with her impish grin filled her head.

"Both Bryan and his brother will be back this weekend," Carlee volunteered, a gleam of anticipation in her brown eyes as she slid out of the booth. "I have to get back to work, but I hope to see you again." Turning, a broad smile split her face as she said in a low, intimate tone Alena couldn't miss, "Morning, Sheriff, Nash. You guys know what you want this morning?"

"Just a cup of coffee and a word with one of our guests here," Randy replied, his midnight eyes on the guilty flush spreading across Alena's face.

"Oh, good Lord." There went those tingles dancing their way down her spine when both men leveled those identical, intent gazes on her, forcing her to mutter aloud without even realizing it.

"Problem, Alena?"

"Nothing you two getting up and leaving won't solve," she returned, as sweet as her cinnamon roll while making a mental note to have a serious talk with her girly parts later about who was in control.

"One would think you don't like us, luv," Nash put in before turning a charming smile upon Carlee when she returned and set a cup of coffee in front of each of them. "Thank you, Carlee, and don't you look pretty today."

Carlee gave his broad shoulder a playful slap. "The gals back in London might fall for that, but we're a bit smarter over here."

Alena sure wished she could lay claim to having an ounce of brains when she heard either that British accent or Randy's low, commanding voice. Trying to ignore the way her heartbeat had accelerated and the uncomfortable dampness in her crotch, she plopped another bite of cinnamon roll in her mouth, this one with a good amount of melted icing on top that had her chewing with slow relish.

"Shit," Randy groaned, the look on Alena's face as she ate responsible for the uncomfortable shift of his cock. Luckily, Carlee's next statement took his attention off the lust she could inspire with the simplest things and returned it to why they had stopped in the diner when they spotted her bright red head inside.

"I was just telling Alena Bryan'll be back this weekend. I think he's planning a get-together the following week, if you two are interested."

"Ask him to contact me, would you?"

"Sure thing."

At least he waited until Carlee left before turning a stark look rife with impatience her way. Alena sipped her coffee and waited him out, refusing to admit out loud she had been probing again.

"Am I going to have to put a tail on you for the rest of your stay, Alena?" And by that he meant either he or Nash keeping close tabs on her.

Wanting a little payback, she presented him with a soft smile and drawled with feigned innocence, "Why, whatever do you mean, Sheriff?" Laying a small bite of roll on her tongue, she took her time licking her two fingers before releasing a low, "*Mmmm*," from deep in her throat.

"Bugger it." This time it was Nash's turn to swear and Randy sent him a quick look of commiseration before scowling at her again, not that he thought his fiercest glare would do any good. He knew Nash, just like him, was picturing that same satisfaction reflected on her face as he, or they, brought her to climax.

"You keep it up, you'll force me to up the consequences for your interference. Which would you prefer, my belt or a night or two in my jail?"

Okay, that just wasn't right. Her body's instant reaction of a gush of moisture between her legs to that threat was as unnerving as standing too close to the edge of a cliff, a cliff she'd been maintaining a precarious balance on since first setting eyes on those two. Both men made her look twice, which said something; the fact they each made her fantasize and want, made her ache, screamed it. She was in trouble.

Attempting to get herself under control, she looked them both in the eyes as she savored another bite, licking her lips this time with a slow sweep of her tongue, first over the top, then the lower, and gained a thrill of satisfaction when they both narrowed their eyes at her and shifted in their seat with obvious discomfort.

"I think I've proven your threats won't deter me. I want my sister back." She hadn't realized how true that statement was or how much she missed the irritating brat until she admitted that aloud.

"If you do, then you should trust Randy to do his job and stop interfering."

It was her turn to narrow her eyes at Nash. "You seem to be in on every step of the investigation. How're my few questions jeopardizing anything?"

Shit, Randy swore as he flicked a quick, silencing look toward Nash. They couldn't let anyone know Nash was Scotland Yard, here to investigate a possible connection to his case. They needed to keep Bryan and Kevin in the dark about that until he could question the brothers together and gauge their reactions to his inquiries. Not only had he known them for a decade, he was a damn good judge of character and would know if they were holding anything back.

"Nash's timing in visiting me is just coincidental to this case going on. He's leaving the investigating to me and my deputies, not pestering the locals for information I already know they don't have."

"So," she replied slowly, having caught, yet again, another telltale look passing between the two of them, "he's just backup for keeping me in line, is that it?"

"And an enjoyable side benefit of my visit it is." Nash's slow, drawled response and unrepentant smile and tone were sexy as hell, damn it. It had become obvious she wouldn't win this argument between them, so that left her no choice but to play nice while Bryan was still out of town, let them relax their guard, then pick up where she left off.

With a sugar-coated smile, she waved an airy hand as she swallowed the last morsel of her cinnamon rolls. "I guess my only option then, is to be patient and trust you, as you want me to."

"That's right." Not fooled for a minute, Randy slid out of the booth, followed by Nash, then they both stood staring down at her a moment before he added, "Behave, Alena."

"They're enough to make a grown woman drool, aren't they?" Carlee sighed in question when she joined Alena in watching the two men walk out.

"Unfortunately. They're not a couple, but there's more between them than Nash visiting an old friend for a few weeks," she hinted, hoping the other woman knew more about the sheriff and the Brit's relationship. Nash showed way too much interest in a case that had nothing to do with him. "What does Nash do for a living?"

"I have no idea. He just showed up one day and Randy introduced him as a friend from 'way back.' I can tell you the two of them have certain... proclivities in common, as I witnessed firsthand at one of Bryan's parties a few weeks ago."

Alena's gaze grew sharp at that remark, and the look on Carlee's face spoke volumes. Feeling her out, she ventured, "Cora mentioned those parties also. Are you hinting that the good sheriff and his friend attend sex parties?"

"Bryan's parties are well-known, and accepted, among the townsfolk. We don't sit in judgment of each other, and several of us, like myself and Cora Sue, enjoy the... activities Bryan's house is set up to provide. But we are careful about keeping them private. A lot of us rely on the extra summer income from visitors and people who own vacation homes in the area, so everyone's discreet. Of course, his place is secluded and has private property signs posted around it. Anyone ignoring them then getting offended at what they might see have no one to blame but themselves. If Bryan catches anyone trespassing, he'll either threaten to shoot, file charges, or invite them to participate if they're so inclined."

The mischief lighting her dark eyes answered the question of whether anyone had ever taken him up on the third choice. "Your secret's safe with me," Alena assured her as she left payment and a tip in cash and slid out of the booth.

"Who knows," she shrugged in nonchalance. "I might be interested in finagling an invite to the next party. They sound like fun." She had never been to a sex party or club, but she had a good idea what went on, who didn't? And if attending one gave her the chance to do some snooping inside the Hirst home, then she'd do what she had to to get that opportunity.

"From the heated looks our sheriff and Nash were giving you, I'd say getting an invite, and having someone to play with, won't be a problem. I'll let you know when the next one is."

"Thanks, Carlee."

Alena strolled down the street to the library next and spent an hour in the peaceful, quiet solitude trying to erase the images of herself engaged in various sexual scenarios with the two guys at a party while flipping through a book on outdoor photography. But not even the helpful tips she jotted down could keep those images at bay for long, and when she stepped out into the bright afternoon sun and spotted Randy leaning with negligent ease against a corner light post, her entire body warmed under his black-eyed, intent gaze.

"Afternoon, Ms. Malloy. Enjoy some reading at our fine library?"

Two could play this game, she thought as she returned his congenial greeting from across the street. "Afternoon, Sheriff, and yes, I did. Thank you for asking."

Ignoring the little smirk turning up one corner of his

mouth, she took her time returning to her car, glancing back once to see him entering the library. Just as she suspected, he was most likely checking up on her.

•••••••

The next morning, Alena woke early, drove back to Main Street and located the bakery, thoughts of warm donuts and two men who were just as bad for her keeping her awake most of the night. Taking a deep breath as she entered, her mouth watered at the yeasty aroma of freshly baked sweets.

"Morning. What can I get you?"

"One of everything?" she teased the gray-haired, short, round woman who beamed at her.

"I like a girl who isn't afraid to eat. Just pulled the chocolate long johns out of the oven. How 'bout you start with one of those?"

"One of those and one cherry turnover for later."

After adding a cup of coffee to go, she exited her now favorite shop in Blue Springs only to come face to face with Nash leaning on her car, taking a big bite out of a bear claw as he gave her a teasing wink. "I see you were of like mind this morning. Damn, but that woman can bake."

So that's how they were going to play this. Well, two, or in this case, three could play that game. Shoving aside her irritation, she bestowed on him a smile as sweet as her little bag of goodies.

"Mind if I join you on *my* car?" Hopping on the hood next to his relaxed pose, she dug her donut out and moaned loud and long with the first bite. "Oh, good Lord. You are so right. This is to die for." She almost laughed when he scowled at her. *Hadn't expected me to be so accommodating?*

"You're in a good mood," Nash commented, wondering what the little minx was up to.

"It's a beautiful morning, I've got a delicious treat in one hand, a cup of hot coffee in the other, and a hot guy next to me. Lots to be in a good mood about."

"You think I'm hot? As hot as Randy?"

Rolling her eyes, she laughed at the light of mischief in his eyes. "You're both hot, and you both know it." Popping the last bite in her mouth, she hopped off her car, waved her hand to shoo him to the side, then stepped around to the driver's door. "You have a nice day, English."

Glancing in her rearview mirror after pulling out, she watched him enter the donut shop. *So predictable*, she mused with a smile.

• • • • • • •

Nash watched out the bakery window as she drove back toward the marina, shaking his head at her contradictory moods. He knew damn good and well she had no intention of stopping her prying, so he wasn't fooled by her congenial acquiescence. But he sure liked the way she kept them on their toes. Almost as much as he had enjoyed reddening that delectable ass. If, by some miracle, she did have a change of attitude, he'd just have to find another reason to turn her over his knee, only next time he wouldn't stop at a spanking.

• • • • • • •

"I can help you with that."

Alena turned at that deep voice, cursing her body's 'sit up and take notice' reaction, and forced herself to smile nice at Randy. She wasn't surprised to see he had picked up where they left off yesterday in keeping tabs on her. "Why, Sheriff, that's very hospitable of you." Handing him the two largest of her three grocery bags, she thanked the high-school checker and let Randy follow her out of the small grocer's to her car. "The citizens and visitors of Blue Springs are lucky to have such a conscientious sheriff."

"All right, Alena. Cut the crap." Setting her bags in the back seat, he glared at her, not happy to discover Nash had been right. She seemed pleased with their tailing her movements instead of put out, which just wasn't right. She was up to something.

She bit the inside of her cheek to keep from laughing aloud at his peeved expression. "Why, whatever do you mean? I just gave you a compliment. I suppose Nash deliberately left out that I find you as hot as him, didn't he? Is that why you're bent out of joint?"

"No, he did happen to mention you said that." And under other circumstances he'd have been thrilled at the prospect of a few nights with her, but mixing business with pleasure was never a good idea, especially given how much he wanted her. "We're both flattered, but I still have to insist you stay out of my investigation into Ashley's disappearance."

Stifling her annoyance, she slid into her car, saying only, "Have a nice day, Sheriff."

• • • • • • •

Needing a break from the irritating night sounds emitting from the surrounding woods as she bobbed on the lake, Alena opted to spend that night at Blue Springs quaint B & B. The queen-size bed with its quilted comforter was more comfortable than the small bunk on her boat rental, and the secluded, two-acre lot two streets over from Main was a lot quieter, yet she awoke Saturday morning as out of sorts as every other morning since she'd driven into this town.

Groggy from another restless night, she rose cursing the happy birds singing outside her window, her sister for leading her on this wild goose chase, and the guys for making her body ache for something she couldn't put a name to. After a long, hot shower, she took advantage of the complimentary breakfast of juice, coffee, fruit, and an array of pastries from the bakery.

"Oh, this is worth ten times what you charge for a night," she complimented her hosts with a sweep of her arm over the table laden with sweets set up in the small parlor. Mort and Edna Wolford, the owners of the three-story, restored Victorian manor, beamed at her as she piled her plate with several pastries.

"We're glad you like it. Please come visit us again while you're here," Edna said, her eyes warm on the younger woman.

"I'm not sure how much longer I'll be around. The rumors about that missing girl have me a bit worried, traveling alone and all." Okay, that was pouring it on a little thick, but she was desperate to find *something* she could give the authorities in Portland to follow up on. Or maybe she was just desperate to get back to her life in crowded, noisy, smog-filled New York City, she thought with longing. At least at home there weren't any men whose erotic threats and intense, soul-probing gazes kept her on edge and awake at night.

"Oh, Sheriff Janzen's on that, and that's never happened around here before. Our town's as safe as they come. If that young girl was last seen at one of those wild Hirst parties, why, there's no telling who she left with or where they went." Mort didn't appear miffed or disapproving about *those* parties, but neither did he seem overly concerned about what might've happened to Ashley.

"Yes, I've heard about some of the private goings-on at that lake house," she admitted. "Thank you for the to-go bag. I've already put my overnight bag in my car. Thanks again."

In a hurry to get away from them before she gave in to the urge to ream them for hinting Ashley was at fault somehow, even though she couldn't argue that point, she left the B & B and returned to the marina where she took out on foot instead of boat. With her little bag of treats, a bottle of water, and her camera, she vowed to spend the afternoon doing nothing, thinking of nothing except taking pictures. Why she'd even brought up Ashley's disappearance she didn't know. Her subtle inquiries into her disappearance had gotten her as far as the endless hours she'd spent spying on the Hirst house, absolutely nowhere. As far as she or anyone else knew, her sister hadn't been seen anywhere except The Well, the local bar just outside the city limits, and at the Hirst house.

When she had signed the rental papers, Bill had pointed out all the well-marked trails around the lake, and had even given her a map, which she'd left on the boat. Having already traversed a few of them, she had a general idea where they led and set off at a brisk pace.

An hour later, she sat on a fallen log to rest, pulled out a blueberry muffin and her water, and refreshed herself before deciding which direction to take next. The dense forest allowed for only swatches of sunlight to peek through the leafy branches, but she still managed to work up a sweat without a breeze to cool the upper seventies temperature.

Taking a long swallow of water, she was enjoying listening to the gurgle of a nearby creek, thrush trilling and squirrels scurrying in the trees overhead when the distinct sound of slapping flesh followed by a high-pitched cry startled her out of her contemplative mood.

"Bryan, please." The soft voice whimpering from close by came on the heels of another flesh-smacking strike.

That voice sounded familiar, the woman's pleas revealing frustration and need instead of coming across as pain-filled or scared. Curiosity more than concern spurred Alena to creep through the brush then hide behind a large tree when she came upon a small copse, the Hirst house sitting just beyond. Tied naked with arms stretched above her to a protruding tree limb, Carlee writhed and cried out as Bryan Hirst laid a switch across her already bright, red-striped buttocks.

Alena cringed with the snap, but her body shocked her by responding much the same as Carlee's, with tightening nipples and moisture-seeping excitement. The canopy of overhead tree limbs kept her shrouded in the dim, quiet woods, making her confident she wouldn't be seen.

Fascinated by their scene, and her growing arousal, she watched him strike her butt again then run one finger over the puffy welt it left behind.

"Very pretty, Carlee. I love how easily your skin marks." He slid his finger between her buttocks and stroked her slit. "And how you respond to the pain."

Carlee jerked against that teasing finger and Alena's own sheath spasmed. When he reached around and pinched her nipple, a low moan slid past Carlee's compressed lips and her hands clenched above her. Alena could recall only too clearly her two spankings, and her response to them, most notable her startling arousal at the exposure and pain of the bare-bottomed one Nash administered.

So engrossed in her recollections and the couple she spied on, she never heard someone coming up behind her until a hard hand covered her mouth and a tall, solid body pressed against her back. A deep voice she recognized whispered in her ear, "You just won't give up, will you?" and her body responded with a surge of shuddering heat.

Randy sighed in frustration as his friend switched Carlee's breast next, catching her nipple and setting off her orgasm. "Bryan doesn't mind an audience, but he won't tolerate spying. Promise to keep quiet and I'll take my hand away. Give us away, and I won't be responsible for the action he'll demand."

When she nodded her head, he slid his hand down her neck and cupped one unfettered breast, her thin tee shirt leaving little to the imagination. Her stiff nipple beaded into an even tighter, pronounced nub when he rubbed it with his thumb.

"I… I didn't plan this," she whispered, finding it difficult to speak with his hand kneading her plump flesh, his thumb rasping over her nipple.

"And I'm supposed to believe that why?"

Bryan bent his head and sucked Carlee's abused nipple into his mouth. The way she laid her head back and moaned low and long gave every indication she enjoyed his suckling.

"Look, I was just hiking and happened upon them," Alena whispered with fierce determination to get herself under control. Unfortunately, Randy took that moment to slip his hand into her loose shorts and found her bare, damp crotch when he palmed her. His low, knowing chuckle reverberated through her as her hips thrust against his hand of their own accord.

Those callused fingers teased the soft flesh of her folds, light strokes meant to titillate and arouse. A tight pinch on her nipple forced her to bite down hard on her lower lip, the quick sharp pain responsible for another uncontrollable thrust of her hips into his palm.

"Maybe, but it seems you're very happy about this *chance* encounter. You like what you see, Alena?" He slid his middle finger past her slit and buried himself in her slick, wet heat. "Christ, what you can do to a man, girl." He pushed his jean-covered erection against her ass to let her know exactly what he meant.

"I... oh, good Lord," she breathed when he took a leisure exploration of her vagina and her channel convulsed around his finger, her body breaking out in a sweat. The press of his cock against her butt had her aching to feel that thick stalk invading her flesh, her clit swelling to almost painful proportions.

Randy shifted the arm wrapped around her waist down then under her shirt to glide his hand up her perspiration-damp waist and fill it with the soft, abundant flesh of her breast, her pointed nipple stabbing his palm. "You are so fucking soft everywhere, and so damn responsive. Do you know what a turn-on that is?"

She had never given much consideration to her abundant figure. Her fondness for everything related to a donut showed in her hips, breasts, and everything in between, as well as her thighs. Since she was comfortable in her own skin, she never tried to conform her figure into something that might draw more attention or men might find sexier. They either liked her the way she was or didn't.

The sweet rush of pleasure that consumed her at his remark was both surprising and unwelcome. Damn it, she *didn't* care if he, or his sexy, British friend, found her attractive or desirable.

"No, I don't, and don't care. Please, *do* something… more," she pleaded when he kept his finger thrusts light and shallow, avoiding all contact with her pleasure button. Right now, that small piece of flesh throbbed with need so intense, it left her shaken. It didn't help when Bryan took that moment to drop his switch, release his raging erection and palm Carlee's buttocks to lift her onto it.

"Hold tight, baby," the big man demanded right before he slammed her down on him, her legs going around his hips to grip him in a tight vise with her feet crossed behind him.

"You could be a lot of fun under different circumstances," Randy whispered in her ear right before he released her breast and covered her mouth again. Her lush body jerked in his arms as he finger-fucked her with hard, deep plunging strokes, rasping over and over her clit until she whimpered behind his hand and her hands clutched his arm with a tight, nail-digging grip. With her hips thrusting against his marauding hand, he whispered in a voice harsh with suppressed need, "Now, Alena. Come for me."

Alena screamed behind his hand as he finally took her swollen bundle of nerves between his fingers and milked the aching piece of flesh until she creamed all over his hand. Consumed with pleasure brought on by days of frustration, teasing, new-to-her painful stimulants, and unwanted attraction to not one, but two men who were so not her type, she basked in the multitude of euphoric sensations sweeping her body and consuming her mind until she finally sagged liked a limp noodle in his arms.

She didn't rouse until Bryan's shout of release erupted right before Randy whispered, "We need to go."

CHAPTER FIVE

"I really didn't intend to go snooping." Alena spoke to Randy's back as he led her back down the trail she had unknowingly followed right to the Hirst property. The tight clasp of his large hand around hers seemed to aid in keeping the small tremors from her climax still going. She hadn't come like that in… well, never. Was it any wonder she couldn't get her befuddled mind to concentrate and or that her happy places still pulsed with lingering pleasure? Now she just had to decide if it was the erotic scene she'd witnessed or the man responsible for her uncharacteristic response.

"Uh huh," came his skeptical reply without turning his black-haired head.

Rolling her eyes, she tried again. "You know, I'm not from around here. How am I supposed to know where these trails lead? I don't know why you don't believe me." She knew that would get a response from him and when he slowed and swiveled to face her with a silent quirk of one dark brow, she flipped him a sassy grin and returned his sardonic brow lift with one of her own.

"You must be one of those women who likes to gab after sex."

"It's better than the silent treatment."

He left her glaring at his back again as he picked up the pace. The aromatic scent of pine and the sound of the lake splashing along its shores somewhere off to their left didn't soothe her overstimulated body like fifteen minutes in a sauna would or distract her like jostling through a New York crowded street resonating with honking cab drivers and grumblings from irritated pedestrians in a hurry.

Trying a different tactic, she asked, "Is that what goes on at those parties, like the one Ashley was seen at? You tie women up and beat on them to get your rocks off?"

He stopped and pivoted so abruptly she almost ran into him, and coming into direct contact with that muscle-packed body again wouldn't help her still tingling senses. "From what I saw and heard, Bryan wasn't the only one to get off. Did Carlee look like she was being abused?"

She didn't have to think about it to give him an honest answer. "No, but I don't think I'd go for the switch. Those welts looked like they really hurt."

"To each his own. Some get off on administering and receiving the harsher pain; others, like you, enjoy milder painful stimulation. Which one of the good townsfolk you've been talking to told you I attend Bryan's parties?"

"I don't want to get anyone in trouble."

His bark of laughter echoed around them as those obsidian eyes warmed with mirth. "Baby, small towns thrive on gossip. It would be pointless to get upset over it, or to try to keep something like the Hirst's occasional sex party secret. I figure it was either Carlee or Cora Sue."

Because she didn't like the way her skin rose in goosebumps from the sound of his deep laugh, the light in his eyes, and the way he called her baby in that slow drawl, she attempted to turn the tables around as they emerged from the woods and made their way toward where he had parked next to her car in the marina parking lot.

"Carlee invited me to the one he's throwing next week. I'm going to see if I can get Kevin to tell me something he may not have told the Portland PD."

Randy swore under his breath before pinning her against her car, his humor replaced with irritation at her dogged insistence. "No, you're not. I told you, stay out of it. There're things in play you could jeopardize."

"Like what?"

"None of your business. Stay. Out. Of. It."

Taking a shot in the dark, she guessed, "Like Nash isn't just a friend? He's a cop too, isn't he?"

Her wild, accurate guess forced Randy to consider his options. It was obvious she wasn't going to quit snooping, and if they didn't keep her under control, she could make a comment like that to the wrong person. They couldn't risk Bryan or Kevin becoming suspicious of Nash's true reason for being here or they'd clam up before he had a chance to talk with both of them. He still didn't think either of them was involved, but given Bryan's overprotectiveness and penchant for bailing Kevin out of trouble, he didn't doubt he, or both of them, would hold back a crucial piece of information that could lead them to Ashley's whereabouts or hint at what happened to her if it reflected badly on either of them.

"You're not going to quit, are you?" he asked her point blank.

"I want to find my sister."

"You got a good idea of what happens at those parties, what might be expected of you if you attend. Bryan doesn't invite just anyone, only friends who enjoy BDSM or alternative sex, including voyeurism, exhibitionism, and the use of restraints. You'd really agree to some or all of that?"

"Yes," she returned fiercely, without hesitation. "I'd do anything, anyone, to find Ashley."

Her answer surprised him as well as her. While she and Ash had never been close, their tenuous relationship more a pain in the ass than a blessing the past ten years, Alena cared about her and ached with worry over what could have befallen her. The not knowing was the worst and she prayed her irresponsible sister wasn't suffering.

"Meet me and Nash at the diner at seven o'clock."

"Why?"

"Because it's meatloaf night. Don't be late."

She watched him with a frown as he got in his vehicle and drove away without further explanation. Hoping that olive branch meant he'd bring her in on what they had going, she started imagining scenes between her and one or both of the guys at a party. When it didn't bother her to picture herself sandwiched between them with others looking on, she had to wonder if she had always harbored a perverted streak or if she just needed the diversion of something different to take her mind off of Ashley.

Returning to her boat rental, she skipped down to the small living quarters, stripped, and squeezed into the compact shower. Letting the warm water soothe her aching muscles from the long trek and body-exhausting climax, she speculated on what Randy wanted to discuss with her. His last look had conveyed both irritation and resignation. He may not like her interference, but he was also attracted to her, which was working in her favor so far. She had to admit, having both men wanting her gave her a heady ego boost. She liked sex as much as any woman her age, but had never craved it the way she had since first setting eyes on those two, and she had never been fortunate enough to enjoy two men desiring her at the same time. They might not like their attraction any more than she liked hers to them, but if they could use it to their advantage to get a clue to her sister's disappearance, why not kill two birds with one stone? At least, that's what she hoped they were thinking.

Turning off the shower, she wrung out her hair, contemplating the lengths she told Randy she would be willing to go to find Ashley. She meant what she'd said, but how much, and to what extent she would go still surprised her. Her attraction to both Randy and Nash made those lengths easier to accept, but they were still beyond anything she had ever done sexually or even considered doing.

She hadn't wanted to step into her mother's shoes when she couldn't cope after her father's death, had been too young to be both older sister and parent to a rebellious preteen and an even more disruptive teen. Every time one of Ashley's stunts had pulled her away from her efforts to get through college, she had resented the hell out of both her and their mother.

But there had been good times between them. One time one of her mother's more lucid periods had happened to coincide with one of Ashley's good spells and Alena had taken advantage of the lull in their constant drama to convince them to take a long weekend with her. It had been fall and they had taken a scenic drive up the coast, stayed in a few historic B & B's and ate freshly caught seafood. Their ceasefire hadn't lasted long, but those few days of fun and peace with her dysfunctional family kept her hopes up they could salvage something of their tenuous relationships.

From her mother's hysterical reaction when Alena finally broke the news to her about Ash's disappearance, followed by worrisome silence since, she feared she'd never get the chance to have anything worth continuing to strive for with either of them. But that didn't bear thinking about right now. She still believed Ash either had taken her self-absorption to a new level or she had gotten herself into another bind she needed help extracting herself from. Which only added to the urgency of finding her that continued to plague her.

• • • • • • •

A few hours later, Alena entered the diner and spotted Randy and Nash seated at a table instead of a booth. Taking note of the crowd, she surmised they had been lucky to get it. Heads turned as she wandered their way and she returned the librarian Maxine's wave and replied to Bill from the marina when she passed his table and he tossed out a casual, "Evening, Alena."

"Hey, Bill." She returned his smile, glad she had the foresight to pay cash for everything once she decided she would have better luck getting answers if she kept her relation to Ashley to herself.

Ignoring the tightening of her abdomen and the warm flush creeping up her neck and over her face at the intense, heated looks from both men, she sat on the chair Nash had pushed out for her. Before she could say anything, her stomach took that moment to rumble in loud protest of having had nothing but pastries today.

"We better let her eat before we talk," Nash told Randy, but kept his eyes on Alena's blushing face.

"I can eat and talk at the same time." To prove it, she reached for a warm roll in a basket sitting in the middle of the table. Taking a moment to slather butter on the soft bread, she took a big bite and closed her eyes as she chewed, moaning from the fresh baked taste. "Oh, good Lord, that's good."

Nash and Randy exchanged a look, silently agreeing they found her enjoyment of the roll damn arousing before Nash warned her with good humor, "Careful, luv, or we'll be skipping the talking and moving right into the demonstrating."

"Demonstrating what?" Though her active imagination immediately conjured up multiple ideas, she preferred hearing the details from them.

Randy chose to ignore her question for now. "You've put us in a difficult position, Alena. Which forced me to put a call in to your supervisor." At her scowl, he held up his hand to forestall the complaint he saw brewing in her eyes. "You're the one who insisted on being brought in on what we're doing so I had to be sure you're able to keep details of an investigation quiet. Deal with it."

Alena sighed, fought back her irritation, and admitted he was right. "Okay, you did what you had to do. I'm sure Captain Price vouched for me."

"He did, which is why we'll tell you Nash is from

Scotland Yard checking out the fact Kevin Hirst and his two closest friends, Brad and Joel, were in London last year when the body of a missing college student was pulled from the Thames."

When her face paled, Nash rushed to reassure her. "That doesn't mean Ashley's met the same fate, it only means it's a coincidence we both feel needs to be considered. And in order to do that thoroughly, my real reason for being here has to be kept quiet. I'm Randy's friend, period. Got it?"

She had never seen such a hard look on English's face before—on the sheriff's, yes, but not Nash's. That alone told her how serious they were. Hearing about the other girl only reinforced her determination to find her sister, and she'd keep their secret and take whatever they dished out if it meant getting something to go on.

"Got it. So, I can go with you next weekend to their party? Will all three of them be there?"

They did that silent exchange again, and she reluctantly fought back her irritation once more as she waited for them to answer. Carlee's approach in time to hear her request meant she didn't have to wait long.

"Oh, do bring her," she encouraged with a twinkle in her eyes and a knowing smirk. "That'll add to the tongues already wagging about the three of you since you've been spotted together multiple times now."

"Just take our order, Carlee, and quit listening to rumors."

"Randy, you know we all thrive on gossip around here. Now, I already know you want my meatloaf. How about you two?"

They waited until she left with their triple order of the special before Nash said, "For once, those rumors might work in our favor. From the little I know about your friend, Bryan's pretty particular about who he lets attend his gatherings."

"Yeah, and even more so in the last few months."

"Since Ashley was there."

Randy nodded, his eyes compassionate as they rested on her face. "Yes. So, to ensure you don't stand out like a sore thumb, or in this case, an alternative sex virgin, we'll go to my house after dinner and see if you can pass a demonstration of what you can expect."

If her traitorous body responded with half the enthusiasm as before with these two, Alena had no doubt she would ace whatever test they had planned for her.

By the time their food arrived, her hunger pangs had taken a back seat to the combined nervous/sexual tension now tightening her stomach. After eating her salad and another roll, she knew she wouldn't be able to swallow another bite.

"I think I'll get the rest of this to go. My appetite seems to have deserted me." No sense beating around the bush; those two knew exactly why she couldn't eat any more.

"Good idea. I'll meet you two out front after I pay up and get your leftovers."

Nash didn't give her a chance to protest Randy's decision when he stood and took her arm in a light, but unbreakable clasp. "Come along, luv, and don't argue."

"Is that all you two can say, don't argue?"

"No, you'll probably be hearing don't come before long." Oh, Nash really did like the fire in her green eyes. Made him wish he'd be the one wielding the belt shortly instead of the scene he and Randy had already planned.

"Seriously?" she gasped, wondering how on earth she'd be able to follow that order. "And if I do?"

"Well, then," he replied with an amiable smile as he held her car door open for her, "we'll have to come up with an appropriate punishment. Follow us," he added before shutting her door and strolling to the police cruiser where Randy had just slid in behind the wheel.

Heart tripping with excitement, hands clammy with nerves, she worked to get both emotions under control as she followed them about a mile out of town to a cabin with an amazing lake view and neighbors close, but not too close.

After they ushered her inside, she didn't have time to do much more than note the wall-dominating stone fireplace and comfortable-looking leather sectional in front of it before she found herself drawn into Nash's arms and up against his rock-solid body. His mouth muffled her gasp of surprise but it took her just seconds to return his kiss and take a taste of him. Her low moan of surrender would have been humiliating if his lips hadn't felt so good moving against hers, his tongue so arousing as they stroked each other.

Just as her body grew pliant against his, she found herself loosened from his tight embrace, turned, and enveloped in another pair of arms that were just as strong in holding her against another ripped body. Randy kissed her with as much ruthless intensity as Nash, and her body responded with equal fervor to his taste. Before she was ready to be let go, he lifted his head to gaze down at her with glittering purpose in his midnight eyes.

"Tonight we'll see how well you obey us before taking the next step to agreeing to let you accompany us next week."

Okay, that's just wrong, she bemoaned when her happy places grew warm and tingly at that statement. Since when was she an 'obey' type of woman? If this kept up, by the time she returned home, she might be forced to seek psychological help.

"All right, what do you want me to do?"

Both men took one step back from her and crossed their arms, but it was Nash who ordered, "Remove your top and bra."

Was it the way they both watched her as she pulled her tee shirt over her head that was responsible for her shaking fingers, or the sharp-edged arousal already making itself known? With a quick flick of her fingers, her bra fell open and her breasts popped out, her nipples already beaded into puckered nubs that were close to being painful.

"Very good, Alena," Randy praised her as they each

cupped one full breast and just held her in their hands. "So soft and full here," they kneaded the fleshy tissue, "and so hard here." Two thumbs rasped her nipples once, twice, three times before they dropped their arms, taking the heat of their touch with them.

"You know when to keep quiet. That's another promising start. Remove your jeans," Nash instructed.

She could've told Nash the only reason she had kept her frustration to herself was because her need spiked so high she feared where more would lead her, but why squash his delusions? Kicking off her flip-flops, she loosened her jeans and wiggled out of both them and her panties, shoving the garments aside with a push of her foot. The cool air from the overhead fans did nothing to lessen the fiery spread of lust enveloping her from head to toe as she stood there and waited out their slow perusal of her complete nakedness.

Nash reached down and shocked her when he ran one finger over her waxed folds, the light caress eliciting a gush of moisture she prayed remained hidden. When both men grinned, their eyes fixated between her legs, she glanced down to see the glistening proof of what that one touch had done to her along the seam of her puffy folds.

"Well, what do you expect?" she snapped, refusing to be embarrassed over a very healthy reaction.

"Calm down, baby. We couldn't be more pleased." Randy's teasing look turned hard when he clasped her hand and led her to the thick, braided rug spread out in between the fireplace and sectional. With a tug, he instructed, "On your hands and knees, parallel to the hearth and sofa."

Okay, I like doggie style, she thought as she got into position, her body on board with everything so far. But when the guys pulled their shirts off then moved their hands to the waist of their pants and loosened them just enough to look even sexier, her mouth and throat went dry as dust. They were both broad shouldered, Randy's black pelt of chest hair narrowing down to a thin line over his six-pack abs to disappear inside his jeans, Nash's light sprinkling of dark brown curls making it easy for Alena to notice the tight pucker around his nipples. *Oh, good lord*, she groaned in silence as she admitted she was doomed to respond to whatever they did to her.

"Um, what…"

"Head to the floor and no talking," Randy interrupted as Nash pulled open the small drawer in the end table and retrieved the new butt plug they had picked up for her.

Before she could comment, Nash knelt behind her and Randy gave her yet another position to get into. "Clasp your hands behind your back, keep your face turned toward the sofa."

She struggled into position, shivering from the sheer decadence of the pose, her cheek pressed to the soft rug, her hands gripped together behind her. The awkward position and self-imposed restraint of her arms worked to enhance her arousal instead of diminishing it, another eye-opening revelation. Nash added to that feeling of lewdness when he knelt behind her upraised butt and pushed her thighs further apart. Cool air wafted over her exposed sheath, sending a shudder of heightened awareness and longing through her.

"Have you ever used a butt plug, anal vibrator, or probe?" Nash asked conversationally as he rubbed the greased round tip of a plug over her anus.

"No, just… *oh!*" The narrow end slid past her tight sphincter without fuss, but as he continued to push, the burn from the stretch of the wider part took her breath away.

"Just what?" Randy reached under her and slid one finger inside her damp pussy to tease her protruding clit with a few strokes aimed at diverting her attention and easing her tension.

"Just fingers." Her breath released on a whoosh when the plug went in as far as it could before the round base held it snugly in place. Between the unaccustomed, full sensation in her butt and the light touches grazing her clit, all her senses soared to high alert.

"Deep breath, luv."

"Damn it, English," she swore when he pumped the plug in and out in a few shallow dips right when she had gotten accustomed to its feel. A hard swat blistered her right buttock, diverting her attention with a different burn. "Okay, I get the point," she moaned when those little plunges set off small licks of pleasure along sensitive nerve endings she had been ignorant of until now.

"Good, then we can move on."

She bemoaned the removal of Randy's fingers until the guys shifted to where she could see them without straining her eyes anywhere but up. Watching Nash lower his zipper until his impressive cock sprang free and Randy removing his wide leather belt then folding it over with obvious purpose had saliva returning to pool in her mouth, forcing her to swallow with convulsive difficulty to keep from drooling. Keeping her mouth shut right then was the hardest thing she'd ever had to do, but Randy's low murmured praise of "Good girl" made her effort worthwhile. Something she'd have to think long and hard about later, much later as she eyed Nash taking a seat on the sofa in front of her and Randy stepping out of her sight.

The erotic vision of Nash sliding his hand up and down his long, thick cock in slow stimulation accompanied the snap of leather across her buttocks, the soft lash just enough to sting and set her pussy to tingling. She kept her eyes steady on Nash's stroking hand through the next swat, and the next. Her shoulders relaxed as the light snaps turned soothing, building a slow warmth across her buttocks. Nash palmed his seeping crown then spread the moisture down his ridged length, a tempting sight that had her salivating to take him in her mouth.

The next swat snagged her attention, the searing heat and pain it left behind zeroing straight between her legs. She bit her lip, concentrated on watching English masturbate, determined to not only prove to herself she wasn't a slave to her body's demands, but to show them she had what it took to accompany them to that party.

"I did warn you'd risk my belt if I caught you snooping again, Alena." Randy laid another, slightly harder stroke below the last one, pleased to see her slit creaming even more. It was always the most independent women who were the most sexually submissive, and despite the trouble she had caused him, she was proving to be a delight to take in hand. "Three more, then we can play."

She clenched her hands when he took aim at the under curve of her fleshy buttocks, gasping when the next one landed across the top of her thighs and cried out when he delivered the last slash across her ass again with a little more swing behind it. Dropping the belt, he released his cock and knelt behind her.

"Do you like watching Nash get himself off, Alena?" Another deep probe with his fingers into her slick heat accompanied his question.

Alena had trouble following his question and forming an answer as the throbbing burn covering her buttocks on down to her thighs had her sheath pulsing in heated response. Or was that from the deep strokes of his fingers inside her, the teasing glides over her aching clit, the soft press against her g-spot? The seeping proof of Nash's pleasure drew her tongue across her lips, made her ache to taste him as he gave her a warm smile and cupped his sac in his other palm. A hard swat right where the belt had landed caused her to jump and curse, but she managed to hold her position and her tongue.

"Answer me," Randy ordered.

"Make up your mind, either I can talk or I can't," she returned, letting her aroused frustration win this time. Another slap reignited the pain, but if he thought that was a deterrent, he wasn't as knowing as she had given him credit for.

"She's got a shit-eating smirk, mate," Nash drawled.

"Does she now?" Sheathing himself, Randy grabbed her

reddened buttocks and thrust into her wet heat. "Let's see if I can wipe it off. No coming, Alena, and no talking."

Crap, crap, crap. Once, just once she wanted to get the upper hand with these two. How was she supposed to keep from going off like a firecracker when each stroke lit up another fuse? The full sensation of having both orifices stretched and filled worked to spike her arousal despite the slight discomfort. She wanted to shut her eyes and bask in his hard possession and these new feelings, but then she'd miss seeing Nash bring himself to orgasm, so she kept them open and took each pummeling thrust with a deep breath and building lust.

A soft cry slipped past her pinched lips as the small tremors leading up to a climax started to ripple around his thick erection, his thrusts increasing until he rammed into her over and over with such force her upper body slid back and forth. Her squashed nipples abraded on the carpet and sent shards of electric zings to her core, adding to the overwhelming buildup of pleasure. Then he used his thumbs to rub the tender spots left from his belt just as Nash erupted with a shout to spew his release into his pumping hand, the sensory overload forcing her to admit, "I can't…"

"Come, Alena," Randy demanded, wincing at the desperation his guttural tone revealed. The tight clasp of her pussy spasming around his dick proved to be too much and as her orgasm creamed his length, he let go with a low groan, the pleasure ricocheting throughout his body so intense he shook with it.

By the time his head cleared, Nash was cleaning himself up and Alena was breathing heavily and shaking from either the pleasure or dealing with what they had just subjected her to. Withdrawing from her snug warmth took effort, but Randy managed to do so and rid himself of his condom and her of the plug then leaned down to help her up. When she fell against him, he could feel her damp body shivering, her hot breath panting against his neck and the rapid beat of her heart against his. Glancing over her red head, he returned Nash's nod then picked her up and sat on the sofa with her in his lap.

"You were wonderful, Alena. We're both proud of you." He kissed his way down her cheek as she lay pressed against his chest, nibbled the soft skin between neck and shoulder and stroked his palm down her chest, her waist, around her hips, down her thigh then took his time retracing his path. Her knees were bent, tucked against his side, shielding her pretty, plump folds. He'd give her that privacy this time since she was new to their demands, but only this time. "I love your body. You're so soft," he squeezed her breast, "so warm," he rubbed her waist, "and so fucking responsive," he kneaded her buttock.

The renewal of discomfort left from the lash of his belt roused her the final stage and Alena opened her eyes to see Nash striding down the hall. She wanted to call him back, couldn't believe how much she wanted him to stay and hold her too. Her orgasm had been so intense she could still feel her sheath contracting with the lingering pleasure. She had never come like that before, never dreamed that much pleasure was possible. This past hour with them had put all her other encounters to shame, and only one of them had fucked her. What on earth would happen when they both took over her body at the same time?

After her off-the-charts climax, she found Randy's embrace comforting, his hard thighs beneath her sore buttocks and his chest hair tickling her still sensitive nipples stirring, and his deep voice speaking such nice words to her soothing. But she needed time to herself to get her bearings. As she pushed up, he surprised her by loosening his arms right away.

"I need to go."

"Okay. I'll follow you back to the marina."

"I'm fine, I don't need…"

"I said I'm following you. Deal with it."

He didn't raise his voice, or even look stern, but his

insistence came through loud and clear nonetheless. "Fine. Mind if I use your restroom first?"

Tugging on her hair, he smiled and pointed down the short hall. "First door on the left."

Alena picked up her clothes and slipped into the bathroom to get herself together. If only that was as easy as putting her clothes back on. "Ashley, what have you gotten me into?" she whispered aloud, worrying where all this would end.

CHAPTER SIX

Randy parked in front of Bryan's lake house wishing he could've brought Nash along for this chat. The Brit had been a cop as long as he had and he could use another opinion that wouldn't be swayed by friendship. Kevin's compact SUV sat next to Bryan's BMW in front of the detached garage behind the house. Anxious to get this over with, he rapped on the front door, relieved he didn't hear anything he'd be interrupting.

"Hey, Sheriff. What brings you out here today?" Kevin asked, holding the door open to invite him in. At least he wasn't balking at having him show up unannounced, Randy thought, putting a positive spin on this visit already.

"Kevin, it's good to see you. Sorry to intrude," he added when he followed Kevin into the great room and saw Joel, Brad, and Bryan gathered around the kitchen table. "I hate to keep bringing this back to you, but I told Portland PD I'd speak with you when I saw you again, and see if you, any of you, remembered anything else about the night Ashley Malloy came out here during spring break."

Damn it, he swore. Kevin and Bryan exchanged a swift, conspiratorial look and the other two boys shifted their eyes away before Bryan responded in a bland tone. "I have nothing else. Kev, Brad, Joel, can you think of anything you might've missed telling the police when they questioned you?"

"No, sorry, Sheriff. We met up with Ashley at The Well and she was the only one of her friends who came back here with us. It was just us and, who else was here that night, Bryan? Other than Carlee?" Kevin asked.

Randy could tell Bryan didn't like how his brother turned the questioning back on him but he hid his irritation well. If Randy hadn't known him so well, he never would've noticed the slight tic in his clenched jaw.

"Just two other couples. You already questioned them, Randy."

"Yes. After seeing her come in with the guys, they spent the next few hours upstairs, so they didn't see her leave. Okay. But, if you think of anything, even if you don't think it's significant, give me a call. You never know where something she said or did might lead us. Appreciate your time."

"You and Nash coming Saturday?' Bryan asked as he walked out with him. "I'm expecting all of the regulars and will have the grill fired up."

"That's our plan. Might bring a friend, we don't know yet."

"Anyone I know?"

Randy understood his frown and his concern over bringing someone new, especially after Ashley's disappearance. Maybe he'd read too much into their discomfited looks. Bryan had always been a stickler about who he allowed to attend his parties, inviting only close friends and making sure anyone they brought were seasoned in the lifestyle.

"No, unless you've seen her around town. Curvy redhead who's vacationing here for a few weeks. We've hooked up and, let's just say we won't ask her if we don't think she'll fit in, but from the few times we've been together, I think she'll like what she sees, and whatever we do." He'd know for sure when they tested Alena's response to an audience.

"I think I have spotted her. Wouldn't mind seeing more of that body myself. You know the score better than anyone. Bring her along if she's agreeable."

Randy pulled away with a sick feeling tightening his gut. Even though he struggled to admit the man he had known for over ten years could be complicit in the disappearance of a young girl, he couldn't deny there was something Bryan intentionally held back from him. Kevin didn't surprise him as he and his sidekicks had been in and out of scrapes since they were twelve. But could they really have had a hand in whatever had befallen Ashley, or did they just fear getting blamed for making a bad decision that led to her disappearance? Whatever it was, they were banding together to keep it from him and without proof, or something other than his gut feeling and a few questionable looks no one else would've thought anything of, he was still at a dead end.

A mile before reaching Blue Springs city limit, he pulled off the main road into the parking lot of The Well, not ready to return to his office and make a fruitless call to Portland. The only bar within a fifty-mile radius, The Well did a good business all week during the summer peak season, and kept busy on weekends during the off season. He spent a fair amount of time here himself, both as a patron and as law enforcement when things got out of hand, which was often during spring break and long holiday weekends. Today, however, there were only a few cars in the lot, which suited his need for a stiff drink and a moment to himself to go over his options.

"Sheriff, how are you?" Zachary, ex-marine turned tattooed biker/bar owner asked as Randy took a seat at the long, beat-up bar counter. It was nice to be greeted by name everywhere he went, he pondered, something he knew Nash was still getting used to.

"I'm good, Zach, but I'll be better after a cold one."

"Bad day, huh?" He popped the cap off a bottle and slid

it right into Randy's open hand.

"Let's just say I've had better." He took a long swallow, not surprised the bartender knew he didn't make a habit of drinking while on the clock. Sometimes, he found it necessary to bend the rules.

"I'll leave you to it then."

Grateful for Zach's ability to read his customers well, he saluted him with the bottle then took another long draw. His thoughts turned to Bryan's upcoming party, and Alena. Her response to them still had the power to move him. Just recalling the tight feel of her slick channel milking his cock had him shifting with uncomfortable arousal. But it was the way she had snuggled on his lap afterward that got to him the most. He never would have imagined a woman of her fire and independence succumbing that quickly to the need to be held after a new experience had stripped her of her control.

Taking a wild guess, he would bet she had never come that hard, never pictured herself getting off on the harsher pain of leather and the helplessness of the position he had instructed her into. But, fuck, what a turn-on her responses had been. A week ago he wouldn't have even considered wishing she'd stay longer, now he couldn't quit thinking about it. *That woman's fucked with me ever since she walked into my office*, he groused, disgusted with the weakness he seemed to have for her, a growing soft spot he knew Nash struggled with also.

"There a reason you're in here drinking alone while on duty, chap?"

With a rueful laugh, Randy swiveled to face Nash as he took the stool next to him. "I was just thinking of you."

"That right?" Signaling the bartender, he called down, "I'll take a pint of your darkest brew, mate." Ignoring the gruff man's muttering, he turned again to his friend. "Your thoughts have anything to do with your visit to the Hirsts, or are they centered around our girl?"

"Both. Bryan and Kevin know something. Whether it's

relevant, or could lead us anywhere, I don't know, but there's something they're both reluctant to reveal. And that just pisses me off."

Nash suspected he was more put out because of his close friendship with the elder Hirst, but kept that opinion to himself. Besides, he'd rather talk about Alena, and what their next step would be concerning her involvement. Watching her take the plug and her response to the double penetration when Randy had fucked her had driven his own orgasm higher. Combined with the way she'd kept her expressive green eyes glued to his cock as he'd fisted himself to climax, he'd had no choice but to erupt in intense pleasure. Those eyes had glazed over with her orgasm seconds later, and his pleasure had shot up another notch watching her come apart under his friend's vigorous assault.

Her acceptance and responses boded well for her to accompany them to Bryan's next gathering, but what she was willing to do in private might not be the same when others were around. They'd have to test that first, something he looked forward to doing soon.

"So, what're our choices? Because I gotta tell you, partner, I'm not leaving here without answers. I have the body of an eighteen-year-old girl strangled to death and a coroner's report outlining abuse of beating and repeated autoerotic asphyxiation haunting me. I owe her and her family answers."

"I hear you," Randy sighed. "Think Alena knows the dismal odds of finding Ashley alive?"

"Given her profession, yes. But given the relationship, she's not anywhere close to admitting the very real likelihood. If we bring her along this weekend, one of us might be able to slip away to do a little snooping."

"Inadmissible if we find anything, even if it leads us in the right direction."

"True," Nash agreed. "But who says we have to tell anyone we found a lead? Bollocks to anyone who questions how we come across whatever there is to find." He respected the laws of both countries, but the tortured look in the dead eyes of Lisa Ames had left him no choice but to do what he had to do to get justice for her.

"First we have to make sure our girl is as up to indulging in public as she was in private."

"I have a plan for that. Let's order another and I'll fill you in."

• • • • • • •

Alena spent the next two days playing tourist and shopping the quaint one-of-a-kind shops as she tried to reconcile her responses to both men the other night and decide what lengths she'd be willing to go to to find answers concerning Ashley's disappearance. She'd told Randy she would do anything to find her sister, and she meant it, but sometimes reality had a way of coming back to bite you on the ass. Of course, if he or Nash were to bite her back there, she seriously doubted she would mind. It'd be futile to deny the way her body came alive under their hard hands and kinky demands. She wasn't a prude, but she'd never imagined herself getting off on spankings or relishing the attention and touches from two men. Nine times out of ten, fantasies were more exciting if left unfulfilled. Not so with those two.

Leaving a small boutique with a new bathing suit that caught her eye from the display window, she glanced up and down Main Street, trying to decide where to go next. She had already spent a few hours in the library on their computer, skyping with friends and coworkers. Damn, but she missed hanging out with all of them, enjoying a drink after work with her coworkers at the local cop hangout or hitting her favorite sushi bar with a group of friends. This place was just too quiet, too peaceful, for her preferences. She thrived on crowds, hustle and bustle, noise, and a variety of entertainment options. Being out on the lake on her small houseboat did relax her and she enjoyed the scenery and people, but she definitely wasn't into sitting idly all afternoon with a pole in the water. She preferred her fish baked, all gross stuff already removed. Swimming invigorated her, but that was the extent of her water sports activities. Snapping photos of the limitless scenic views she had discovered floating around the lake had turned out to be a pleasant diversion, and she had even taken to clicking quick shots around the small, close-knit town.

Without too many more options, she popped into the bakery, picked up two glazed caramel twists that had just come out of the oven, and savored the first one as she strolled down to the beauty shop to treat herself to a manicure, waving to people she recognized along the way. The afternoon was warming up nicely, so maybe she would spend it sunbathing, something she couldn't do in New York due to a lack of private outdoor space at her downtown apartment. Funny how privacy didn't concern her around here. Maybe these laidback people were rubbing off on her more than she thought. Or maybe it was just two of them who had her daydreaming about some outdoor activities that had nothing to do with getting a tan.

"Welcome back, Alena," Cora Sue greeted her as soon as she walked in, licking her fingers from icing as she swallowed her last warm bite of sugar-laden decadence. "Why aren't you out enjoying our pretty lake this afternoon?"

"I intend to after a manicure," she responded, glad Cora didn't seem to be too busy. "Do you have time now?"

"Sure. Just let me ring up Maisy here."

Maisy appeared to be in her early to mid-forties and greeted Alena with a warm smile as she stepped up to the counter. "I've seen you with our sheriff and his friend, haven't I?" she asked with a shrewd look in her eyes.

Resisting the urge to roll her eyes, Alena kept her reply as evasive as possible. "They're very friendly to visitors."

Both women laughed before Cora Sue smirked, "Yes, they are, but Randy doesn't make a habit of sitting down with visitors at the diner or carrying their grocery bags out for them."

"Oh, good Lord," she muttered. "Please don't read anything more into their interest other than that of being friendly." God, she really couldn't wait to get back home where the only ones who knew her business were those she chose to tell. Blue Springs' gossip grapevine was worse than Facebook.

"Just you be careful." Maisy patted her arm. "Our sheriff's a great guy, and that Brit is a handsome, friendly fellow, but they've been known to party at that Hirst lake house, and well, I know Cora Sue here's told you what goes on at those parties." With a twinkle in her eyes, she glanced askance at the beautician, adding, "Most likely she's spoken from having seen them there herself, isn't that right, Cora Sue?"

"Hey, I'm a single, healthy adult. Nothing wrong with getting a little crazy now and then. You and Ron ought to try spicing things up a bit once in a while. Come this way, Alena, let's get you done so you can enjoy that new swimsuit I see peeking out of your bag. It's going to be a warm afternoon."

"Nice to meet you, Maisy," Alena tossed back as she followed Cora. Taking a seat behind the small table, her curiosity got the better of her. "Is everyone around here okay with the sex parties held at that place?"

Picking up her right hand, Cora gave her a rueful smile. "Oh, there're a few older folks who mostly ignore the rumors. Those of us who have gone to one or two make it known everything is safe and consensual, and kept private as long as no one ventures onto his private property. Honestly, they've been going on so long, we don't think anything of them, and if an out-of-towner happens to hear or see something that shocks them, we all band together to dispel any negative feedback. There have been more than a few who've been interested, such as you."

Alena grinned at the comic wiggle of her eyebrows. "I'm

from New York, remember? I don't shock easily." She was tempted to bring up Ashley again, but she promised the guys she'd stand back for now.

"No, I could tell that right away. Soak your fingers in here for a minute while we pick a color." Cora pushed her hand into a small bowl of sudsy water. "Maybe, if you're lucky, you'll get invited to the next one."

That's what I'm counting on. Alena kept that to herself. The last thing she needed was any more rumors and speculation about the three of them wagging around town. She just hoped the guys wouldn't make her wait much longer before letting her know what their plan was. She only had two weeks left before she had to get back to work and she didn't want to return home empty-handed.

An hour later, her wish was granted when her cell phone buzzed just as she returned to the marina and jumped aboard her compact, floating hotel room. They had both programmed their names and numbers in, and her heart took a sudden leap at seeing Nash's pop up.

"Hello," she answered, wincing at the breathless sound of her voice.

"Hello, luv. We'll meet you at the pier at Hirst's private dock in about an hour to discuss this weekend."

She liked how he got right to the point as much as she liked the way he called her love in that sexy accent continued to fire her up on all cylinders. "You mean the same place where Randy threatened to lock me up if he caught me moored there again? That place?"

His throaty chuckle had her nipples peaking and her hand tightening on the phone.

"Yes, that place. See you soon."

Almost giddy with anticipation over what they might have planned that would bring her one step closer to her goal, she went below and changed into her black bikini, not above tempting them into giving her what she wanted. Then she took the multiuse, semi-sheer swim cover-up in a vivid splash of floral colors and wrapped it around her hips, leaving one end to hang down her right leg. No sense in making them work for what she wanted to give to them, she mused, especially if it would get her closer to Kevin Hirst and possible answers.

Taking the boat out, she floated once she reached the middle of the lake. Lounging on a small chaise, she read to kill time, waving to a few people she had come to recognize as they sailed by or hailed from the shore. The afternoon really had turned out warm, the light breeze just enough to keep from getting uncomfortably hot. Having fair skin to go along with her red hair, she had applied a generous amount of sunscreen and had given herself twenty minutes to lounge before moving on to their meeting spot.

Thirty minutes later, warm and relaxed, she maneuvered up to the dock just as the guys pulled up. It was a good thing she had already decided to go with this strange fascination she seemed to have developed for both of those men and ride it out until she left. The way her happy parts grew warm and tingly every time they showed up told her she'd be fighting a losing battle if she didn't admit she wanted them almost as much as she wanted answers about her sister's whereabouts. Still, that didn't mean she would let them walk all over her.

"Why is it okay for me to be here when you order me to and not when I want to be?" she asked, placing her hands on her hips as they stepped aboard and came toward her with those identical looks on their faces that sent heat rushing through her veins to pool between her legs. She got more turned on from one look from them than she did during an entire session with her vibrator, which was both exciting and disconcerting.

"Because we're the boss."

Narrowing her eyes at Randy, she ignored the ridiculous little thrill those four succinct words elicited. "Only because you've left me no choice. It's either jail, cooperate, or go home with no answers."

Nash did love the way those green eyes spit fire at them.

All that lotioned, sweat-slick skin had his fingers itching to touch her. "So," he asked, stepping right up to her, "will you cooperate to get what you want?"

"I thought I already proved I would the other night. What's this next test you mentioned?" And did they intend to put her through it now, here? She cast a hasty look around the quiet shore, then her eyes widened when she caught sight of Bryan and Carlee exiting the side door of his house and moving to the large grill sitting on the small patio. A younger version of Bryan who had to be his brother, Kevin, joined them. Her suspicions went haywire when she turned back around and the two of them shuffled close enough to crowd her against the rail.

"Did you really mean it when you said you'd do anything to go with us next Saturday?" Randy drew her against him, his body as warm as his whispered breath against her ear. "Think long and hard before you answer this time."

He took her mouth in a no-holds-barred kiss that had her toes curling into the deck, the feel of Nash's hard body pressing behind her adding to the immediate sensory overload that set her heart tripping over itself in excitement. Yes, she meant it, but it sure helped that she wanted these guys with every fiber of her being. Clutching his bulging biceps, she moaned into his mouth, her tongue dueling with his until he bit it, causing her to pull back and glare at him even though that small bite of pain egged on her arousal.

Before she could complain, Nash spun her around, his mouth taking over, his tongue soothing the sting as his lips slid over hers with just enough pressure to elicit another soft moan from her. Damn, but they could kiss. Before she was ready for him to, he lifted his head, the look in his glittering blue eyes probing and intent.

"Prove it, Alena. Do what we say, here, now, knowing they'll see. Bryan's skeptical of allowing an unknown newcomer to come to his private party, even if Randy and I vouch for you. Are you willing to show him you're submissive enough to do as you're told, mind the rules, and keep quiet about what you might see and do there?"

Being sandwiched between the two of them, feeling the press of their clothed bodies against her bare skin, drew her answer a lot quicker, a lot easier than if they weren't touching her. "Yes."

Nash breathed a sigh of relief as he stripped her of the bright wrap around her hips while Randy loosened her swim top behind her neck. His cock throbbed with such painful insistence already, he feared he wouldn't be able to free himself safely from his zipper. The thin straps fell, followed by the minuscule cups that had held her generous breasts. She had the nicest rack he'd seen in a while and those berry nipples proved too tempting to ignore, even though he was veering off script by bending and drawing one into his mouth for a deep suctioning pull that had her gasping and clutching his shoulders to keep her balance. He fucking loved how responsive she was.

"Nash."

Randy's low, frustrated growl reminded him of their plan and he pulled up then released her nipple with a pop, both men eyeing her breast as it swayed and the pink tinge spreading across her face that had nothing to do with the sun. Clasping her shoulders, Nash spun her toward the rail and bent her over.

One minute Alena was enjoying the pleasant tugs on her nipple that elicited shivers up and down her spine, and the next the lake water shimmered below her as she found herself braced at the waist against the rail. With her hair tied up in the back, she could see them take up a position at her sides, the swaying of her dangling breasts when they pressed against her again adding to the ignominious position they maneuvered her into. With an abrupt yank, her bottoms were shoved down to pool between her feet and leave her buttocks vulnerable to the lake breeze, hot sun, and their hard hands.

She knew what they intended before the first dual, sharp smacks landed on her cheeks and she jerked against the stinging heat. Biting her lip, she refused to cry out, or look up to see if the Hirsts or Carlee were watching, or question why what should be humiliating was so damned arousing.

"There'll be more than three people watching this weekend," Nash warned her as they both slapped her again, her skin warming nicely under his hand, her slit already glistening with proof of her arousal. The restless shift of her hips drew a smile from both of them, her impatience a come-on they couldn't resist. "Think you'll be able to bend over like this in a room full of people who have an up-close seat to what we do to you? *Without* complaining," he added with the next smack that set those soft, round globes to jiggling.

With the now familiar burn spreading over her butt and her sheath pulsing in tune to the painful throbbing encompassing her entire backside, she had no choice but to gasp, "Yes!" in acceptance. The truth was, at this point she doubted she could deny them anything, anytime, anywhere. Which would have her balking if she wasn't in such dire need that increased with each blistering smack.

"Oh, good Lord," she moaned when they shifted their aims to belabor the tender skin of the under curves of her buttocks. The steady barrage of double swats became almost too much to take in. Receiving twice the heat and pain all at once tossed her into a spiraling downfall that both excited and scared her.

"I hope so, Alena, because if you screw up, you won't like the consequences."

Nash sent a significant look between her legs where the visible proof of her pleasure couldn't be missed, asking, "Are you sure of that, Randy?" as they delivered a couple of slaps on her thighs before palming her reddened flesh.

"With this one, I've never been sure of anything."

"I'm right here." Swiveling her head around, she glared at Randy. "And I've been good these past few days."

"Yes, you have, luv." Squeezing her red buttock, Nash grinned at her yelp and futile attempt to jerk her hips away from their hands. Pressing her soft flesh in a hard pinch, he taunted her with "Tsk, tsk," then let Randy help her rise as he took care freeing his raging erection.

For two days, he had been walking around semi-hard, the vivid picture of her kneeling with her face pressed to the floor, eyes glued to his fisted hand around his cock as his partner plowed her from behind leaving him aching for his turn. Palming his thick girth, he squeezed his dick too hard for comfort in an effort to get himself under control. Unfortunately, with Alena facing him in all of her glorious nudity, held secure against Randy's chest with an arm wrapped just under her lush breasts, not even that discomfort could lessen his tormenting need.

"You've got a body made for fucking, but I suspect you've heard that enough you already know it." The surprise on her face took him unawares. Surely men had told her how desirable she was?

"No, that line's a first for me. But since I'm a sure thing, it was unnecessary." She didn't need empty compliments from men, especially men she wouldn't see again after another two weeks. She'd had plenty of rejections, no doubt, but there were enough men who weren't picky about body shapes to keep her happy as well as her bedside buddy. Although, as she struggled not to drool over Nash's cock, hard and seeping with its readiness to fuck, she knew she would never reach the heights these two could take her on her own.

"It's not a line. Neither of us need to toss out platitudes to get what we want. You should know that."

Randy's growled admonishment accompanied a sharp bite on the sensitive spot where her neck met her shoulder.

"Okay, fine, just... *please*." She all but whimpered when he added a pinch to her right nipple to go with the little throb in her shoulder. Then her mind became completely frazzled when he lifted her right leg under the knee and pushed her thigh out to the side, the move parting her bare folds and affording Nash an excellent glimpse of her wet pink channel.

"You want him, Alena? Look over."

Randy's demand came with a nudge under her chin, and she saw Bryan, Kevin, and Carlee sitting at a picnic table, burgers in hands and their avid gazes on the three of them. "I…"

"Right here, right now. Yes or no?"

Between that low, gravelly voiced demand, her hot, throbbing buttocks, the titillating decadence of outdoor exposure, and the lust reflected in Nash's eyes, there could be only one answer. "Yes."

Nash almost crumpled from relief as he sheathed himself and stepped between her legs. "Clasp your hands behind your neck," he ordered as he slid two fingers inside her gaping pussy. Finding her soaking didn't surprise him, but the quick, tight clench of those slick walls around his fingers did. Between the tiny contractions pulling at him and the glazed look in her eyes, he suspected she could explode in climax with just the lightest touch in the right place.

"Good girl," he praised her when she obeyed without comment. With her arms raised and elbows bent, her breasts were lifted in prominent display, the pebble-hard nipples pointing in blatant need toward him.

He and Randy had talked this scene through, and with a nod at his friend, Nash reached behind her and gripped her still warm buttocks, spreading them for the invasion of Randy's fingers first. He chuckled when she closed her eyes on a low groan.

"Like that, do you?"

"Damn it," she snapped, her eyes flying open again to glare up at his smug face. "Can't we get on with it?" Those two thick fingers invading her anus stroked slow and deep until her dark channel burned and throbbed as much as her pussy and her butt, the three erogenous zones pulsing with such need, it turned her lightheaded.

Nash shifted enough to land a blistering swat on her labia and exposed clit, the slap echoing around them as loud as her startled cry. "Forget who's in charge already?"

"That would be impossible." It took supreme effort on her part to get herself under control, her spiraling need coiling that much tighter, that much higher with another painful incitement.

"Is this what you want?" He slid into her one slow inch at a time, torturing them both with his slow entry. When she struggled in his tight hold of her ass, he gave her buttocks a hard squeeze, another reminder to behave.

"Ow! Don't I get credit for keeping my arms in place?" Sheesh, these guys were strict, and why did that increase her excitement instead of dampening it?

"Of course you do, baby." Randy's whisper in her ear set off a shiver of goosebumps down her body as he nipped then licked her lobe. "Here's your reward."

He lifted her right leg even higher, pulled her thigh out even further, then Nash followed with several fast, deep plunges.

"*Yes*," she cried out, and would have been mortified over her exuberant, loud response if his strategic aims didn't have her coming undone with the sweetest explosion of ecstasy she'd ever experienced.

Between the thick rod ploughing her sheath and the deep, thrusting invasion into her back hole, the tight clench of large hands on her buttocks, and being sandwiched between the two of them, what choice did she have but to let go and follow where they led her?

CHAPTER SEVEN

By the time Alena came down from the incredible high of her climax, Nash had already adjusted his pants. Randy removed his fingers from her ass, his arm now a steel band around her waist, his denim-covered cock still pressing with scratchy insistence against her buttocks. Standing naked between two fully clothed men added to her heady aura, turned her on in a way she'd never been before. A quick glance toward the shore revealed her audience still watched and what she could detect of their looks from this distance, they were in no hurry to return inside the house. Between their voyeurism, Nash's smug look, and the hard press against Randy's body keeping her arousal simmering, the need to exert some control over the situation, if not herself, exerted itself.

Pulling out of Randy's embrace, she shocked them by grabbing the cushion off the lounge, tossing it at Randy's feet, and dropping to her knees before him. "Can't leave you hanging, now can we?" She smiled with teasing promise as she reached up and took her time undoing his jeans, taking care when she lowered the zipper over his thick bulge.

"No, I certainly wouldn't want that." It took every ounce of Randy's control to let her keep the lead, to hold back from clasping his hands on her bright red head and pushing his erection past those plump lips. The sparkle in her eyes drew a smile from him, the warm grip of her hand wrapping around his shaft forced an indrawn breath, and those soft lips closing around his cock head provoked a low groan.

He thought holding her for Nash to fuck had been difficult to endure, but her talented mouth and tongue were proving to be a bigger threat to maintaining his rigid control. A slow stroke with her moist tongue along the sensitive area just under the crown sent a lightning bolt of heat straight down his dick to set his balls aflame. With a suffering moan of surrender, he reached up and pulled off the band holding her hair back, tunneled his fingers through the long strands then tightened his hands on her skull.

"More, baby."

That deep, guttural demand excited Alena as much as having him in her mouth and knowing Nash and the others watched. Even so, she refused to relinquish complete control over the situation. Suckling his smooth crown, she reached behind him and shoved his jeans down far enough to grip his taut buttocks. Both globes clenched under her hands as he pushed past the tight clasp of her lips into her mouth. Swiping just once over his seeping slit, she took a slow, tongue-licking journey down his ridged root, taking her time lapping around his girth, stroking each thick, pulsing vein while taking as much of his length in her mouth as she could. When his tip bumped her throat, she breathed a sigh of relief as he loosened his hands and allowed her to pull back with ease.

Moaning around his shaft, she fed with ravenous intent as both of them battled for control of her movements. He tried to hold her head still, but her assault, as she intended, proved too much for him. She pulled up as soon as his grip eased, tormented his cap again with tantalizing sweeps of her tongue over and over his oozing slit until he all but shook before her and his low curses colored the air around them.

"Problem, mate?" Nash asked from behind her, his dry tone laced with amusement.

"Yeah, she's too fucking good at this and I'm not... *fuck*," he hissed when she took him deep again before releasing him and nibbling down his shaft until she could draw one testicle into the warm cavern of her damp mouth.

She wanted to laugh, but held back to feast on his balls, as that seemed to rev up his engine as much as sucking his cock. Kneading his buttocks had him quickening even more, and when she shifted her right hand between his cheeks to graze over his puckered back hole, another curse accompanied the drawing tightness of his sac.

Not yet ready to give him what he wanted, she took his cock deep again, licking his pre-cum before nipping her way down his shaft.

"What the hell, Alena?" Randy struggled with the way the slight sting from her sharp teeth eased his orgasm back even as his cock grew harder. Looking up from her bright, bent head, he told Nash, "Our girl knows a few tricks of her own."

"I'd be surprised if she didn't."

He wasn't fooled. Nash may look and sound unaffected as he leaned against the rail with his arms and feet crossed in a relaxed pose, but the bulge tenting his slacks gave him away.

"True." Tightening his hands, Randy ordered, "Enough," then took full control by holding her head immobile for his short, jabbing thrusts into her mouth, intent on getting back where he was before she'd short-changed him.

She tried, but this time there was no loosening of his hold. Warmth infused her entire body from his show of strength and control, her sheath seeping as much as his cock, her nipples beading into painful pinpoints of renewed need. Her traitorous body responded with as much enthusiasm as it had to the invasion of Nash's cock fifteen minutes ago, as if she hadn't had relief in days instead of just minutes.

Taking the easy way out, she worked his cock like a pro, sucking with hard pulls as he withdrew, licking, stroking with fast swirls when he shoved back in, never relinquishing her hold on the head of his cock. His quick jerks heralding his climax set her core to spasming, the first taste of his orgasm on her tongue had her squeezing his ass in an effort to keep him there, right there until he let go with a shout. Working to swallow every drop, she managed to ignore her own unrelieved state to bask in the knowledge she had driven both men to lose control, an experience almost as heady as her own climax.

"You can't say I didn't pass this test also," she stated with confidence as she rose on shaky legs and reached for her swimsuit.

"No, luv, we most assuredly can't say that. Sheriff, do we have our own sub for Saturday?"

"You're in, Alena, but remember, Nash's true identity stays between us and leave any subtle questioning up to us. You're along for observance only, agree?"

"Agree. Thank you."

• • • • • • •

The next few days dragged for Alena. She was anxious for Saturday to roll around so she could get her first chance to meet Kevin Hirst and his friends—the last known people to have seen Ashley before she'd disappeared. Any sign from them they knew more than they were letting on would be welcome. She'd take any lead, no matter how minuscule, at this point.

Exiting the donut shop with a gooey cherry turnover in her hand, she rehashed her call to her mother last night with a grimace. Her tone slurred, she had begged Alena to find Ashley, sobbed over the grief of not knowing. That was one time she hadn't blamed her mother too much for numbing her sorrows with alcohol. The not knowing had worn her down also, kept her awake at night as she'd fretted over her sister's whereabouts. Even though she still believed Ash had exerted her typical willful negligence and had taken off with someone of short acquaintance then found herself in trouble, that did little to ease her mind. Her sibling had been a trial for the past eleven years, but she would never wish harm to come to her, and refused to even consider someone might be hurting her at this very moment. The most she could hope for was her safe return and a hard enough learned lesson to straighten her out.

Sinking her teeth into the turnover, she cast a look around her, experiencing another irritating stab of disappointment when she didn't see either of the guys lurking about, keeping tabs on her. How could she have grown accustomed to having them cramp her every movement in such a short time? She hadn't seen or heard from either of them the last three days, not even from a distance. It didn't help she could still feel a twinge of soreness from both of them spanking her, just enough of a reminder of the heated pain that had led to a scorching release to make her want more and question her sanity for about the millionth time since meeting those two.

She tried masturbating to thoughts of previous lovers, memories of encounters she had always thought were awesome sexual experiences. But those memories paled in comparison to the pleasures both English and the sheriff had given her with their hard hands and even harder cocks. She swore if they ruined her for anyone else, she would make them pay, she just wasn't sure how she would do it. The encounter on her boat showed her all too clearly the hold they had on her. It was just sex, she knew that, but amazing sex, especially new experiences she never dreamed she'd get off on. She would get over it, and them, when they found Ashley and she returned home. Just thinking of New York, her challenging job, her friends and the hangouts they liked to frequent, sent a wrench of longing through her that equaled the pang she experienced every time she found herself searching for a glimpse of the guys. If she didn't get away from this small town soon with its friendly residents and panty-dampening sheriff and his friend, she would go nuts, or nuttier than they had already made her.

Taking her time, she strolled to the end of the street and found a bench in the city park to sit on and finish her breakfast. Sipping her coffee, she smiled at the toddlers romping on the elaborate playset, their mothers keeping a close eye on them. Lifting her camera, she snapped a few shots, then took one of an older couple walking hand in hand with their toy poodle along one of the paths lining the woods. She never went to any parks at home, was either too busy on the weekends or found the effort it would take to get to one after work not worth it. And, of course, she would not venture into one after dark, not even with a group of friends. There had been too many early morning calls for her to do her job at a crime scene that had occurred the night before in a park, sometimes involving multiple victims. Strange, she mused, that she had never felt the slightest fear being out on her boat, alone, at night. Other than Ashley's disappearance, this area seemed devoid of any real crime.

Finishing off her last bite, she tossed the wrapper in the trash bin and stood just as Mort and Edna from the B & B waved to her.

"Morning, dear," Edna called, her hand clutched in her husband's and a smile on her lined face. "Nice to see you again. Stop in sometime before you leave and we'll treat you to breakfast."

"Thank you, I'll do that." Bemused over the nice overture, Alena made her way back to her car while pulling out her phone and placing her weekly call to Portland PD. A few minutes later, she drove back to the marina, frustrated and even more anxious for Saturday to get here. Even though the odds of learning anything at a sex party were slim, it was at least a possibility, which was all she had right now.

· · · · · · ·

"Here you go." Carlee set Alena's plate of fried chicken in front of her.

"Thanks, Carlee, this looks great." Bored out of her mind this evening, Alena returned to town to avoid giving in to the temptation to spy on the Hirsts again, wishing now she hadn't promised the guys she would behave. She did enjoy taking a ski lift ride up the small mountain slope and the abundance of vistas it afforded her for photographing, but with the evening looming and nothing to do, she came to the diner to make sure she could face Carlee again without wanting to hide in mortification. Carlee took the worry out of that when she greeted her as if she had never witnessed her and the guys going at it three days ago.

"I haven't seen you with the sheriff or Nash lately. Everything okay?" she asked in her straightforward way.

"You mean not since our little show the other day?" Alena surprised herself with how easily she could bring up her exhibitionism and *not* feel awkward or embarrassed.

Carlee chuckled. "I should thank you for that. Bryan jumped me the minute you pulled away. I'm surprised the picnic table held up."

The picture made her smile, but she couldn't help asking, "In front of Kevin?"

"Wasn't the first time." Her easy reply came with a nonchalant shrug. "Bryan began slowly introducing his brother into the lifestyle when he turned eighteen. Because of his avid interest, he didn't want Kevin exploring on his own. Since his stepfather walked out on Kevin when he was eight, Bryan's taken his role as the much older big brother seriously."

Alena wanted to bring up her sister in the worst way, but couldn't risk her own relationship with Ashley getting out, let alone determined to keep her promise to the guys. "Randy and Nash invited me to the party Saturday. I know

I'm going to feel a bit awkward in front of them."

Squeezing her shoulder, Carlee spoke to reassure her. "I doubt either of those two will give you a chance to worry about it, but why don't I check out of here in about thirty minutes and we'll go have a drink and girl talk."

"I think I might need more than one drink to go along with that girl talk," she admitted with a rueful grin.

"Works for me. Eat up and I'll be back."

"Thanks, Carlee." A night out was just what she needed, and she looked forward to cutting loose, and to the girl talk.

· · · · · · ·

An hour later, Alena sat with Carlee at the scarred bar top in The Well and eyed the tattooed, redneck-looking bartender with amusement. He and his bar were as vastly different from the impeccably styled bartenders in the trendy clubs she usually frequented as the quiet, quaint town of Blue Springs was from the hustle and bustle of New York. The roadside bar vibrated with country western tunes Alena cringed at hearing, but as she sipped her second whiskey sour, her mellow mood made allowances for the grating twangs patrons were line dancing to.

"So, not only are you going to attend a sex party for the first time, but with not one but two super hot guys. You've got guts, New York."

She switched from people watching to give Carlee a wide smile. "You have to have guts to survive in New York. Now be honest," her two drinks gave her the courage to ask, "could you pick between the sheriff, who with one look from those black eyes could dampen a nun's panties, or the Brit, who could get your motor running after one sentence uttered in that sexy accent?"

"Hell, no," she admitted on a deep sigh of regret. "That's why I hate your guts."

Alena laughed at that outright lie. "You're a jealous bitch."

"Damn straight. I gotta tell you, I played with our good sheriff at Bryan's parties years ago, and whew!" Carlee fanned herself with dramatic waves of her hand. "If I wasn't so freaking obsessed with my guy, I'd insist on joining you. Never had a four-way. You?"

Sputtering on a giggle, she replied, "I've never had a three-way, just each of them with the other watching."

"Well, like I said, they'll make sure you'll be too busy to be uncomfortable for long Saturday night. I think this'll be a small group as his big summer bash isn't planned for another two weeks. That one you won't want to miss."

Since that would be the day before she was supposed to return home, Alena hoped she would have something to celebrate by then instead of the dead-end leads that had brought her here in the first place. "I'll try."

"Try what?"

Both women swirled to see Bryan standing behind them, his brother Kevin, and two other younger guys taking seats at a nearby table. Alena's heart beat double time at finding the people she had been eagerly awaiting an introduction to suddenly right in front of her. Nothing had ever been more difficult than resisting the urge to demand what they knew of her sister's whereabouts. Instead, she kept quiet and let Carlee make the introductions.

Jumping off her stool, Carlee threw her arms around the big guy, exclaiming, "I thought you were busy tonight."

"I was, now I'm not."

Alena watched him slide his hands down Carlee's back to grip her buttocks and lift her to meet his descending mouth. She glanced away to see Kevin who, with his wavy brown hair and hazel eyes was the spitting image of his brother, watched them with a small smirk. He happened to shift his look to her at that moment, and sent her a friendly wink. But there was something... off in those eyes, a look the brother didn't have, a calculating gleam that made her uncomfortable as she remembered he too had witnessed that scene on her boat a few days ago.

"Meet Randy's hook-up," Carlee said as she pulled away from Bryan, tossing Alena a wicked grin. "He's invited her to come to the party with him and Nash."

"I've seen you around the lake and town with Sheriff Janzen, not to mention moored at my private dock. I've known Randy for a decade and have never known him to take up with a tourist. I'm Bryan Hirst, your host for Saturday night." His smile was friendly, his eyes twinkling with remembrance. "I'm looking forward to seeing more of you."

She took his outstretched hand and found hers engulfed in his huge palm. Thinking of the time she saw him wielding a switch on Carlee's bound body, she had trouble reconciling that stern man with this affable, teasing person. "Not much more to see than you already have. I'm Alena."

Grinning, liking her candor, he squeezed her hand before releasing her and inquiring, "Just Alena?"

"May as well keep it simple since it's doubtful any of you will see me again after I return to New York."

"Like I said, I've never known my good friend to take up with a visitor. He's always been strictly by the book and playing footsie with the town's income goes against his nature. What'd you do, cast a spell on him?"

He was digging, but she didn't know why or what for. Maybe he was just suspicious by nature. "If I had spell-casting powers, I wouldn't waste them on getting a man's attention. Most men of my acquaintance aren't worth the effort."

"Ouch. I hope you'll feel differently this weekend."

"She'll have fun. What're you and the kid up to?" Carlee asked.

Uncaring of who might see, Bryan reached out and pinched Carlee's distended nipple, her thin top doing little to disguise the small bumps of her areola or her puckered nipple. "I'm trading them for you. Alena, can I give you a lift to your lodgings?"

Alena noticed he didn't wait for Carlee to agree, just

assumed she would. Giving a mental shrug, she supposed if Carlee didn't mind his high-handed assumption then she shouldn't either. "Thank you but I drove and I'd like to finish my drink first. I'll see you Saturday, Carlee." Spinning around on her stool, she waved her off.

"Later then," Carlee called back, returning her wave and laughing as Bryan all but hauled her out of the bar.

On her return swivel around, Alena almost toppled off her seat when she came up against Kevin, his two friends standing next to him wearing expectant grins before they picked up their drinks and returned to their table.

"Sorry, didn't see you had come up," she mumbled. Up close, his good looks were hard to ignore and she could see why her sister had been attracted to him, but his knowing smirk as he eyed her with blatant appreciation for having seen what was under her clothing set her on edge.

"I'm full of surprises. Would you like to join us for a drink? We hate to see a pretty girl drink alone."

Both Randy and Nash had praised her by saying 'good girl,' and she easily recalled the warm flush those two simple words had given her at the time. Why did hearing 'girl' from this kid have her gnashing her teeth? The desire to put him in his place warred with not wanting to miss this opportunity, so she shoved aside her irritation to give him a flirty smile and a small dig. "If you can remember I'm a woman, not a girl, then I'd be happy to join you."

The quick flare of hot anger that tightened his face almost sent her toppling off the stool again as she leaned away from him in a reflexive move, but he masked it so fast she wondered if she had imagined it. Picking up her glass, she took a big swallow, relishing the burn as it went down her throat.

"My apologies," he returned in a smooth tone. "I usually hang out with college girls. Can I buy you a refill?"

"Thank you, no. I'm already at my limit to drive safely. So, where do you go to school?" She took another sip of her whiskey, stalling before going to their table to give the light dizziness she experienced all of a sudden a chance to subside. Her drinks must've been stronger than they tasted.

"USM in Portland. You from around here?"

"New York," she replied, sticking as close to the truth as possible. After swallowing another sip, she took a deep breath to shore up her nerve, slid off the stool, then ventured, "That's the college that missing girl attended. Did you know her?"

"Let's not put a damper on the evening by bringing up depressing topics," he crooned, running a finger down her cheek in a soft stroke that was at odds with the hard look in his eyes, a look that proved she'd touched on a nerve. But was it due to guilt or just reluctance to talk about a disturbing subject?

She didn't get a chance to ask or speculate further before he bent and whispered in her ear, "Come join us, sweetie. Don't worry, I haven't told Joel and Brad about the little show you put on for me the other day."

His tongue dipped into her ear following that snide insinuation and Alena pulled away in disgust, her abrupt jerk back sending the room spinning in circles. With a gasp, she clung to him until her woozy head cleared somewhat, heat infusing her body at the press of his erection against her stomach. His low chuckle drew a shiver up her spine, and to her astonishment her nipples beaded into taut, painful buds, her sheath swelling with moisture. "Oh, good Lord," she breathed before she could stifle the exclamation. What the hell was wrong with her?

"Problem, Kevin?"

Alena recognized the bartender's voice with relief, then Kevin's reply followed by low chuckles from his friends had ripples of both fear and excitement crawling under her skin.

"A little too much to drink, Zach. I'll give her a ride."

"Yeah, I bet you will, Kev."

"Can it, you two," Zachary snapped at Kevin's friends before turning back to him. He had already phoned the sheriff since he had heard the rumors about Randy and

Nash's involvement with the redhead. "Just take her outside and wait for the sheriff."

Bewildered, Alena felt as if her mind had detached from her body, but she managed to toss back the rest of her drink as Kevin went to grab the glass. Jerking away, she heard it shatter on the wood floor. "Oops," she giggled, this time leaning against him instead of pulling away.

"Out!" Zachary swore as he retrieved a broom.

The cool evening air did nothing to dispel the sudden heat flowing through her veins, the press of the hard male body against her side tossing timber on those flames and threatening to burn her up. "Are my guys here?" she asked, needing them, wanting them in the worst way.

"Now, what do you want them for?"

I need them, she wanted to say, but instead she went with Kevin toward his sporty SUV, trying to focus her fuzzy brain on why she shouldn't be leaving with him. A brief moment of clarity fought its way through and brought her to an abrupt halt. Pulling back, she tried focusing on his handsome face swimming before her, registering the smug look even with her senses addled. "I don't know you, I'm not going with you. People disappear when they leave with you."

"What'd you say?" he asked sharply, his hand digging into her upper arm.

Wincing at his tight grip, she struggled to think fast, which was difficult to do with her body burning up and her head twirling in dizzying circles. Somehow, she managed to come up with a good excuse for her blunder. "I'm from New York. *Nobody* from New York leaves a bar with a stranger. They might never be seen again." Even through her blurry vision she noticed his scowl had disappeared, replaced with a taunting smile as he opened the passenger door.

"This is Blue Springs, not the big city. You're safe here, with me. Come on, get in."

A sigh of relief found its way past her spiraling confusion

and over stimulated senses when she blinked against the bright glare of flashing blue strobe lights. They were here. "Let me go, my guys are here and I want to go with them." Suddenly she was free of his brutal grip and stumbling toward Randy and Nash as they strode toward them.

"What's going on, Kevin?" Randy demanded, his arms going around Alena's trembling body.

"Just doing a good deed, Sheriff," he drawled, insolence dripping from every word. "She had a little too much to drink and I offered to take her to wherever she's staying."

There was something wrong with that explanation, but the fire raging through her body demanded Alena's total concentration. Nash had moved next to Randy and settled a reassuring hand on her shoulder, his touch searing through her thin shirt with the burning heat of a branding iron.

"Take me home," she whispered, praying they knew she meant their place. She ached for them with every fiber of her being and her little bunk on her little boat just wouldn't do for what she craved.

"We'll take her," Nash's voice came from above her head, just as hard and implacable as Randy's had been.

"Good enough. I'll see you at Bryan's party."

As soon as Kevin walked back inside The Well, Randy pushed her back at arm's length and demanded, "You want to tell us what's going on?"

"Don't know, don't care. Take me home, to your place." Grabbing their hands, she tried tugging them toward their vehicle, but they didn't budge. "Damn it," she whimpered in frustration, her body's needs so intense they bordered on painful. The itch crawled just under her skin, spread throughout her body, and left her a mass of gluttonous craving. "You have to take care of this!"

Nash cupped her nape, urging her face up to shine a penlight in her eyes. "Fucking bastard drugged her," he bit out, glaring at Randy.

'Oh, good Lord, complain later, fuck now."

"Let's get her back to my place and we'll deal with this.

I have a feeling we're all in for a long night."

"God, I hope so," she breathed in relief as they led her to the Tahoe and opened the back door for her. Alena had no idea what was happening with her, all she knew was she had never needed anything, anyone as badly as she needed sex with them. "I want to sit up front with you," she complained, desiring to be as close to them as possible, her skin on fire for the soothing touch of their hands, their mouths.

Both men swore again then mild-mannered Nash pushed her head down and nudged her inside before slamming the door on her curses.

CHAPTER EIGHT

Randy clicked his phone shut with a low curse as he pulled out of the parking lot. "Zach didn't see anything. She sat at the bar with Carlee for about an hour with several people coming up and ordering drinks close enough to have slipped something into hers. Then Bryan arrived with Kevin, Joel, and Brad, but he was busy at the other end and didn't see anything then either. Even if we had her blood drawn and tested, that won't tell us who did it."

A soft, frustrated groan from Alena in the back seat drew Nash's head around to see her face flushed and her hands busy rubbing over her breasts as if she were trying to alleviate an ache. Turning back to Randy, he didn't bother to hide his anger as he told him bluntly, "You're going to have to come to terms with the likelihood one or both of the Hirsts are in this up to their neck."

Before he could respond, Alena scooted forward and reached for both of them over the seat. Trailing her fingers up their necks, she tickled their ears then grumbled when they shifted away. "C'mon, guys. Let's just pull over and play. I don't want to wait until we get to your house," she cajoled.

Randy slapped her hand and Nash bit her finger when

she reached for them again. "Behave, Alena," Randy snapped.

"Ouch! That hurt. Do it again." This time she demanded their attention.

"We've created a monster," Nash sighed, tugging on her hair before giving her a light push to sit back.

"Yeah, and whatever someone gave her turned her into a hungry demon, one we're going to have to deal with for hours before it'll wear off. Alena," he growled when she slid a hand into the neck of his shirt.

"God, I love it when you snarl at me like that. It gets me all hot and bothered. But, since you're being cranky, I'll just play with Nash. You want me, don't you?" she whispered in Nash's ear then teased the shell of his ear with her tongue.

"Not going to happen, luv, not while you're impaired." He gave her another light push and sent her toppling back in her seat. "Look, we're at the sheriff's house. You can go in and sleep it off."

Before they could stop her, she flew out of the back seat and whipped her top over her head before she reached the front door. Laughing, she shook her wild hair back as they stomped up the steps to the porch, reaching behind her to unhook her bra. "C'mon, guys. I'm burning up."

Unlocking the door, Randy ushered her inside just as her bra dropped off and her full breasts bounced free. Then she threw herself at him, pressing those lush curves against his body, leaving him with no defense except right and wrong. "C'mon, baby, you'll feel better after you sleep it off," he said, his tone gentle and rife with regret as he eased her arms from around his neck.

Anger, desperation, and need flashed across her face and filled her eyes as she jerked out of his hold and pivoted to Nash. "Help me, English, please." She reached trembling hands to his waist, her intent clear.

Her whispered plea tore at him, but Nash wrapped his hands around hers and held them in a tight grip. "It wouldn't be right, deep down you know that."

Jerking out of his hold, Alena fought against the threatening tears their gentle, *understanding* tones wrought, the fire raging through her body turning her frantic for relief, however she could get it. "Fine. I don't need you, either of you."

Her nipples had puckered into even tighter, more painful nubs when she'd freed her breasts from the tight confines of her bra. Having two pairs of hot eyes on her nakedness added to her excitement, fed the arousal pulsing like molten lava through her veins and pooling between her legs. Hands going to her waist, she took a quick, desperate look around the room and spotted the large leather sectional in front of the rock fireplace she remembered Nash jacking off on.

Shoving her jeans down, she bragged, "I've been taking care of myself for a long time, and I can do so now."

Nash exhaled a sigh of defeat, eyeing her bouncing buttocks as she hopped out of her jeans and flopped down on the sofa, her hands going straight to her breasts, squeezing the soft flesh so hard he winced along with her. "We're going to have to do this, you know."

"Yeah, I know," came Randy's disgruntled reply.

"You don't want her hurting any more than I do."

"We're the ones who'll be hurting an hour from now."

"But we'll have a clear conscience." Striding to her, Nash grabbed the hand she had moved between her splayed legs, hauled her up then bent and tossed her over his shoulder, landing a sharp smack on her ass when she cursed and struggled.

"A lot of good that'll do." With a sigh, Randy resigned himself to their fate. Nash was right, he wouldn't be able to sleep himself knowing she was suffering and in dire straits they could help with. "The loft, I've got the biggest bed."

The burn on her butt matched that in her pussy, and when Alena bounced on the soft bed Nash tossed her on, her hand automatically went back between her legs to work at soothing it. Fear lurked in the back of her fuzzy mind, a sliver of knowledge warning her something was off, not right with her, but the ravenous hunger controlling her body overshadowed everything else. The bed dipped with their weight as the guys joined her, one on each side, their hard-bodied nearness her final undoing.

"Now, now, now," she chanted over and over, turning to one then the other, confused and distraught over how to get what she craved.

"Let's give her something else to think about for a few minutes." Nash grabbed her restless legs, wrapped his hands around her ankles and pulled her legs up and over her head, elevating her hips and leaving her ass available for Randy to torment.

"Damn good idea, and position." Randy swatted her upturned ass with hard, rapid smacks, peppering both cheeks as well as the backs of her thighs. Her buttocks clenched with each swat, but that didn't make them any less soft and bouncy.

Mindless with the pleasure-pain he heaped upon her butt, Alena fisted her hands in the sheets as she lifted her hips for each scorching hot slap, wanting, needing more, relishing the fiery burn building across her buttocks and thighs. She forgot about the heat throbbing in her nipples and sheath as she embraced this new distraction from the pain of her unrelieved arousal. "More," she pleaded incoherently, "please, don't stop."

"Maybe this wasn't a good idea," Nash admitted as he looked under her bent back legs and took in her glazed eyes and flushed face, her constantly jerking hips making it difficult to maintain his hold on her ankles without hurting her.

"Good or not, we're in it now. Switch with me, my hand hurts."

She whimpered when Randy ran a hand up her quivering thigh, the lull in hard swats more painful than her throbbing buttocks. "Please," she begged again, even though the discomfort had worked to escalate her need instead of temper it. Why hadn't she remembered that? Then the painful swats started again and she closed her eyes in relief. Her folded-up position with her legs held over her head would have been uncomfortable if not for the riot of sensations bombarding her from all angles.

The small bedside lamp cast shadows on the walls, the litany of steady slaps on bare flesh echoed along with her soft whimpers and their heavy breathing. Her cheeks were a mass of throbbing flesh by the time he slowed his hand, pulsing with hot pain she was coming to realize did nothing to alleviate the stress of her vibrating, out-of-control body, even though it was more than they had ever subjected her to.

"She's burning up back here." Nash slowed his swats and switched to light slaps aimed at teasing the pain into lingering instead of adding to it.

"Let's give her what she needs then."

Her legs were lowered and then their hands and mouths were on her body, touching, tasting everywhere. Lips suckled her nipples, the relief almost painful. Her thighs were spread over theirs, leaving her wide open for their fingers to delve in between. "Yes!" she cried out when one of them rooted out her clit and milked it between two fingers, those mouths never letting up on her nipples.

Sensation after sensation whipped through her, hot need driving her into a frenzy of lust. With a sudden burst of pleasure, she exploded in ecstasy, the orgasm erupting fast and hard only to leave her still simmering when it subsided just as quick. Then Nash released her nipple and kissed his way down her waist, over her smooth mound to bury his mouth between her legs and the out-of-control spiral began anew.

"Again, Alena."

Randy's dark, commanding words barely penetrated the fog of pleasure surrounding her, but that deep tone still had its usual effect, sending additional ripples of pleasure skittering along her overly sensitized nerves. Without a word between them, Randy pinched her nipple just as Nash nipped at her engorged clit, the twin pinpricks of pain tossing her right back into the maelstrom of overwhelming pleasure. Next time, she swore, she wanted to savor the feel of his mouth on her labia, his tongue stroking deep, laving her throbbing clit over and over, but right now, whatever demon had possession of her body wouldn't allow for that luxury.

"*No!*" she exclaimed when they both pulled back, but she needn't have panicked. Within seconds, they had positioned her on her side facing Randy, Nash sandwiched behind her, her leg draped over Randy's hip, his mouth covering hers as fingers invaded both her vagina and anus.

"Don't fret, luv," Nash's sexy voice whispered in her ear. "We'll keep going until you're too tired to hurt anymore. Trust us."

She did; it surprised her how much she did. She retained enough of her faculties to realize by now they weren't going to fuck her, the scratchy press of their clad bodies indicated that much. They pulled their fingers back and a moan of denial slid from her throat into Randy's mouth. She lost control of her bucking hips as she strained between them, eager for their penetration again. When it came, it forced her to pull her mouth from his on a gasp of both pleasure and discomfort from the invasion of three fingers in each orifice, stretching her, filling her.

"Too much?" Randy asked, watching her closely.

"No, never too much. Just, *please*." She had no idea what she wanted at this point until they finger-fucked her in tandem, one thrust in while one retreated, a continuous stroking over sensitive, swollen nerve endings. The pleasure became excruciating in its intensity, never completely assuaged no matter how many times they drove her up.

Lights exploded then went dark, pleasure rippled between her nipples and her crotch then abated. Over and over until she finally lay sated between them. All three breathed in heavy pants, the dark room a cocoon of safety as much as the press of their bodies against her. She fell asleep knowing something significant had occurred tonight, but was too exhausted to try to figure it out.

"The hell with it." Randy lay back, made quick work of lowering his zipper over his raging hard-on and breathed a sigh of relief when he tightened his hand around it.

"Well, if you're not heading for a cold shower, neither am I." Nash had his cock in his hand in seconds, his shaft jerking in pleasure at his tight-fisted hold.

"Shit, English, I've seen your junk before so why wait? God, jacking off never felt so good."

"Agreed, but only our girl can call me English."

"Lecture later, kind of busy right now."

Nash's low chuckle was followed with their mutual groans of pleasure as neither wasted any time getting the relief they needed. Their heavy breathing and Alena's soft snores were the only sounds in the room until low curses and moans heralding their climaxes took their place.

• • • • • • •

"Think she'll remember much?" Nash eyed Randy over the rim of a steaming cup of coffee as he leaned against the butcher block kitchen counter the next morning.

Shrugging, Randy glanced up toward the loft where they left her still sleeping soundly an hour ago. The late morning sun warming his back from the kitchen windows did nothing to dispel the cold he experienced whenever he thought of what could have happened to her had Zach not called him to come get her. "Depends on what he gave her. What I really want to know is why she broke her promise. She had no business being at The Well with Hirst in the first place."

Nash knew Randy fought against admitting either of the Hirsts were involved with Ashley's disappearance, and blaming Alena for last night would be a typical response instead of looking too closely at Kevin or Bryan for answers. "I thought Zach said she was there with Carlee."

Running a hand through his hair in frustration, Randy released a pent-up breath. "Yeah, he did, but she could've left when they did."

Nodding, he admitted, "Yes, she could have, but are you more upset because of what *could've* happened or because all arrows keep pointing to your friends? Because, mate, I know I had trouble sleeping thinking of her with anyone but us in the state she was in."

Hell, if Nash could admit to growing feelings, Randy guessed he could be man enough to also. Seated at his kitchen table with a large, three-paned window affording him a view of his back yard and the woods beyond, he pictured taking Alena outside as she leaned over the picnic table. The image stirred his cock and urged him to shift in his seat. Turning to look at Nash, he said, "Just the thought makes me want to smack something, or someone. Good enough for you?"

Nash smirked. "As long as it's not me. Coincidentally, I'm not as anxious to get back to London anymore, which is something I don't take lightly."

"I'm in no hurry to boot you out, in fact…" He paused when they both heard the upstairs bathroom door close. "Looks like we're about to find out what she does and doesn't remember about last night."

• • • • • • •

It was a good thing Alena heard the guys' distinct voices coming from downstairs when she opened her gritty eyes and found herself in a strange bed and strange bedroom. Vague images flitted through her memory of last night, or what she thought was just last night. Her leaning against Kevin, the strange combination of fear and lust his nearness had elicited, then both Randy's and Nash's angry voices, the press of their bodies igniting just lust, no fear. Given the blurry memories of lying between the two of them in this bed, her nakedness didn't surprise her. What did was the soreness she experienced in every muscle, every joint, and both her vagina and rectum as she rolled out of bed.

Stumbling across the dark brown carpet toward the bathroom, she relied on the sunlight shining down from the large skylight to turn on the faucet. Bending, she splashed cold water on her face, wishing she had the guts to take her time and thaw out the chill invading her from the inside out in the huge, walk-in shower with its multiple showerheads she knew would feel like magic. But delaying facing them, and the truth of what happened last night, would only add to her angst. The only thing she could attest to with any certainty this morning was that neither Randy nor Nash had fucked her last night; that is, not with their cocks.

She found her clothes lying on an old, comfortable-looking recliner facing a corner fireplace. Concentration proved difficult, which worried her as much as their moods this morning. She remembered Carlee leaving with Bryan followed by Kevin and his friends coming up to her at the bar. After that, the memories were disjointed, filled with heated arousal so strong it made her ache. Recalling the sense of safety replacing her fear when the guys arrived, she knew she owed them her thanks. Explaining herself might be more difficult.

She wasn't completely in the dark today. Having worked for several years with the NYPD, she knew enough to know she had been drugged last night. It baffled her how someone could have distracted her long enough to slip something in her drink, but she had to admit she hadn't been as diligent last night in staying aware of those around her as she always was when at a club back home. Equating the friendly ambience of this small town with safety had been a stupid mistake, one she wouldn't make again. Her sister's disappearance from this area should have been enough of a red flag that all was not as it seemed, especially where the Hirst brothers were concerned.

Descending the stairs one slow step at a time, she glanced around the lower floor of the log cabin, surprised at the spaciousness and homey feel of the place that was at complete odds with her six hundred square foot apartment. Shifting her gaze to the wide open kitchen, her heart did a crazy flip at seeing the guys eyeing her with looks of concern, followed by her body's usual heated response. *Oh, good Lord*, she bemoaned in silence, tightening her hand on the wood banister. How on earth could she be reduced to a puddle of lust so quick from just looking at them again after the decadent excesses she suspected had happened last night? Was it because they hadn't fucked her that she could still want them so much, or was their chivalry the cause of that funny feeling in her chest that worked to increase her desire?

Neither would do. She had no wish for a steady relationship, let alone two long-distance ones, and nothing would keep her from going home as soon as possible. It must be a silly fluke, just a simple, basic response to all that testosterone and the intent, probing looks in their eyes she couldn't get used to. No one had ever bothered to peer at her so closely, to really see her, let alone two men almost every time they saw her.

Nash set his cup down and met her halfway across the room. Palming her face, he gazed into her eyes several moments before announcing, "A little wary, but back to a clear, pretty green. Much better," and then bending to give her a light kiss that curled her toes.

"Good, then she can come sit down and explain why she was with Kevin Hirst last night after promising to stay away from him."

"Don't worry, luv. He's as concerned as I am over what happened last night. That's why he's so cranky."

Nash's small smile eased her apprehension when she looked over and saw Randy's dark scowl.

"I didn't plan it." Stepping away from the comfort of Nash's embrace, she padded to the table and accepted the cup of steaming coffee Randy pushed over to her as she sat down. "Thanks." Waiting until she took several fortifying sips of pure, courage-building caffeine, she took a deep breath and admitted, "But I remember wanting to take advantage of his unexpected interest after Carlee left with Bryan. After that, everything is..." She waved her hand and shook her head, finishing with, "fuzzy."

"After witnessing our scene a few days ago, his interest shouldn't have been unexpected," Randy drawled, pleased with her honesty even if she should've left when Carlee had. But hindsight never amounted to a hill of beans, so he let it go. She was all right, that was the important thing.

"Yeah, I got that much. He... he gave me the creeps, that's all I really recall with any clarity. I know I was drugged, but honestly, I have no idea who, or even when someone could've done so. It could've been him, or either of his friends as they were at the bar together when I had my back turned to tell Carlee good-bye. I'm sorry, and thanks for your... intervention." She couldn't help teasing them with a wicked grin and saying, "If you give me a little time to recoup, I'll be happy to make last night up to you."

Tugging her hair, Nash returned her grin. "You need to rest up. Tomorrow we go to Bryan's party and you can make up to us there. But thanks for the offer."

"Is that why neither of you fucked me? Because you're waiting for the party?"

Randy raised one midnight brow at her blunt inquiry. "Maybe because we didn't want you feeling differently this morning. Taking advantage of someone who is impaired is illegal, and wrong."

Alena sputtered on a laugh that felt good after the stress of the morning. "You both know me well enough to know that wouldn't happen. I haven't run from anything you've done to me yet and I think I remember begging for it."

"Beg tomorrow night, when you're free of drugs, and we'll give you everything you've been pushing us toward."

The heat in Nash's blue eyes indicated he looked forward to hearing her plead again. "How are you going to question Kevin, Bryan, or the other two if you're both busy with me?"

"I don't intend to question them at the party. That would definitely send up a red flag. *If* an opportunity comes up for one of us to slip upstairs unnoticed to do a little unauthorized snooping, we'll take it. If not," Randy shrugged and gave her a hard look, "then we don't do anything. This is my ball game, Alena, and you're just a spectator. Don't forget it."

Taking the last swallow of her coffee, she rose on legs still shaky and took her cup to the deep farmhouse sink without bothering to reply. She knew the rules, and had no intention of breaking them. Then again, she had no intention of going home empty-handed either. Rinsing out her cup, she set it down then turned around to find them both eyeing her with that look that revved up her engines on all cylinders. This ridiculous reaction she continued to have to both of them bordered on insane and she needed to find a way to appease it once and for all in the next ten days.

"Apparently, I need my rest before I see you again, so would one of you mind taking me to my car?"

Randy stood and snatched his keys off a pegboard. "C'mon, breakfast is on me for both of you. Then I want you to fill out a report before returning to your boat. It won't do much good, but I want an official record of your complaint and condition."

She knew exactly how little that would do without an eyewitness or better recollection on her part. She just hoped word didn't get back to the cops she was familiar with in New York. There were several who were good friends and a few on and off bed partners who would flip out if they knew she had been a victim of a date rape drug. As much as she enjoyed the special bond she had with her fellow coworkers, she didn't need the drama of their overprotectiveness.

"That's an offer I can't refuse," Nash stated as he moved toward her and snatched her hand. "Let's order the works, you know, just because we can."

"Problem is, I'm so hungry, I think I can eat the works this morning, followed by a donut of course."

"Of course, luv."

Randy rolled his eyes at their backs as they stepped outside, but a small smile played around his mouth.

CHAPTER NINE

Daisy Mae was not at her desk when they arrived at the sheriff's office after breakfast, and by the time Randy had written up Alena's report and walked her out with Nash, there still had been no word from her. For all her immature, flighty ways, she'd always been punctual. Randy tried not to worry, but was beginning to think he needed to write that in as part of his job description. He'd spent a good portion of this past week fretting over agreeing to let Alena accompany him and Nash to Bryan's party, worried over whether she could, or would handle what would be expected of a willing participant. If she balked at all, Bryan would notice and wonder why they had brought her. As most dominant men were, he was very astute and diligent at reading women; he had to be to host those parties safely as well as legally.

With his association with Bryan teetering on the line and his growing feelings for both Nash's friendship and Alena's affections causing some disquieting thoughts, it now appeared he'd have to add stressing over his receptionist to his long list of concerns. His only hope for a return of sanity to his daily life was for everything to go back to normal when he cleared Bryan and Kevin of any involvement in Ashley's disappearance and Nash and Alena returned home.

And Daisy went off to college. And assuming he didn't miss them. And they found Ashley safe, and unharmed. Yeah, piece of cake; all he had to do was wait for a miracle and he would get his life back on an even keel. Of course, if all that happened, he'd have to keep an eye out for flying pigs.

"So, what do I wear to this party tomorrow?" Alena asked as he held open the car door for her.

"As little as possible. Makes it easier to strip you."

"She can still blush, mate. I'm betting by the end of the evening she'll be over that."

Nash grinned at Randy over the roof of his vehicle, both of their smiles stretching wider when she gave a little huff and ducked into her seat.

Shutting her door, Randy turned serious, telling Nash, "I'm going to check on Daisy Mae then head out on patrol. You might pop in and check on Alena this afternoon, you know, just to make sure she's not suffering any lingering effects and still wants to go tomorrow."

"Okay, Papa, will do," Nash returned dryly, his blue eyes glinting with humor.

"Stuff it, English."

"I told you, only…"

Alena interrupted them by sticking her head out the window and announcing, "I'm fine and nothing will keep me from going tomorrow. Now, can we go?"

"You heard her. She'll behave. Let me know how Daisy is."

Nash no sooner climbed behind the wheel and drove off when Daisy's mother, Barb, pulled up, her faced lined with worry and anger, her distraught daughter sitting next to her. Gut tightening in dread at the look of terror and anguish on the young girl's face, Randy hastened over to open the door for her. One glimpse of the small bruises around her neck had his own anger churning. The picture of Nash's victim that he carried everywhere with him came to mind. The dark bruising around that young woman's throat, the cuts and abrasions on her wrists and ankles silent testimony she hadn't been a willing participant in the autoerotic asphyxiation game the autopsy report stated she had endured and was, after multiple attempts, the cause of death.

Opening the passenger door, he took a gentle clasp of her upper arm and helped her to stand. "Where are you hurt, Daisy Mae?"

"Can we go inside, please?"

Her tremulous whisper broke his heart and he led her inside, Barb following behind with a tissue clutched in one tight fist. Leading them straight back to his office, he shut the door then eased Daisy Mae into a chair before attempting to remain professional by taking a seat behind his desk.

"What's going on, Daisy? Barb?"

When Daisy just started crying, her mother reached over and squeezed her hand, her voice hard, her eyes teary as she said, "Her friends brought her home from a party last night. Claimed they heard her scream from the woods and when they ran to help, they saw someone wearing a hoodie running off. They found her with her blouse torn, drunk, drugged, or both." She turned a scowl on her daughter even though worry and love still shone in her eyes. "She knew better of course, but that doesn't ex... excuse..." Her voice broke and she turned a pleading look to Randy.

He didn't like the coincidence of Daisy's assault coming on the heels of Alena's drugging. Just what the hell was going on in his usually peaceful county? Keeping his tone kind but brusque, he tried to get Daisy's version. "Daisy Mae, I need to hear it from you."

Swiping a trembling hand across her eyes, she squared her shoulders and looked up at her boss. "I don't remember much, Sheriff. A whole bunch of us went to The Well, but I only had Coke. Zach, he's a real stickler for making sure no one underage drinks there. You know that."

"I do, so I assume you got hold of alcohol at this party."

She hedged but didn't try to avoid the truth. "Yes. Some

older college people joined us, and I remember dancing with several, but we always watch the drinks at our table for each other. After someone suggested moving the party to the lake, we all left. After that it gets fuzzy."

He hated to ask the next question, but saw no way around it. "Give me names, especially of the college kids." Grabbing paper and pen, he jotted them down, recognizing most of them as local high school graduates who returned for the summer each year. Then she gave him the three names he had been dreading hearing, the knots in his stomach getting tighter as he added Kevin's, Joel's, and Brad's names to the list. "Is that all of them?"

"Only the ones I can remember, and, of course, there were several I didn't know. I'd guess over thirty people were there."

Exhaling a frustrated sigh, he leaned back in his chair and ran his hand through his hair. "Okay, hon. Now the hard part. What happened in the woods?"

A small smile kicked up the corners of her bruised mouth. "Not so hard as that's the fuzziest part of the whole night. One minute I'm sitting with some friends, sipping a beer and the next my back hurts from being pressed down on the hard ground by... I don't *know*!" She tried, but the tears broke through her resolve to be strong. "He... he was heavy and he sounded so... so mad, really, really angry. I can only recall a hard, whispered voice and hands around my neck. As soon as he squeezed, I bucked. I don't remember screaming, only gasping for air, and fear, terrible, terrible fear."

Barb wrapped her arm around her daughter, her anguished face on him as she rocked Daisy back and forth. "There's nothing you can do, is there?"

"I can question her friends who found her, and everyone on this list, but unless I get an unimpaired eyewitness as to who took her into the woods, no, I won't be able to pin this on anyone. Be thankful, both of you, that you weren't hurt worse, or raped. You got lucky this time, Daisy Mae. Make sure you're not in a position for there to be a next time. I'm writing an order for blood testing, but it's doubtful anything will show up now. Go to the clinic and give this to the lab and get a physical." He ripped off the order and handed it to Barb. "I'll call ahead for you and attach the results to my report along with my interviews."

"Do, do you *have* to question my friends?"

"It's my job, even if it's a long shot I'll get anything useful to go on." And he had never shirked his duties, no matter who he was forced to bring to task. That was the hardest part about being responsible for enforcing the law in such a small, close-knit community; everyone wanted a favor when caught in a wrongdoing.

"My friends wouldn't hurt me," she returned in a stronger voice.

"Someone at that party wasn't your friend. You've only given me sixteen names. I might get more from some of these. There's a chance, a slim one, I'll get enough to proceed."

He could tell she was second-guessing coming in to him, didn't want her friends interrogated even though they knew what had happened. Walking them back out, Randy wasn't pleased about the long, frustrating day ahead of him, given the odds of learning anything fruitful. Determined to get the interview he dreaded most out of the way, he slid into his cruiser and drove to Bryan's lake house.

"Sheriff, I bet you're here about Daisy Mae," Kevin greeted him as soon as he stepped out of his cruiser and strode toward the three boys seated around the fire pit in the side yard.

"Word travels fast. Why that still surprises me, I'll never know."

Joel held up his cell phone. "Between texting and Facebook, it's all over about her visit to you this morning. We saw her when some of her friends helped her out of the woods back to our party. Is she okay today?"

"Shook up, bruised, and traumatized. Any of you see

who she left with? I really want this guy." Randy lasered each of them with a hard look, letting his gaze linger on Kevin the longest. He couldn't detect any signs of guilt or subterfuge on their faces, and he knew what to look for.

"Last time I noticed her, she was standing by the water with two other girls, not sure of their names though," Brad said.

Kevin took a long pull on his beer, his direct gaze bordering on insolent. Lowering the bottle, he swiped the back of his hand across his mouth then asked, "How's the other woman today? Alena, isn't that her name?"

For the first time, Randy allowed himself to look at all three boys as suspects instead of kids he'd known since they were adolescent teens. He didn't like it, but his job of keeping the citizens in his county safe demanded it. "She's recovering from whatever drug someone gave her illegally. The same with Daisy Mae. You wouldn't know anything about what's circulating around here, would you?"

"We're law-abiding citizens now, Sheriff. We've left our teenage hellion days behind us."

Kevin's insolent drawl and their identical smirks didn't sit well with him, especially after he recalled the ravaged look on Daisy Mae's face and the vulnerability in Alena's eyes that morning. "Yet, you three are the common denominator between Ashley Malloy's disappearance and the two druggings last night. How do you explain that?" Despite the warm afternoon temperature, Randy experienced a cold chill from the glacial looks he received from all three young men.

"Coincidence," Joel said as he rose to retrieve another beer from a cooler sitting by the back door. As if by cue, their scowls turned to small smiles, their looks once again affable.

"C'mon, Randy. You've known us for years. We may have sowed a few wild oats as teens, but we'd never do anything to hurt someone else. You saw how careful we were at the last two parties. If Kev's brother trusts us, you should too."

Joel made a good point. Bryan had allowed his brother and his friends to participate in his parties this summer, and Randy hadn't seen any behavior that sent up a red flag, and he had kept a close eye on all three as it was their first time to party with Bryan's friends even though he had hinted he'd been educating the guys in the lifestyle a little at a time. His gut continued to tell him these three were innocent of any wrongdoing concerning Ashley, but his cop instincts urged they, or at least Kevin, knew more than they were letting on.

"You think of anything, no matter how trivial, contact me," he stated, leaving the trust issue unsettled for now. "And no driving or boating until that alcohol has worn off."

By the time Randy finished his interviews he had no more information than he had when Daisy left his office. Irritation left him disgruntled, both worry and anger over Daisy's and Alena's spiked drinks last night putting him in a foul mood. After checking in with his deputies, he went home, grabbed his pole, and drove to his favorite spot on the lake.

Unfolding his camp chair, he sat, baited his line and tossed it in, then reached into his cooler and snatched a beer. After taking a long draw, he released a sigh and tried setting aside his impatience with the lack of answers to now two plaguing investigations. Spending time in the idyllic privacy of the small cove with no one around to bother him always soothed him when his job's demands took a toll on him, which, given the low crime rate in Blue Springs, wasn't often. He and his deputies covered the county, but that consisted of small towns and rural areas. Over the last decade, he'd had numerous drug busts, thefts, and more than his share of teenage shenanigans and car accidents. Then there were the heart-wrenching cases of drownings, missing hikers who were eventually found dead from either exposure or falls, and substance abuse overdoses that always put him and his staff in a funk for days.

But nothing had ever frustrated him more, or tore at his

gut more than Ashley Malloy's disappearance and the lack of leads for him to work with. Was it the unsettling possibility Bryan and Kevin were holding back on him, the problematic intrusion of Alena's and Nash's presence and his growing affection for them, or just the sad reality that the young girl was most likely dead and never to be found responsible for his heightened emotions over this case?

The scuttle of squirrels scampering in the trees behind him, birds tweeting out a litany of chirps, and the splash of softly rolling waves along the shore usually bestowed a calming effect on his rioting emotions, but not today. With a decade-long friendship on the line, a new one fated to be temporary due to distance, and a woman who could be everything he'd ever wanted for a long-term relationship but was destined to walk away soon, was it any wonder he found himself out of sorts?

A tug on his line drew his attention and he reeled in a trout big enough to serve both him and Nash tonight. Given the big argument the two of them had had when the Brit first arrived and insisted their cases were related due to Kevin, Joel, and Brad being in London last summer when his victim went missing, it still surprised him they came to a quick, amicable agreement of wait and see and now got along so well. Yeah, he'd miss the irritating son-of-a-bitch, he thought with a rueful grin as he tossed his catch into a bucket then rebaited his line.

"How the hell can you look so content playing with smelly fish, mate?" Nash frowned at the flopping, slimy creature, his delicate shudder drawing a laugh from his friend.

"City boy," Randy scoffed. "I was just thinking of you. And no, before you ask, I didn't find out anything today."

"Didn't think it'd be that easy after all this time. There are still no leads back home, according to my partner, so our only choice is still for one of us to try and sneak away for a little unauthorized snooping tomorrow night."

"But?"

"But, I'm not sure our girl really is ready for what we'll put her through. Playing on her boat with a few people watching yards away is a lot different than in a crowded room of strangers."

Alena possessed a hidden vulnerability that clashed with her independent, feisty nature, especially where her sister was concerned. Nash suspected she took her responsibility as the eldest sibling seriously, and worried she was blocking the reality of her long disappearance. She pulled at him, this fiery redhead who had repeatedly surprised the hell out of both him and Randy with determination and her unguarded, exuberant responses to their demands. He wanted her, and that worried him too because they were both leaving soon and it was doubtful their paths would cross again.

"She's handled everything we've dished out. She might be uncomfortable, but I've no doubt she'll not only respond, but embrace whatever we do." Giving him a shrewd look, Randy added, "I think you're more concerned about your response to her tomorrow than hers to anything we might do."

"What makes you say that?" he asked sharply, frowning at his astute observation.

"Because I feel the same way. But," rising, Randy reeled in his line, "one problem at a time, *mate*. Right now, I'm thinking our girl needs something new to wear to her first sex party."

"Why? She'll be naked right after we arrive." And he looked forward to stripping her in public and laying claim to that soft, round body, he thought, his cock stirring at the images popping into his head.

"Yeah, but I saw a little number the other day that I'm dying to see on her. Come on, we'll stop in at the shop and you'll see what I mean."

Nash shoved his misgivings aside for now. Randy was right, tackling one problem at a time would be the best way to move forward. With little leave time left for him, and, he suspected, for Alena, they needed to make the best of what time remained for both of them. If there was evidence of Kevin or his friend's involvement in either his case or Ashley's, their only chance to find it was at these parties, at least for now.

"Okay, but if this dress keeps me up tonight, you're the one I'll take my sleepless night out on," he warned him as they ambled back to their cars.

Laughing, Randy clutched his pole and bucket with his catch in one hand and slapped his friend on the back none too gently. "Deal."

• • • • • • •

Alena sat between Randy and Nash in the cruiser and gave her short sundress another tug. As with every other time, the soft, stretchy knit slid right back up, revealing the very edge of the black satin thong they had surprised her with along with the dress. She never wore thongs; what was the point? They weren't comfortable and presented no effective hygiene coverage. But even worse, the constant brush of cool satin against the bare flesh of her labia aroused her to the point of dampness and stiffened nipples. With the green knit clinging to her breasts, every little bump on her areolas surrounding her turgid peaks could be detected.

The tight fit of the three of them in the front seat didn't help her exalted state of awareness even if the press of hard, thickly muscled arms on either side of her added a touch of comfort. The way their much larger frames dwarfed her made her feel small even though she was far from petite. Strange how their nearness eased the anxiety she'd been stressing with all day. The new, slutty part of her was excited about tonight, but the part she knew best, her independent, 'I control my body, not the other way around' part cringed at spending an entire evening pretending to be something she wasn't.

Liar. Releasing a frustrated sigh at that taunting inner

voice scolding her, she yanked on her dress again. Okay, she liked it when they took over, got off on their piercing looks and rough demands. But in private she could talk back, refuse, or tease them and, according to the lecture they had given her along with the dress, she couldn't do any of those things without 'consequences.' At first that hadn't bothered her; after all, she had enjoyed the consequences they had meted out thus far, but when Randy added that a punishment may be given by their host, she had balked. It took her a while to come to terms with how much she wanted both Randy and Nash and how much she enjoyed their dominant sexual control, she knew she didn't want that from anyone else, especially Bryan who might be harboring information about her sister.

They just pulled off the main road circling the lake when Nash clasped her hand, preventing her from tugging on the hem again. "Why do you keep doing that when you know by now it won't do any good?"

"It's bugging me. I hope we don't plan on sitting much tonight."

Both men laughed before Randy stated, "Baby, *everything* will be showing eventually, so fretting over a peek at your panties is a waste of time."

"I know that," she grumbled as they drove through the open gates to the Hirst property and parked behind several other vehicles lining the circular drive in front of the house.

"C'mon." Randy took her hand and helped her out. "Behave and everything will go fine. You can do this."

His confidence in her evoked a warm glow, and when Nash picked up her other hand, her usual self-confidence returned. Following a stone path to the back yard, the first person she spotted was a young woman tethered naked with her arms stretched above her to the low-hanging branch of the towering tree she had spied Carlee bound to last week. Bryan stood next to her, arms crossed as he watched his brother with a close eye working the flogger over her back and buttocks.

There weren't a lot of people, maybe twenty, which helped ease the tension from her shoulders. Smoke billowed from the large grill, the tantalizing aroma of sizzling hamburgers permeating the pine-scented copse. The incongruity of watching a few people laugh and joke in front of the grill and table laden with side dishes while one woman sank to her knees with a push on her shoulders from her lover and proceeded to take his cock into her mouth wasn't lost on Alena. Before she could tease the guys about it, Carlee turned from chatting with another woman and came running when she spotted them walking over.

"I heard what happened the other night after I left with Bryan." Throwing her arms around Alena, she whispered, "Are you all right?"

Giving her new friend an awkward pat on her back, she attempted to reassure her. "I'm fine, Carlee. Randy and Nash took good care of me afterward."

Pulling back, Carlee's grin split her face. "I'll bet they did." Turning to her two escorts, she asked politely, "May I borrow Alena for a few minutes to introduce her to a few people?"

"Ten minutes, luv, then we want you back."

Nash bent and kissed her, hard, before she could vent her automatic ire over needing their permission to socialize. Getting naked and fucked publicly just might be the easiest part of tonight, she judged as she leaned into him and returned his deep, tongue-probing kiss with enthusiasm and an increase in dampness between her legs despite her annoyance.

Releasing her plump lips, he whispered, "Don't fret, we'll have your back tonight."

Nodding, gratitude replaced her pique as she realized just how seriously these people took their dominant play. She tossed him a grateful smile then followed Carlee over to the circular bench surrounding the unlit fire pit where two other women sat. She knew she had it bad when, after only a few minutes of idle chitchat, she found herself chomping at the bit to be back with the guys. Cindy and Diane, Carlee's friends, and their significant others were staying the weekend with Bryan, she learned, the three couples having partied together on a regular basis for several years. Feeling like the outsider she was as they reminisced about past get-togethers, she let her attention wander around the secluded yard, admiring the creative ways Bryan had outfitted common outdoor furniture with bondage restraints. Padded lawn chairs and lounges bore attached cuffs on the legs, long straps dangled from the picnic table benches, and there was an oddly shaped swing hanging from a sturdy tree branch that set her imagination to working overtime.

"It's fun," Carlee said, nodding toward the swing. "You should get Randy and Nash to let you try it."

"Try what?"

Alena swiveled her head around to find them behind her, Randy smiling as though he knew exactly what Carlee had been referring to. "I don't think so."

They surprised her by letting her get away with that statement, which brought out her suspicion as they each reached a hand down and lifted her to her feet.

"We have something else in mind for tonight," Nash told her before nodding to the other women. "Thank you for keeping our girl company, ladies, but we'd like her back now."

"Your girl?" She wasn't sure how she felt being labeled both a girl and theirs, but as they led her over to the food table where two men were conversing with Bryan as he manned the grill, her stomach took that moment to let everyone know she hadn't eaten since a late breakfast.

"Here, try some of these snacks until the burgers are done." Randy put chips, cheese and crackers, and fruit slices on a small plate and handed it to her before introducing her to the other two men. "Alena, this is Chuck Melton and Jon Adams. Gentlemen, our guest tonight is vacationing on the lake."

Chuck eyed her full figure displayed in the clinging knit dress with appreciation. "Nice to meet you, Alena." Turning to Randy, he asked point blank, "You sharing tonight?"

"How dare... *ow!*" Her gasp of outrage burst out before she could suppress it, but the quick lift of her dress and hard smack Nash delivered to her butt shut her up fast. If it weren't for her need to find her sister and the way the tingling burn on her buttock zeroed down between her legs, she would have marched out of there that minute.

"Apologize, Alena."

She leveled an icy glare at Randy, but caved under his unrelenting, black-eyed stare and mocking raised brow. Taking a deep breath, she faced to the other man. "I'm sorry. I'm new at this and still unsure about the rules." God, it hurt to say that, but then both Randy and Nash bent and kissed her cheeks, the warm look of approval in their eyes causing her heart to trip in a way she didn't have time to question too closely right now.

Holding the plate Randy gave her with one hand, she nibbled on the finger foods as the men conversed as if nothing untoward just happened. Maybe for them, that little incident was nothing, but for her it was an eye-opening lesson on how this night was going to proceed.

Oh, good Lord. Her silent groan accompanied the next lesson a few minutes later when Nash slid his hand under the short dress that barely covered her butt to caress her buttocks. Then Randy added to her torment and embarrassment by reaching up and scooping her right breast out of her halter top with careless ease, his thumb rasping her turgid nipple in an absentminded caress as they continued their casual talk.

The crunchy chip she had just bitten into lodged in her throat before she managed to swallow it. Their large, callused hands wreaked havoc on her senses and despite the secret, illicit thrill sweeping through her from the public exposure and her heightening arousal, she found being the object of so much male attention both disconcerting and arousing. The close presence of the guys aided in allowing her to just stand there and let them fondle her in front of several other men who were strangers to her. This exhibitionism, though tamer thus far than what they had exhibited on her boat, seemed so much more personal standing this close to her audience and she couldn't help but squirm under the heated looks in the men's eyes.

"Pretty breasts, responsive too. You never answered Chuck about sharing."

Nash squeezed her buttock as Randy kneaded her breast, the rougher touches heating her core and diverting her attention from the way Jon's eyes never looked away from her bare breast as she held her breath waiting for an answer. No matter what they said, she *would not* let anyone touch her other than Randy and Nash. She felt nothing for any of these men other than titillation from having their eyes on her.

"Sorry, but no, we're not sharing." Nash palmed her soft flesh for added reassurance.

"Maybe when Kevin is done with Mandy you can talk her into joining you and Diane," Bryan put in over his shoulder as he flipped burgers and kept an eye on his brother.

"You're here with someone?" Alena exclaimed in surprise before she could stop herself. When all five men laughed, she cringed, mortified over revealing her inexperience in such a way. Of course these people weren't into fidelity, what was she thinking?

Randy leaned down and whispered in her ear. "No, baby, their relationships aren't exclusive, but ours is, as long as you're here." This time it was his turn to squeeze her flesh softly in reassurance.

A warm flush spread up her face, but Alena wasn't sure if it stemmed from the pleasure his words evoked or the pleasure their caressing hands were responsible for. The sudden removal of their hot palms sent a shiver of longing down her spine for a return of their touch. Instead of lessening, her need for them seemed to get stronger the more they were together, something she needed to get under control and soon.

"Burgers are up," Bryan announced, piling thick patties on a plate and setting it on the long table with the other food.

Much to her chagrin, Randy left her breast hanging out as he maneuvered her down the food line, slapping her hand away when she tried to cover herself. "Leave it," he ordered, setting a hamburger on her plate.

As several more people came out of the house, Alena noted with relief she wasn't the only one exposed. Seeing a few other women bouncing around topless and unconcerned and one completely naked save for the minuscule thong covering her mound, she didn't feel like she stood out in the crowd.

She happened to look across the yard just then and noticed Kevin releasing his playmate, Mandy, her white skin bearing multiple pink stripes that she must relish from the small smile on her face as she looked up at the younger man. Even from a few yards away, Alena could detect the tightening of his jaw and when he shifted his eyes from Mandy to her, the look he leveled on her nudity sent fear, not pleasure, crawling under her skin. It was gone so fast, replaced with a bland expression and nod in her direction, she was left wondering if she had imagined the malice in those dark eyes.

A shiver went through her, catching Nash's attention as he took her elbow to escort her to a picnic table. "Cold?"

"No, it's nothing." At least, she hoped so, she prayed as she sat between the guys and dug into the juicy burger. Putting the incident out of her mind, she concentrated on fueling up for the next few hours. If her damp crotch was anything to go by, she sensed tonight would be memorable whether Randy or Nash unearthed a lead or not.

CHAPTER TEN

Fifteen minutes later, Alena had just begun to relax and enjoy the banter around the table after having gotten used to her exposed state when Randy and Nash took her elbows and stood.

"Kevin did such a good job wielding that flogger, it put me in the mood for leather." Randy didn't bother keeping his voice down and the faces around the table revealed avid interest in his announcement. She wondered if her excitement stemmed from those looks or the way the guys had stroked her skin all through their meal and kept her teetering on the fine edge of arousal.

When they stopped at the tree where Kevin had had Mandy tethered to the dangling rope with attached cuffs a short time ago, her heartbeat sped into triple time. She had to force herself to recall the thrill she had experienced when Randy had held her immobile for Nash to fuck. She wanted to feel that rush again, but tethered to that limb, her skills from self-defense training would be of little use, unlike when Randy had had a hold of her. Stalling, she whispered to both of them, "When are you going to check out Kevin's and Bryan's rooms?"

"Since Kevin is inside, now is not a good time. Relax,

Alena. The later the evening gets, the more engaged everyone becomes and less aware of others," Randy told her as he and Nash each lifted an arm and attached the cuffs to her wrists. "There. You're just the right height for this station."

Her sandaled feet remained flat on the grass even with arms stretched taut above her, with no give left in the rope. When Nash reached behind her and untied the halter top of her dress, she glanced across the yard, her face flaming at the number of looks aimed her way. "Keep your eyes on us, luv." His soft instructions accompanied the push of her dress down her body and out from under her feet.

"I don't think that'll help."

"You said you could do this," Randy reminded her as he reached out and cupped both her breasts in his palms, lifting them for his descending mouth. After taking a slow swipe with his tongue over each distended tip, he raised his dark eyes to her face. "Well? Yes or no?"

That was the sheriff, she mused, unable to suppress a small smile at his impatience. Straight and to the point without any sugar-coating. "Of course I can do this," she quipped, grateful her voice didn't reveal her misgivings.

Chuckling, Nash murmured, "That's our girl," before latching onto those plump, enticing lips he had yet to feel around his cock.

They took her over; there was no other description for it. Hands plumped her breasts and fingers tweaked her nipples as they feathered light kisses down her neck followed by sharp nips on the tender spots between shoulder and neck. Those small stings made her sheath clench and moisten, but the sharp slap on her right buttock that jerked her hips forward, right into the delving hand between her thighs, triggered a deluge. She closed her eyes and cried out with the next smack, pain and pleasure doing its usual dance along her nerves.

"*Please*," she pled when Randy didn't penetrate her aching vagina.

"Quiet, luv, or we'll have to gag you," Nash admonished in her ear before biting her lobe, then soothing the sting with a stroke of his tongue.

Her eyes flew open, whether from the threat or that bite, she didn't know as she gasped, "You wouldn't!"

"Oh, but I would."

The wicked gleam in his cobalt blue eyes signaled his hope she would test him, but there was no way she'd give him the chance to follow through on that threat. She admitted being bound turned her on, giving them the control over her to do as they pleased without having to worry about anything, but there was no way she'd let them suppress her voice. She needed to keep some control for herself.

Narrowing her eyes at them, she stated, "I get brownie points for trying."

"We can give you that."

With his eyes on hers, Randy shifted his palm against her labia, pressing just hard enough to stimulate another gush of cream from her core. Nash delivered two rapid, painful smacks on her buttocks, once again pushing her soft flesh against that rough palm. Alena bit her lip to keep from begging or complaining as they kept up the teasing torment of slap/rub until she ground her hips against Randy's hand with small whimpers of frustration, the escalating burn spreading over her butt increasing her arousal to a feverish pitch.

Unable to hold back any longer, she released her throbbing lip from between her teeth on a long moan of pure frustration. "Damn it, *please* do something!" The rapid beat of her heart pulsed between her legs, inside her pussy, leaving her to ache for both of them.

"Is this what you want, baby?" Randy crooned. Separating her damp folds, he rooted out her clit and bent to suckle one stiff nipple.

She was about to say yes when her vaginal walls clamped around the sudden invasion of his fingers, but when he just teased all around her aching clit, his touches so light she could barely feel them, all she could do was curse.

Nash laughed outright at her inventive language. Sliding his arm around her waist, he shifted to her side and lifted until her hips were elevated and her feet dangled off the ground. Randy joined him in peppering her pretty pink ass with a barrage of hand smacks that had her screaming either in outrage or pleasure, neither of them sure which.

The embarrassing position, with Nash holding her tight against his side and Randy leaving his fingers embedded inside her as he shifted to her other side and joined in tormenting her buttocks, would have mortified her if she hadn't been in such a needy state. The fire they ignited across her cheeks and thighs fed the burning embers of lust Randy refused to stir into a full-fledged blaze.

By the time they released her, she'd become a quivering mass of deprivation, her arousal left to simmer unfulfilled as they freed her hands from the cuffs. Randy reached up and kneaded her tense shoulders, leaning over her to ask, "You okay?" in a concerned voice just as Nash took her wrists between his hands and rubbed the pink skin.

"Oh, good Lord," she muttered. How could she be put out with them when they went and behaved with such solicitous intent?

"I think that means she's okay," Nash returned with a wry grin.

Randy pulled up her thong then picked up the dress they'd bought her. Slipping it back over her head, he posed another simple question. "Better?"

"Than walking around here naked? Yes." Even though there were now several naked guests, she felt more comfortable covered since it looked like they were done tormenting her for now. Good thing there was more than one way to relieve the persistent itch they left her with. "You'll have to excuse me for a minute. I need to find the restroom."

The look they exchanged didn't bode well for her plans.

"There's a powder room right inside the side door. You get yourself off while you're in there and I'll take a switch to you," Randy warned her, his tone as dark as his eyes.

"How... never mind." Pivoting away from their identical *knowing* smirks, she practically stomped with disgruntlement to the house, wondering how she could have thought she'd get away with anything with those two. If she didn't need answers to Ashley's disappearance so bad, and if she didn't still want them with such longing, and if she weren't so desperate for relief, she would have told them to take a flying leap and would have ignored the threat that had made her skin crawl with unease. She wasn't sure she wanted to find out how painful that could be.

The cool interior of the house did nothing to calm the riotous heat still flooding her pussy, pushing her to make quick use of the bathroom so she wouldn't be tempted to linger and relieve herself of more than just her bladder. She doubted they would know if she gave herself a quick orgasm, but the thought of disappointing them prompted a strange feeling of letdown, something she didn't want to examine too closely. Add in the switch threat and the desire to return with them next week before she left and it became easier to wait for them to get her off than risk those consequences.

Eager to return to them, she stepped out of the bathroom without looking and slammed into a hard body. "Oh, sorry..." Looking up, she tried not to shrink back from finding herself held in Kevin's light grip.

"No problem, Alena. I wanted a moment with you anyway to see how you're doing after the other night. You were really out of it."

That good-looking face reflected nothing but friendly concern, but she still didn't trust him. There was just something about him that gave her the creeps. She had seen him with his friends, and other girls, and no one else exhibited any reservations about him. She knew Randy thought him innocent of any wrongdoing concerning

Ashley except maybe holding back something that might reflect badly on him or his brother. She also knew Nash was convinced Kevin and/or his friends were involved with his case. From what she gathered, the guys had agreed to disagree for now over the possible involvement of either of the Hirsts.

That didn't mean she had to go along with their truce, and before she could stop herself, she replied, "I'm fine, thank you. Rumor has it you and your friends are always around when a woman finds herself in trouble."

And there it was, that flash of menace in his brown eyes she could've sworn she saw earlier. He masked it so fast, she had to blink a few times, but the way he tightened his grip on her arms confirmed she hadn't imagined that look. "Let go of me," she demanded, managing to keep her voice cool and controlled even though she was shaking inside.

"Sorry." He released her immediately and stepped back, contrition written all over his face. "You took me by surprise. I haven't heard that rumor and usually I hear them all when I'm here." Shrugging, a rueful grin tugging at his mouth that didn't fool her for a second, he added, "Just bad luck, being in the wrong place at the right time, I guess. Enjoy the party." He flipped her a two-finger, egotistical salute and look before turning toward the door, as if he didn't have a care in the world.

Leaning against the wall, Alena breathed a sigh of relief when he slipped outside. God, whatever had possessed her to say something so revealing? The guys would take a switch to her for sure if they knew she had provoked him. She hadn't meant to, but that smug look on his face got to her, especially when she pictured him peering at Ashley that way. After getting herself under control, she opened the side door and noticed Randy and Nash conversing with a group around the fire pit that included both Kevin and Bryan. Realizing this was an opportunity they may not get again tonight, she shut the door and followed the short hall out into the great room, ignoring the immediate spasm of guilt over breaking her promise. Her sister had to come first.

Two couples were so thoroughly engrossed in fucking, one on the long sectional and the other on the floor, she had no trouble skipping up the wide staircase unnoticed. The second floor took her by surprise as the two rooms with the doors open held nothing but padded benches and a double bed. There were distinct sounds of leather slapping bare flesh and soft cries of either pleasure or pain emitting from behind the closed doors of the other two rooms and the bathroom was empty. Surmising the staircase at the end of the hall led to Kevin's and Bryan's private quarters, she quickly dashed up them before she could change her mind. As astute as the guys were, it wouldn't take them long to come looking for her.

Luck was with her when the first bedroom proved to be Kevin's, if the University t-shirt tossed on the bed and college texts piled on the desk were any indication. Having no idea what to look for, she did a quick visual check then rummaged through a few dresser drawers before a door shutting too close for comfort scared her into peeking out into the hall. An eerie feeling of eyes on her brought on a shiver from a sudden chill. After checking the hall for anyone else lurking, she ran to the staircase and hastened down to the second floor only to come to an abrupt halt at the bottom step.

"What the hell are you doing up here?" Bryan demanded, his eyes glaring daggers at her, his big hands fisted on his hips.

Alena darted her eyes away from that look, noticed the second floor bathroom door was closed and thought fast. Nodding to the door, she said, "I was looking for another restroom. I *really* had to go."

That excuse failed to placate him. "Guests aren't allowed up here without their escorts, and *no one* is allowed on the third floor, not for any reason. I know Randy told you the rules before bringing you here."

"I did. What's going on?"

Shit, what the hell had she gotten herself and them into?

The guilty look on Alena's face didn't bode well for her, and Randy feared she would have to bear the brunt of the consequences for whatever she had done.

"Says she went up to the third floor looking for an unoccupied bathroom. You know my rules, Randy."

"Yeah, I do. Alena, I did warn you there'd be consequences you won't like if you didn't follow the guidelines I gave you." Turning to Bryan, he stated with forceful purpose, "Keep in mind she's new to all of this or you'll force me to step in."

Alena wondered at the quick grin Bryan gave Randy as he said, "It's like that, is it?"

"Just remember."

Nodding, his stern look reappeared when Bryan faced her again. "Six swats with my paddle. Downstairs, now."

Alena gaped at his retreating figure as he took the stairs before turning her astonishment on Randy. "If you think…"

"What I think," he bit out in an angry whisper, stepping up to her and snatching her clammy hand, "is you lied just then and this is *all* your fault. You went snooping, didn't you?"

"I had to. You two were busy gabbing and almost everyone was outside. What was I supposed to do, let a perfect opportunity slide?" she hissed as he led her to the stairs.

"Yes, because, as it turned out, it wasn't so perfect, now was it?"

Jerking to a stop halfway down when she noticed there were a lot more people inside now than when she had come upstairs, she tried to find a way out of her predicament. "Why can't you punish me?"

He heard the shame in her whispered voice, and the fear even though she'd never show either one. Randy hated she had put him in the position of having to let Bryan punish her. Some women didn't have a problem with someone other than their significant other reddening their asses, but he suspected Alena still struggled with coming to terms with her submissive nature, that it took her by surprise, as did her desire for both him and Nash. With a sigh of regret, he squeezed her hand and told her the truth.

"I'd give anything to spare you this, baby, but the only way to do that is to leave, and that would make Bryan suspicious enough he wouldn't let you, me, or Nash return next week. So, I'll leave it up to you. Your choice."

The unguarded look of caring on his face and the fact he would give her the choice settled her anxiety and made the decision easy for her. Sucking up her nerve, she nodded. "Let's get this over with. Where's Nash?"

"Right here."

He stood at the bottom of the stairs with that same expression on his face, and her heart did that funny little flip again that worried her so much. "Okay, I'm good then."

The significance of that simple statement after she knew they'd both be by her side wasn't lost on either man, but both knew she didn't realize the connotation. Nash took up a position at one end of the narrow footstool Bryan had pulled into the center of the room, and Randy stood to the side as he guided Alena over it.

Refusing to let the guys see just how apprehensive she was, Alena lowered herself over the stool, grateful Bryan hadn't ordered her to strip. Her gratitude took a quick nosedive when Nash guided her hands to the bottom of the stool's legs, shackling them as hands behind her pulled her thighs apart and wide, cool leather straps were wrapped across each bent knee. Put on display in a room full of mostly strangers, bound on her hands and knees with the stool cushioning her abdomen and her head dangling over the side, she had never felt so vulnerable. That is until her hiked-up dress was lifted even higher and her minuscule thong lowered to mid-thigh. An automatic jerk against her restraints set her heart to fluttering in panic, but she managed to fight it back with herculean effort. She would not, absolutely refused to shame the guys in front of everyone by balking now.

"Six swats, and that's a light sentence," Bryan said from behind her.

Nash cupped her face in his large hands as Randy rested his warm broad palm on her lower back. Looking up into English's approving blue eyes, hearing his softly spoken praise, 'good girl,' made the humiliation and pain of the first swat bearable. He bent and covered her mouth with his, swallowing her cry from the next smack, the blistering pain now encompassing both cheeks. Alena concentrated on kissing him back, clinging to his lips like a lifeline while trying to ignore her surprise and shame at her body's usual reaction to the red-hot throbbing, a response the damp swelling of her labia could attest to. She didn't want this man spanking her, didn't want him in any way, but her body was not as discriminating in its preferences.

The next two swats were hard enough to send the stool sliding forward an inch, but Nash anchored her until he released her mouth and face to slowly lower his zipper over his enticing erection. The sight of his glistening cock head jutting toward her mouth made her forget all about her shame, the audience, and the growing discomfort spreading across her butt.

"Make him feel as good as you did me the other day," Randy whispered in her ear as he rubbed comforting circles on her lower back, "and we'll make you feel good."

The last two swats were administered as she opened her mouth for Nash's cock, her gasp muffled by this thick length. He returned his hands to her face, holding her head, taking the control from her. She didn't care.

The soft murmurs of conversation resuming around her indicated her audience had moved on. Randy soothed the heat enveloping her buttocks with soft strokes over the abused flesh and Nash's low groans of approval afforded her as much pleasure as she was gifting him. Closing her eyes, she basked in her own arousal, the constant simmer from their teasing touches earlier brought to the boiling point from the heat of those punishing swats.

"Suck hard, luv," Nash dictated as he took his time pulling back, the warm, wet suction of her mouth and tight clasp of her plump lips driving him insane. He knew that luscious mouth would feel like heaven and hell wrapped around him. She swirled her tongue under his cap, licked that super-sensitive area in a wet caress that spiraled straight down to his balls. Cursing his lack of control, he shifted forward, groaning as she stroked every bulging vein. Caressing her cheeks with his thumbs, he brushed down to the corner of her mouth with the right digit, tracing her lips wrapped around him, his touch including his cock. A ripple of pure pleasure spread down his cock as he put pressure on his engorged, slippery flesh with another slow withdrawal.

God, that's hot, Alena groaned to herself when she felt his thumb tracing her lips and knew he had to be stroking the flesh she sucked on. Then her concentration on Nash's dick flew the coop when Randy glided his palm down between her buttocks and grazed her anus with one finger. Before she could assimilate his intent, he breached her back orifice with one long finger, the tantalizing caress stimulating those forbidden nerves into overdrive. His low voice as he conversed with someone added to the surging pleasure, even though she should have been abashed at the offhanded way he stroked her ass while holding a casual conversation with another guest.

Pulling on Nash's hard flesh again, she tried concentrating on getting him off as Randy continued to stroke her rectum, but all of her pent-up frustration from their earlier play came rushing back in a flood of body-encompassing sensation. When Nash stroked one broad palm down her neck to slip inside her dress and cup one dangling breast, the final spark lighting the firecracker of her orgasm came with the tight pinch and pull on her nipple. The darkness behind her closed lids exploded in colorful lights as she mewled in ecstasy around the hard stalk pumping in and out of her mouth.

Shaking with the force of her climax, she was barely aware of his quickening length, his faster, deeper plunges into her mouth until he spewed his seed down her convulsing throat.

Randy exchanged a startled look with Nash. He could feel the clutches of her orgasm through the thin membrane separating her rectum from her pussy, heard her soft, muffled cries around Nash's cock, and saw her body shudder repeatedly with the pleasure. Just from his finger stroking her ass. Okay, maybe the way they had teased and tormented her outside without letting her climax had something to do with her response, but it was still one fucking awesome experience. He couldn't have been more proud of her when she accepted and took her punishment without arguing, even if her snooping still pissed him off. He could understand *why* she had grasped the opportunity, but that didn't mean he condoned her breaking her promise.

Pulling out of her ass, he palmed one red, warm buttock as Nash withdrew his spent cock from her mouth. Despite the pleasure she'd just experienced, he knew she would need comforting after that intense scene most women would have found too degrading to respond to, no matter how turned on they were. And he had no problem giving her whatever she needed, the deep emotion responsible for squeezing his chest something he needed to come to terms with sooner rather than later.

Alena felt their hands freeing her from the restraints then lifting her as she worked to clear her befuddled senses. She should be used to those powerful orgasms by now, but she continued to become flummoxed by the heights they could take her to. Unfortunately, she couldn't wallow in stupefied pleasure for long as reality had a way of sneaking back in and biting her on the ass in a way that was not nearly as much fun as if the guys had bit her. The comforting embrace of Nash's arms cradling her against his wide chest as he settled her on his lap did little to dispel the cold replacing her inner warmth as she replayed the last twenty minutes.

How could she have let herself go under such degrading circumstances? When she pictured Bryan as the one standing behind her, wielding the paddle, she found the lingering soreness covering her butt more degrading than arousing. Then to climax in front of a room full of strangers just from anal finger-fucking only added to the humiliation burning her face. Had she been alone with the guys, she knew she would have had no problem accepting her responses and would be enjoying the aftershocks of pleasure still pulsing through her body. She could recall with vivid accuracy the excitement of her previous exhibitionism and voyeuristic activities, and she couldn't, wouldn't deny the thrill that swept through her earlier when the guys played with her outside. Why was she so despondent now over her responses?

"Let go, luv, you'll feel better," Nash encouraged her, tightening his arms around her.

"What're you talking about? I'm fine." But when both his and Randy's face swam in front of her, she realized she wasn't fine, and had to blink rapidly to hold back the floodgate of tears threatening to burst. "Oh, good Lord," she muttered, "this is ridiculous."

"It's normal to question yourself, baby. But just so you know, even though I'm going to blister your ass myself for going back on your word, I'm fucking proud of you. We both know that wasn't easy for you."

"I came, didn't I?" she snapped, so confused by her conflicting emotions and their solicitous behavior she couldn't see straight.

Cocking his head, Randy regarded her with solemn contemplation for a moment before glancing at Nash and getting his confirmation nod. "Yes, you did, and we think maybe you need to come again."

Before she realized their intent, they lifted her dress over her head and stripped her thong down her legs. Cool air wafted over her skin, raising goosebumps until Nash shifted her to lean back against his chest and Randy moved to kneel between her legs, spreading her wide enough to accommodate his broad shoulders. Instant warmth erased her chill when he cupped her buttocks, lifting her hips to meet his descending mouth as Nash's hands came around to cup her breasts.

The first touch of his lips on her bare labia sent her reeling back into that pleasurable vortex where nothing else mattered. The scratch of his five-o'clock shadow against her inner thighs provided extra stimulation she didn't need. She brought her hands up to grip Nash's thick forearms, a whimper escaping her compressed mouth with the slow glide of Randy's tongue up her slit.

"Relax, we'll do everything, you just enjoy."

Nash followed his whispered suggestion in her ear with a swirl of his tongue over the sensitive whorls and a sharp nip on her small lobe. A ripple spread from her nipples down to her crotch, his tight pinch of both nubs coming just as Randy released his hold on her right buttock and ran a finger up one side of her clit and down the other. That 'not nearly enough' graze had her shifting against his mouth with a low moan of frustration, but she needn't have worried. Wrapping his lips around her aching bud, he suckled the tender piece of flesh into his mouth as Nash continued to torture her nipples into reddened peaks, proving they weren't going to make her wait this time.

The deep plunge of two fingers accompanying his marauding mouth set her off again, the pleasure sweeping her senses in a deluge of sensation so strong, she hardly felt the tightened clasp of their hands gripping the soft, full mounds of her breasts and buttocks to anchor her. Squeezing her left cheek tighter, Randy proved relentless, delving deep with both tongue and fingers, sucking hard then soft on her clit over and over until she went mindless with the sensory overload. So wrapped up in the two of them and the climaxes ripping her up with pleasure, she never heard her own scream, wasn't aware of the smiles aimed her way or saw the glares Kevin, Joel, and Brad leveled at her from across the room.

Her head began to clear when Randy feathered those talented lips over her labia, soothing touches that eased the heart-pounding come-down from multiple, brutal orgasms. She became aware of her nipples throbbing in soreness and the soft brush of Nash's thumbs over the tortured tips, a gesture that worked to both pacify and arouse, his hard chest a comforting embrace, his shoulder beneath her head a much needed support.

Randy rose above her, leaned over and took her mouth with his glistening lips, letting her taste herself as he freed and sheathed his raging erection with one hand. Always thinking, Nash released her breasts and slid his hands under her slick body to grip her buttocks and lift her pelvis for his penetration.

Bracing his hands on the back of the sofa, Randy released her mouth, murmured, "Excellent," and plunged, deep and hard. The soft wrap of her legs around his back added another lift to her hips, easier access for his pounding strokes. "Again, Alena," he demanded on a harsh breath as he jackhammered into her slick heat over and over.

Funny how she experienced no qualms about accepting the exalted sensations they drove her to this time, or the avid interest from the other guests. Unable to refuse his demand, Alena let go, wondering how on earth she'd ever find her sanity after the mania of the past few hours.

CHAPTER ELEVEN

"Where are we going?" Alena managed to rouse enough from her stupor to notice Randy had driven past the turnoff for the marina and kept heading toward town.

"You need to come back with us," Nash said.

Wrapping his arm around her shoulders, Nash pulled her closer to him. As much as she appreciated their comfort and insight into her frayed and confused emotions, she wanted to be alone, needed time to herself to sort out her feelings and desperately needed to put their unorthodox relationship back into perspective of what she required from them.

"No." Pulling away from his embrace, she turned to look at Randy. "Take me back to the marina and my boat. I don't want to go home with you."

"Alena..."

Holding up her hand, she demanded, "Now, Sheriff."

They both heard the slight tremor in her voice and Nash gave Randy a slow nod, though neither was too happy when he wheeled around and drove back to the turnoff. Pulling into the lot, Randy put the cruiser in gear and twisted to face her in the dim light cast from the lone street light he parked under. "You sure you'll be okay?"

Alena hoped her smile worked well enough to ease his

gruff concern. Unlike Nash, who did nothing to disguise his worry on her behalf, Randy masked his with his usual rough grumble of annoyance. Why she liked that as much as she did Nash's sexy accent was just one more thing she needed to work through, and soon.

"I'm sure, and I'm sorry for tonight. It was just too good an opportunity to pass up."

"I think you said something similar about meeting Kevin at The Well. Does that mean if another good opportunity arises, you'll leap on it?"

"I'm not planning to," she told Nash with straightforward honesty, "but I'm also not promising I won't. I guess it'll be up to you whether I go to the party next week with or without you. Let me out, please."

Nash opened his door and slid out without arguing, but cupped her nape and drew her up for a hard, possessive kiss before telling her, "See you soon."

With her mouth tingling and feeling their eyes on her back, she strolled toward her docked boat and climbed aboard. She didn't hear them drive away until she went below and flipped on the small lamp by her narrow bunk that didn't look very appealing at that moment. She really missed her double bed with its soft mattress and downy comforter, the quiet hum of her air conditioner and the louder street noises of her busy, congested city. That was the only explanation she could come up with for the sudden loneliness assailing her as she slipped under the sheets with a sigh. Tomorrow, she thought on a drowsy sigh, she would work all this nonsense out then.

• • • • • • •

Even though she managed to get a good night's sleep after the physical and emotional stress of the night before, Alena woke sore and edgy, her emotions still bunched in a cluster of unanswered, confusing questions. How much she had liked both Randy's and Nash's attentive regard following her explosive climaxes worried her. Unlike her, they knew what she needed and hadn't hesitated to give it to her. She also didn't care for how badly she wanted to go home with them last night, regardless of the desire to be alone with her confused jumble of thoughts. Nothing could come of their strange three-way alliance. Even if she wanted a steady relationship, which she didn't and never had, she would be returning to New York and Nash to Great Britain in a short time. As soon as they found Ashley, the tenuous thread holding them together would be severed, and sex, no matter how mind-boggling, wouldn't be enough to overcome the obstacles they'd have to hurdle to keep this thing going, whatever it was.

Swearing if Ashley didn't get her act together after this debacle she'd wash her hands of her once and for all, Alena stepped into the compact shower and stayed until she drained the small hot water supply. When that didn't work to ease her aches and pains, she snatched a glazed donut saved from her bakery run yesterday, slung her camera around her neck, and went in search of a new trail to hike, confident the exercise would be what she needed to both ease her tense muscles and get her mind focused back on the reason she still hung around this back woods town.

"Morning, Alena," Bill called out, waving to her as she hopped off the boat onto the pier. "Nice afternoon for a hike."

"Speaking of which," she replied, strolling toward his small office/shop where he was pinning something on the outside information pegboard, "can you point me in a new direction today?"

"Sure. You haven't taken the east trails. They'll lead you along some stream beds and you might get a glimpse of both deer and moose. This warm weather keeps them close to the water. But I have to caution you again about going out alone. Never a good idea."

"I'm from New York, remember?" she teased him. "Trust me, there's nothing lurking in those woods that'll scare me, and I'm pretty good about taking care of myself. What's that about?" She pointed at the flyer he had tacked up when she saw it advertised a town annual celebration of some sort.

"Blue Springs Summer Bash. Been going on for over thirty years, least as I can recall. Rides, games, a parade, and food. Folks'll bring covered dishes that'll make your mouth water. Everything closes for the day, ends with fireworks over the lake Thursday night. You won't want to miss it."

She wasn't so sure of that, but kept her cynical view of what these small town residents considered fun to herself. "I'll think about it."

His weathered face creased into a frown of concern as she turned to leave. "Heard what happened the other night at the bar. Glad you're okay, but that proves you can't be too careful."

"I've got your number in case I run into trouble. Thanks."

Waving, she headed toward the trails as she continued to marvel over the fast spread of gossip in this place. Given their penchant for escalating rumors, it surprised her that her full name hadn't been unearthed by Bill, or one of the other town folk by now. Of course, paying for everything in cash helped keep her anonymity, but the way gossip traveled, she figured someone would have done some snooping right after she had arrived and given her away.

Over the past few weeks, she'd discovered she enjoyed traipsing through the woods, snapping pictures of anything that caught her eye. When she needed a diversion from her stressful job of photographing all the bad things people were capable of doing, the scrapbook she planned to make would fit the bill nicely, remind her there was still beauty in the world despite all the ugliness.

Biting into her soft, sugar-laden donut, she let the warm, pleasant afternoon and the late breakfast decadence lighten her mood. The quiet peacefulness of the woods proved soothing to her frayed nerves, but she still had no answers to her plaguing feelings by the time she retraced her steps back to the marina two hours later. She kept thinking the woman who got aroused from the hard swats a stranger delivered to her butt wasn't her, neither was the person who responded so quickly, so openly to nothing but ass finger-fucking. It felt as if a stranger had invaded her body the moment she'd stepped into the sheriff's office and laid eyes on the two of them, an alien who showed no signs of leaving soon. When she realized how much she was looking forward to the next party, she finally came to the conclusion she liked kinky sex with the guys, and the best thing she could do would be to enjoy them while she had the chance, before she returned home and the real world crept back in.

After stowing her camera, Alena drove the short distance to town, parked in the small lot at the end of Main Street, and took her time ambling down to the library. A nice long chat via skyping with her friends ought to go a long way in taking her mind off two hot, caring, out-of-reach men and her wayward, uncontrollable responses to them. She knew if she just kept her eye on her goal and the real reason she remained here, these strange, undesirable feelings would go away as soon as she got her answers and returned to normal life.

She didn't see either Randy or Nash on her way to the library, but waved to a few people she recognized by face if not name. By the time she finished catching up on what everyone had been up to, she was so homesick she had to fight off the urge to jump in her car and drive back home that night. Lost in her nostalgic thoughts, she didn't realize she'd strolled close to the beauty shop until she heard Cora Sue greet her.

"Hey there, Alena." Cora Sue looked up from watering the colorful flowers potted in front of her shop. "How'd you enjoy your first party at Bryan's, and more important, how'd you enjoy our sheriff and his hot friend?"

Alena couldn't prevent the wide grin spreading across her face. The mischievous twinkle in Cora's eyes and friendly, open banter helped ease the loneliness that had crept in while talking with her friends and hearing about the fun they had going out last weekend to their favorite sushi bar and club.

"What? Are you telling me every detail of the other night hasn't made it to your ears yet? I find that hard to believe," she teased her right back.

Laughing, Cora squirted her sandaled feet with the hose. "Okay, *maybe* Carlee hinted at a few things when I stopped in for lunch earlier." Fanning herself in an over-dramatized manner, she said, "*Whew*, girlfriend, you know what a lucky bitch you are? I'd give anything to have been strung up in your place."

Jumping back, Alena laughed with her. "Okay, that part was all good, eventually, but not… how much did she tell you?"

"Just that you seemed to have a good time and the guys took good care of you. Said even she was jealous of the attention they gave you."

She wouldn't mention the humiliating chastisement if Carlee hadn't. Maybe there was a slim chance that part of the night wouldn't get around. Strange, she mused, that she didn't find the spankings either Randy or Nash administered nearly as embarrassing as those swats from Bryan.

"Well, I'll be gone soon and you'll get them back. Make sure you take good care of them for me."

"Oh, no worries there. Make sure you come around Thursday for our annual summer celebration."

"Will do," she assured her as she picked up her tread, thinking nothing sounded less appealing right now. Born and raised in the city, she never could fathom the draw of small town celebrations. Thinking of the Macy's Thanksgiving Day parades and New Year's Eve bashes she'd attended over the years, fishing contests, softball tournaments, and a small high school band marching down Main Street just couldn't compete.

A dinner crowd filled the diner so she ordered to go and

returned to her boat to eat after assuring Carlee in a quiet, aside conversation she was okay with everything that had gone down the other night. It was nice of Carlee to worry and care, even if it was her boyfriend who had given her such grief.

She fell asleep a few hours later wondering at the discontent plaguing her after spending the day like she always had, part in solitude and part with others.

One minute she was drifting off to sleep to the constant clicking beat from crickets and the occasional owl hoot, and the next waking to choking fear as a startling, heavy weight landed on top of her. Inky darkness revealed nothing except her small nightlight had been turned off, but she didn't need to see to feel warm breath fanning her neck and the painful press of a gloved hand over her mouth, robbing her of breath.

"You've been snooping where you don't belong and people around here don't take kindly to that."

The insidious voice whispering in her ear turned cold fear to throat-gripping, icy terror as she struggled to free herself from his crushing weight. Her strength-robbing efforts only managed to amuse him, more so when she wiggled her arms loose and went for his eyes only to encounter the soft knit of a face mask.

"Want to mark me, do you? I'm too smart to let a cunt get her claws in me."

Suddenly her mouth was free, but before she could gather enough air to scream, his hands locked around her throat, the tight squeeze cutting off her air and sending her terror to a new level. Lights danced behind her eyelids as panic overrode the pain and threatened to take her under faster than his chokehold.

A shudder of revulsion rippled throughout her when her assailant rasped his tongue over her ear right before she barely managed to hear him snarl, "Back off, bitch, or next time I won't stop."

He cut her breath completely with the next squeeze,

turning off the meager flickering lights of awareness and plunging her into total oblivion.

• • • • • • •

Consciousness made a slow return as Alena roused to disoriented darkness and silence. The gentle bobbing of the boat, which she'd begun to find soothing, had her fighting back nausea. Residue shock and lingering fear kept her immobile for several moments as she strained to hear any movement or breathing other than her own. The crickets still sang their night chorus, the owls still let everyone know they were awake, but of her attacker she heard nothing.

Rolling over, she fumbled for the switch to the small nightlight next to the bunk, then squinted against the meager glow it shed. She became aware of the throbbing ache in her throat every time she took a breath and the devastating reality all her self-defense classes and safety awareness ingrained after years of working with the police came to naught when she needed it the most. The swiftness and surprise of her attack rendered her helpless from the moment that heavy body had covered her, something she was struggling with as much as getting out of bed.

Tears filled her eyes and clogged her sore throat as need for supporting human contact slammed into her. For the first time since arriving in Blue Springs, she didn't want to be on this boat alone, didn't want to be alone period. Finding her shorts, she slipped them on, not bothering to change out of her NYPD tee shirt she slept in. Grabbing her purse, she climbed the few steps to her deck, peering topside and taking a cautious look around before dashing to the pier on wobbly legs.

Other boats were moored all along the marina and she was sure there were people bunking in a few as she did, but she didn't want strangers, she wanted the guys. This time, her desperate longing for them didn't scare or irritate her; it became the driving force behind keeping her panic under control. Tomorrow, she reasoned as she made it to her car and sped toward Randy's cabin, she'd question and worry about the motive behind her attack. Tonight, she wanted the sheriff and English to do what they did best, drive her demons and reality away with the temporary respite of painful pleasure.

• • • • • • •

"Shit, now what?" The desperate pounding on his front door sent Randy scrambling into a pair of jeans and down the stairs from his loft bedroom where he met Nash coming out of his room.

"Bloody hell, chap. Doesn't your dispatch phone when there's an emergency?"

"Of course they do," he snapped. After seeing Daisy Mae back behind her desk this morning, her youthful face still ravaged from her ordeal and trying without success to get her to take a few more days off, then spending the better part of the afternoon at a six car pile-up on the state highway a few miles away, he wasn't in the mood for a hysterical midnight caller. "Go back to bed, I'll look into whatever bug's crawled up someone's ass."

"I may as well help you out so we can both get back to sleep sooner." The sheriff's quick temper never bothered Nash. It took a few weeks, but he finally realized his gruff attitude masked a very caring cop who took all aspects of his job seriously.

"I'm coming, just hold on," Randy called out as the pounding continued. "What's so fu... Alena? What the hell... Nash!" he snapped out as she collapsed with a sob in his arms.

Nash took one look at her white face and red marks around her neck and a cold rage unlike anything he'd experienced before swept through him. He had never had a problem keeping his emotions in check on the job, not even with the case that brought him here and had haunted him for over a year. But seeing the terror in Alena's green eyes and fearing her explanation, it took tremendous effort for him to tamp down the urge to grab her and demand answers. Closing the door, he stated, "I'll pour her a shot. Go sit down."

Alena couldn't believe how fast her tension let up as soon as she saw the guys. The second she fell into Randy's arms, heard Nash's sexy accent, everything in her settled. Knowing she was safe helped ease the last of her fear. Remaining glued to Randy's side as he settled her on the couch, she accepted the glass Nash held out to her and downed the alcohol in one long gulp, the fiery burn helping to numb her sore throat. When Nash sat on her other side, sandwiching her between them, she breathed a sigh of relief and laid her head back because she couldn't decide which shoulder she wanted to lean on the most.

Appreciating their patient silence, she finally told them what happened. "Someone pinned me in my bed, choked me, told me to quit poking my nose where it doesn't belong, then... then squeezed... until, until everything went black." The sheer terror of thinking she was going to die came rushing back, making that last part difficult to get out. Their low curses were music to her ears and managed to draw a small smile from her.

"Didn't we..."

"Not now, mate," Nash interrupted Randy's lecture, seeing the anger and concern written on his face that he could commiserate with.

"Yes, you did warn me, but yell at me tomorrow, okay?" Holding up her hand, she continued, "It was pitch black, I felt a ski mask when I tried to rake my nails down his face, he was heavy, tall, and whispered so low I'd never be able to identify his voice. I'm sorry, and I'm really, really tired."

She murmured that last sentence, but it was enough to spur them into rising, Nash scooping her up as Randy led the way up to his room. Laying her down, he said, "I'll be right downstairs if you need anything. Randy'll be..." He turned a questioning look up to him.

"On the couch. We'll talk more in the morning."

With the release of his arms, Alena gained full awareness with both anger and panic threatening her composure. Jerking up in the big bed, she exclaimed, "You're leaving?"

"You want us to stay?" Randy asked, surprised.

"Well, of course I do, why do think I'm here?"

Nash didn't hesitate to shuck his pants and slide in next to her. "We'll be right here, luv. Go to sleep."

Randy was slower in joining her on the other side, but when he did, the king-size bed went from big and lonely to crowded and comforting. She relished the press of their naked bodies against her even as she remained clothed. Surrounded by all that hard, male flesh made her realize this was the first time they had stripped entirely in front of her. And she liked it. But as the minutes ticked by and they did nothing but roll on their sides, wrap an arm around her and hold her close, frustration and escalating need overrode everything else. As much as she appreciated their consideration, that's not what she ached for right now.

Taking matters into her own hands, she slid her palms over their hips, only to be brought up short when they clasped her wrists and returned them to her waist.

"Go to sleep, Alena." Randy squeezed her waist, emphasizing his order.

"Rest now, luv. We'll work this out tomorrow."

Not one to give up, she waited them out, feigned sleep, and as soon as they were relaxed, breathing heavy but not quite asleep, she reached down again and didn't stop until she attained her goal. *It must be latent hysteria*, she thought when giddiness assailed her at finding them hard, hot and pulsing, their cocks silk-encased steel rods. She didn't let the uncharacteristic emotion bother her. They wanted her. They were ready for her. And that's all she cared about right now. Wrapping her fingers around their thick lengths, she gripped them in a tight hold when both men attempted to shift away.

"Let. Go."

"No," she told Randy, turning her head and seeking his mouth in the dim light. Stroking their rigid erections, she licked his compressed lips then moved fast when he parted them on a low groan. Stroking his tongue and molding his lips, she worked their cocks up and down with her fists, cupped their smooth, mushroom-capped heads, smearing the damp pre-cum leaking from their slits then using the moisture to ease her way back down.

"I don't know about you, mate," Nash rasped on an indrawn breath, "but I'm through arguing with her."

"Good enough." Cupping the back of her head, Randy held their fused mouths together as he took over the kiss and pointed above them, a gesture letting Nash know where he was headed. Plundering the depths of her moist mouth, he released a sigh of relief when Nash plucked her hand from his dick. Much more of that and this would be over before she thought she wanted it to. He just hoped they weren't making a mistake giving in to the strong demands stemming from her fragile state.

Alena moaned from both the abrupt loss of their thick flesh in her hands and the sudden jerk of the light blanket baring the three of them. A shiver rippled up her spine when cool air caressed her bare butt as her shorts were stripped off. Pulling her mouth from his, she pleaded on a ragged whisper, *"Please."*

Randy whipped her top over her head, tossed it to the floor, and filled his hands with her lush breasts. "Come morning, just remember this was your idea. Above me, Nash, there's a silk tie."

His grip unbreakable, Alena had no choice but to let Nash raise her arms above her until she felt him bind them to the vertical slat with a swath of silk. Randy released her breasts, cutting her protest short with the quick shift of their bodies. Nash slid under her as Randy helped to maneuver her to her knees, his guttural, succinct order of, "Spread them," spiking her arousal as she positioned herself over Nash's face.

Yes, she groaned in silence, admitting this was what she wanted, what she needed; for them to take her over, drive her into pleasurable oblivion where she could forget her fear and her failures. Closing her eyes, she leaned her head back, let the ends of her hair tickle her shoulders as hands coasted up her spread thighs, thumbs caressing then spreading her labia. She shuddered from the close, intimate exposure, aching for a touch as the seconds ticked by without one.

"Please," she whispered without opening her eyes, wondering why they waited, why they enjoyed tormenting her so much.

"She did ask nicely." Randy knelt next to her, looking down at Nash whose head lay nestled between her spread legs.

"Yes, she did. You want my mouth on your pussy, Alena, then give it to me." Nash followed that succinct order with a sharp nip on the soft flesh of her inner thigh then blew in between her spread folds.

Her eyes flew open at those new stimulating sensations, his instructions both embarrassing and exciting. With her need so great, she wouldn't let the mortification of lowering herself down to his face stop her from attaining her goal of mindless oblivion. A soft cry slipped past her compressed lips at the first touch of his lips caressing the sensitive skin of her inner folds, the slow rasp of his tongue over her clit sending a rippling wave of heat straight up her core. Her nipples tightened into aching pinpoints. The scratch of his unshaved face against her inner thighs aided in the escalating sensations consuming her as he stabbed his tongue in repeated thrusts deep inside her.

"Feel good, baby?" Randy's low voice urged her to shift back into his caressing hand over her buttocks. "Want more?"

Swiveling her head, she looked directly into his midnight eyes and answered without hesitation. "Yes, now, please."

His low laugh and Nash's diabolical hum had her tensing in anticipation. When the first slap landed with resounding impact on her right buttock, the sharp, tingling pain ignited a firestorm inside her, fed by the insertion of deep, probing fingers exploring her vaginal walls. And then they gave her what she came here for, what she craved so much.

Randy delivered a steady volley of hard smacks covering her buttocks, reaching in front of her with his other hand to roll her nipple between two fingers, pinching a little harder with each slap. Nash delved deep with his fingers as he continued to lave her clit too lightly to get her off, just soft enough to keep her teetering on the edge. The distinct slurp of wet suctioning coming from between her legs gave away the extent of her arousal as the throbbing, heated pain continued to build across her butt and spread to her sheath.

Randy swatted the under curve of one cheek, murmuring in her ear, "So soft," he squeezed her buttock, "and so warm." He slapped the tender skin of her sit spot under the other cheek before rubbing the offended areas.

With her entire body aching for release, vibrating in unfulfilled lust, she ground her crotch against Nash's mouth, desperate for the touch that would give her what she wanted. A blistering sting that set her nipple to throbbing forced her to lift back up a fraction and blast Randy with a startled, angry glare. "What was…?" She noticed the open drawer in the bedside table, then the small, flexible bamboo strip in his hand along with the wicked grin on his face.

"It's actually called a clit spanker, but it works great on nipples too."

"Oh, good Lord," she moaned when the burn encompassing her tortured nub sent a fresh gush of moisture into Nash's marauding mouth. "That's just… wrong."

"I think it's just fucking awesome," Nash managed to pull away from his feast long enough to counter.

"You're just fucking awesome," Randy praised her before bending and taking her mouth in a deep, probing kiss.

Alena clung to his mouth a moment, leaning into the kiss

and him, for both titillation and comfort. When he released her with a bite on her lower lip, there was no time or functioning brain cells left to continue the banter as they seemed to have silently agreed to end her waiting. Closing her eyes, she basked in the immediate pleasure of Nash suckling with hard, strong pulls on her clit as Randy set up a slow, steady repetition of butt slaps accompanied by light taps from the little spanker on her nipples, back and forth between them in another slow, steady torturous litany of pain-induced pleasure.

She screamed as pleasure ricocheted throughout her body, the convulsing spasms going on and on, the ecstasy all consuming. Her body still shook with pleasurable, tiny contractions when Randy moved to release her wrists then bent his head to suckle one tortured, throbbing nipple. The strong pulls from his mouth egged on the pain from the mini-spanker and her arousal as Nash scattered a combination of kisses, licks, and tiny bites all over the bare flesh of her labia, literally eating her up.

They didn't give her time to bask in the lingering pleasure as they both shifted, their large hands arranging her boneless body alongside Nash's, lifting her top leg over his hips in a position that left her buttocks spread and her pussy in alignment with his probing cock. With Randy's tall, muscled body pressed against her back, she lay snuggled between them as they threw her right back into the vortex of out-of-control, spiraling pleasure.

CHAPTER TWELVE

"Take a deep breath, luv," Nash suggested right before slipping into the furnace of her tight pussy. She closed around him in a greedy clasp, her slick walls caressing his length in small, milking contractions as soon as he was balls-deep inside her. "God, you feel good."

He pressed her head to his shoulder, the image of her scared face when Randy opened his door searing him anew. He swore when he caught the bastard who terrorized her he'd give him a taste of his own medicine before assisting the sheriff in locking his ass up. With her soft body wrapped around him and his cock enveloped in her equally soft pussy, he prayed he had the strength to hold back long enough to assist Randy.

"Another deep breath now." Gliding his hands down her damp back to her warm ass, he gripped her buttocks and spread them even wider.

"Thanks." Randy probed her anus with short, jabbing strokes, using two then three well lubed fingers before pushing with slow precision inside her tight channel. "Do you still want this, baby? Want us?"

A muffled "Yes" came from where she kept her face buried in Nash's shoulder, followed by an impatient shift of her hips.

"Good enough." Nash pulled away from her tight clasp long enough to give Randy time to slowly take her ass. When his partner finally said, "I'm good, let's do it," he pressed back in as Randy pulled out. Having done this together only twice before, it surprised him how quickly and easily they fell into a tandem rhythm, and, from her mewling cries and spasming vagina, how fast she responded to their dual penetration.

"I can feel her contractions already... *shit*, she's tight," Randy swore as he shifted forward again.

"Tell me about it. Hell, why wait."

Alena was lost. Lost in sensation, in knowing total possession for the first time, in their deep voices echoing around her, and in another 'rob your senses' climax. Pleasure ripped through her overheated system with lightning speed and heat, the deep plunges of their cocks, first one then the other, taking her to a place she'd never been before. Under normal circumstances, she would never allow herself to be taken over, possessed so completely by one man, let alone two. But these weren't normal circumstances. As their sweat-slick bodies rubbed together, their harsh breaths mingled, and their releases were felt and heard by all three of them, she shoved aside all concerns and worries for the temporary respite of falling into pleasure one more time.

• • • • • • •

She woke alone to sunshine brightening the room and a sore body that brought back a rush of memories from the night before. Rolling over with a groan, the ache in her rectum reminded her of the pain of Randy's anal possession followed so swiftly with indescribable pleasure. Their slow, deep thrusts had driven her into orgasm so fast she barely had time to adjust to the new experience and sensations of double penetration. But, as always, with the dawn came reality, and a lift of the last dregs of shock that had kept her befogged mind from facing what happened on her boat that drove her here in the first place.

Now that she could think with a clearer head, she knew, without a doubt, someone at that lake house knew something about Ashley's disappearance. Her assailant's words proved someone had seen her snooping the other night, and with her sister's case the only crime worth threatening someone over in this area, the odds were against her attack not being connected to Ashley. The common denominator between the last people who saw Ashley, Alena's drugging, and her attack last night were Kevin, Brad, and Joel, who had been around when all three events occurred. She didn't believe in that much coincidence.

Crawling out of bed, she gathered up her discarded clothes and stumbled into the connecting bathroom. A long, hot shower sounded wonderful, but the towel racks were empty. Thinking the narrow cedar door led to a linen closet, she almost drooled when she opened it and saw a cedar-lined sauna, a stack of towels folded neatly on a shelf to her right. After indulging in the small, steam-filled enclosure for ten minutes, she took a quick shower and felt marginally better by the time she left the loft and followed the guys' angry voices down the stairs.

"You can't tell me you're still willing to make excuses for them?" Nash growled, glaring at Randy across the kitchen counter. Randy's relaxed pose of leaning on his arms on the butcher block top didn't fool him for a second. The glitter in his friend's dark eyes gave away his frustration.

"No. Bryan or Kevin knows something, but that doesn't mean one of them was behind the attack on Alena."

"I don't understand your continued defense of these people. *Everything* points to Kevin being involved with Ashley's disappearance and that's still too much of a coincidence not to keep him at the top of my suspect list for my victim, especially after Alena's recount of how she was choked just until she lost consciousness. Are you forgetting my ME's report that gave evidence Lisa Ames suffered through multiple episodes of autoerotic asphyxiation before finally being choked to death? Damn it, Janzen, she deserves justice, and her family needs closure." While he could admire Randy for his loyalty to his friend, turning a blind eye to the facts was not acceptable.

"I know that, Nash," Randy replied with a sigh. "And trust me, I'm as upset over what happened to Alena as you. Don't forget, Daisy Mae also suffered a similar attack and there were over thirty people at that party who could've been the perpetrator. I've known Bryan for over a decade and I'm telling you he wouldn't be behind what happened to those girls. He went overboard spoiling Kevin after his stepfather walked out on him when Kevin was just eight, which included being overprotective, I'll give you that, but I saw how strict he was with that kid the last ten years, how he drilled right and wrong into him during his teens. Kevin was wild, but not purposely harmful to anyone."

"But he would cover for his friends, wouldn't he?" The three of them—Kevin, Brad, and Joel—had been the best of friends, according to Randy, since grade school. Since they'd arrived in Blue Springs, he hadn't seen any of them alone; they were always together at either the lake or hanging around town.

"Yeah, I'm pretty sure he would, which…"

"Which means he would hide any proof there is of Ashley's disappearance." Alena entered the kitchen with a fierce look and firm voice that told Nash the pathetic victim of last night had been replaced with the sister determined to find answers. Letting Randy handle that statement, he turned to the refrigerator, pulled out a small bowl of fruit, and set it next to the plate of assorted donuts he had picked up earlier.

"He *might*, but we don't know that for sure. How are you this morning?" Randy looked her over carefully, then nodded. "You slept well."

Releasing a pent-up sigh, she scooted onto the high stool

next to his and almost drooled when he handed her a napkin and slid the plate of donuts toward her. "I did, and now I wake up to my favorite breakfast. Thanks, guys." Snatching a long john dripping with chocolate icing, she bit into pure sugar sweetness, closing her eyes a moment to savor the gooey treat. Those two really knew how to get to her, in more ways than sexual.

"Eat that before you get another one." Nash set the small bowl of fruit next to her, grinning when she opened her eyes and scowled at the strawberries and bananas then at him.

"Why?" Damn, all that healthy stuff would ruin everything.

"Because it's good for you and that's not." He pointed to the one small bite of her donut she had left.

Narrowing her eyes, she ignored the tickle both men's intent, probing looks were responsible for. She started to retort they weren't good for her either, but couldn't, in all honesty, claim that. Last night they had been very good for her fragile state of mind, even though they had made it clear they didn't want to go that far.

"Maybe I need comfort food after what you put me through last night," she baited them before popping the bite into her mouth and reaching for another. The sharp rap on her hand had her snatching it back from the plate and leveling a glare at the sheriff's smug face. "That wasn't nice."

"Never claimed to be nice. Eat your fruit and I'll get you a cup of coffee."

"Oh, well, since you put it that way…" She dug into the fruit, refusing to admit how good it tasted. After taking a sip of the steaming mug Randy set in front of her, she asked, "What're your plans now, regarding Ash's disappearance?"

"Yes, what is our next step, chap?" Nash drawled with a sardonic lift of one eyebrow.

"My first inclination is to send you two back home, but since that is a battle I'm sure to lose, I say we go with our original plan. I can't question anyone more than I have without reason, and without a description, or anything else to go on from your attack, I don't have that. Since you said your assailant wore gloves, Alena, you would know dusting the boat for prints will be futile, but it'll be done anyway. Tomorrow is the annual Blue Springs Summer Celebration, which Bryan always follows on Saturday with his biggest get-together. There'll be twice as many guests, which will give us more of an opportunity to slip away." Randy narrowed his dark eyes at her, pointed his finger, and stated with quiet authority, "Nash and I, not you."

Touching her fingers lightly to her sore throat, she had no problem agreeing to that. "Got it, believe me."

Nash strolled around the counter, surprising her by bending and spreading a row of soft, soothing kisses around her neck. "There, all better, luv." Cupping the back of her head, he devoured her mouth in a searing kiss, before saying, "Gotta run. Promised some town folk I'd help with preparations for all the events tomorrow."

Randy snorted. "Sucker."

Alena clenched her hands into fists to keep from touching her lips and reaching for Nash to pull him back down for more. Would she ever be completely sated with these two?

Snatching another donut, she swiveled to Randy. "You're not helping? It's your town."

Instead of cupping her skull, he fisted her hair and held her head immobile for his kiss, which was just as hard and possessive and Nash's. The slight tug on her scalp set her nipples to tingling and her hips shifting on her seat in uncomfortable dampness.

"I have to work, thank God," Randy answered as soon as he released her. "Meet us for lunch later, if you're up for it, otherwise make yourself at home."

They both strolled out, just assuming she would be staying at the cabin for now. Since the thought of returning to her boat tonight sent a shiver of fear crawling under her skin, she didn't argue with them. With them was where she wanted to be, at least for the next few days.

· · · · · · ·

At noon the next day, Alena found herself standing on Main Street along with what looked to be the entire town, clapping and smiling as the parade of floats, high school band members, and different clubs marched by. She stood next to Carlee in front of the diner, glad Randy had to be on duty and Nash was busy helping elsewhere for now. Her displeasure and frustration with the two of them for refusing to sleep with her last night continued to bristle today. Most women would have found their excuse she needed to rest and 'heal' after her first ménage considerate. Given her never-ending, constant state of needy arousal when around them, she found it damned annoying. Didn't they realize she would only be here another few days? She'd think they would want to get in as much sex as possible, like she wanted to do. But, oh no, they had to go and be all chivalrous and do what was *right*. Thinking of returning home and going back to her occasional hook-up and spending a night having vanilla sex with one of her friends with benefits didn't make her inclined to see it their way.

"Come on, Alena, lighten up. They'll be banging you again in no time, you lucky bitch."

Shifting Carlee a rueful look, she sighed in defeat. "Yeah, okay, I guess I am being unreasonable." Confessing the reason for her irritability to Carlee during her late breakfast this morning felt good. She hadn't realized everything closed for the day of celebration except the diner, which only opened until eleven serving breakfast.

"Ya think? Dressed like that, you're sure to get their attention." She eyed Alena's new ass-hugging bright yellow shorts and clinging halter top with envy. Nudging her with her elbow, she added, "Maybe you'll even get in trouble again Saturday night and treat us to another scene."

"Scene? What'd I miss?" Cora Sue sidled up next to

them with a lascivious grin.

"Sex, just sex, now watch the parade, you two," Alena stated.

Alena couldn't help but become more lighthearted as they joked during the rest of the parade and her temporary friends filled her in on the activities planned for the day. When Nash showed up as the three of them were walking down to the park thirty minutes later, her heart did that funny little skip and she forgot her annoyance with him. His bright blue gaze showed blatant appreciation after lingering on her braless chest, her nipples puckering in noticeable response aiding in setting aside her pique.

"Come on, luv. I've signed us up for the three-legged race."

Nash took in her rosy cheeks and sparkling green eyes along with the prominent outline of her nipples and the way her top clung to the full roundness of her breasts, glad to see her mood had improved from this morning. She had no idea how difficult staying out of her bed last night had been for him, and, he suspected, Randy. The more time he spent with her, the more he wanted her. Knowing his partner felt the same added to the pleasure of having her close. But they were also concerned as to where this would end shortly. The thought of returning to Scotland Yard didn't appeal to him as much as when he'd first arrived in Blue Springs almost two months ago.

"You're kidding, aren't you? I've never been in any kind of race, let alone a three-legged one."

"I'll do it with you, Nash," Cora Sue volunteered with a look that gave amused double meaning to her offer.

"Thanks, but I think us two amateurs ought to stick together. I've never done this either."

Fifteen minutes later, Nash and Alena tumbled to the ground in a heap of tangled legs, her lush body a soft cushion beneath his as they laughed with uncontrollable mirth at their ineptness.

"We came in last, English!" she exclaimed, looking up at

him in delight.

Giving her a swift, hard kiss, he slipped his hand between their bodies and grazed her nipple with a light stroke. When she jolted against him with a low groan, he pulled back with a smile. "So we did. Let's see if we can do something else with better success."

Reaching for his hand, she frowned but let him help her up. "Now you're being as mean as Randy, and you used to be the nice one."

"I *am* the nice one, but I can't resist teasing you and getting that look of irritated arousal in return. That's such a turn-on." Tugging her hand, he pulled her over to a tug-of-war contest. "Let's join the underdogs. They look like they could use our help."

"I doubt if I'll be any better at this than hopping around with you, but what the heck. I'll give it a try."

God, he loved that brave, 'take the bull by the horns' attitude of hers, that willingness to try anything once. Was it any wonder both he and Randy had fallen for her so fast? Her stubbornness with insisting on being involved with finding her sister had been as admirable as it was frustrating. He wondered if Ashley knew what a gem of a sister she had, and worried over how Alena would cope if the outcome of this turned out to be as bad as they feared.

Shoving aside concerns he couldn't do anything about right now, he settled her in front of him at the end of the line on the rope pull, wrapped his arms around her, and placed his hands in front of hers on the thick hemp. "That's my girl," he whispered before laughing and calling out loud, "Pull!"

Once again they landed on the ground, only this time the heap of losers tangled together contained seven bodies instead of two, all of them laughing in good-natured defeat. Struggling to disengage herself and stand, Alena brushed off her now dirty new shorts then fisted her hands on her hips. "That's it. From now on, I'll be watching from the sidelines. Preferably with one of those funnel cakes I saw at a booth."

"You've been a good sport, luv. Let's get you a treat and you can cheer Randy and me on as we join the softball game in about fifteen minutes."

A few hours later, Alena sat at one of the long picnic tables, hot, sweaty, and tired, trying to recall when she'd enjoyed a day more. It worried her how much fun she'd had with her new friends and the guys all afternoon as she participated in the games and activities of the small town's celebration. She enjoyed her funnel cake as much as she'd delighted in trying to out cheer Carlee when they discovered their guys were on opposite softball teams. Cora Sue had wisely remained neutral. The competitive side of Randy and Nash she hadn't been privy to before surprised her as neither seemed to have a problem sharing her. She liked it as much as she liked having sex with them, which left her unsettled in more ways than one. She really needed to get home soon, back to normal before she forgot how much she wanted her normal again.

"I don't think I'll ever be hungry again," she groaned, pushing aside her empty plate. A large tent had been erected to keep the food-laden tables out of the sun and she had managed to take a sampling of damn near every wonderful homemade dish before taking a seat in between Randy and Nash. Whoever knew home-cooked food would taste so good?

"Not even if we have donuts again in the morning?"

Randy's knowing glance drew a smile from her despite the discomfort of her over-full stomach and concerns about her growing feelings. "I might be able to muster up a small appetite for donuts. It'd help if I got a little exercise later tonight." This time she gave him a knowing look.

"I have been itching to rid you of that top," Nash said as he shoveled in the last of his potato salad. "Especially after you got plastered with that water balloon."

Both men trailed their eyes down to her still damp halter where her nipples proceeded to pucker, again, from those heated looks. Squirming in her seat, she cast a conscientious glance at the park full of people milling around. For a small town, everyone seemed open-minded and nonjudgmental about her obvious relationship with both men, at least those who weren't oblivious to their sexually charged looks.

"You can rid me of everything once we're back at the cabin. So... ready to leave?"

Randy laughed outright at her eager response. "Sorry, baby. I have to stick around until the fireworks are over, and you're sticking too. Excuse me."

Fishing his phone out of his pocket, Alena noticed his jaw tighten the longer he listened to whoever called. "Are you sure? Okay, got it. I'm on my way." Snapping the phone closed, he stood, braced his hand on her shoulder, and gave it a brief squeeze as he spoke to Nash over her head. "I need a moment with you. Wait here, Alena."

She knew that tone, and that look. Something had come up, something that put a cold knot of dread in her stomach. They walked several feet away, had a few words that caused Nash's face to turn grim, and then Randy strode away without looking back at her.

"What?" she demanded as she rose and faced Nash.

"Let's go back..."

"No!" Shrugging away from his outstretched hand, she glared up at him, insisting again, "What happened?"

Nash released a frustrated breath, unable to refuse the plea in her eyes, even though he really wanted to. "That was the state patrol. Some hikers found a car down an incline that matched the description of Ashley's. They have to dig out the brush around it to get to the license plate or inside for the registration. Might take a while."

Panic threatened to bring her dinner back up, but she swallowed the bile filling her throat, concentrating on the thread of hope he gave her. "Her car, not her?"

"No body, Alena, and no sign of her around the wreck. Let's go back to Randy's..."

"No," she said again. "Take me there."

"Not a good idea. We can't help, we'd only be in the

way." He hated seeing the desperation etched on her face. Unlike her, he doubted they would find her sister anywhere near the car, or at all without help. He wanted to be there for her whenever they found Ashley, *if* they found her, and wanted to either celebrate or mourn with her. If there was ever a woman who needed someone to lean on, it was Alena.

Pivoting, she went around him, speaking over her shoulder. "I'll find them myself, somehow."

Cursing, he stormed after her, grabbed her hand, and kept a tight hold. "You are so stubborn. Come on then."

They strode at a brisk pace to where he parked in front of the sheriff's office, Nash hoping Randy didn't kill him for caving in to her. Pulling out his phone, he texted for directions without telling Randy he would be bringing Alena with him.

Holding open the passenger door, he warned her, "The sheriff's going to be pissed and don't expect me to run interference. This isn't a good idea."

"I can hold my own with Randy. Let's go."

It took them almost an hour to get to the deep ravine lined with official vehicles, their flashing lights a beacon guiding them to the right spot. Alena kept quiet as Nash drove, thinking of anything and everything except the possibilities of what had happened to Ashley or where she could possibly be. Jumping out as soon as he pulled to the side of the road, she ignored his call for her to wait. Tripping down the steep slope, she didn't feel the painful scratches on her bare legs and arms as she struggled through the brush toward the small group of state police and Randy.

"Anything?" she gasped when he whirled and caught her as she stumbled next to him. Ignoring his angry, black-eyed glare, she peered down the slope, watching as a heavy chain attached to a tow truck slowly cranked the car back up, tail end first.

"What the hell, Nash?" Randy clasped Alena's arm to keep her from tumbling down the hill. "You never said…"

He stopped when Nash held his hand up and shook his head with a significant look toward Alena. Taking a closer look, he saw the despair in her green eyes, the dimming of hope that had been there since she first stormed into town demanding answers.

Reining in his irritation, he tugged her next to his side. "Alena, baby, come away. There's nothing to see, nothing to do."

"What do you mean? We need to look for her."

"Yes, *we* need to look for her, law enforcement and experienced hikers and searchers who know this area." He didn't tell her the slim chances of finding anything, or anything positive. She knew what they were, he was sure; she just refused to acknowledge it. "We've already sent out inquiries to the nearest hospitals again, checking to see if a Jane Doe has been brought in within the past two months since we first checked with them and calls are going out for volunteers to scout this area. Trust me, we're doing everything we can."

He also didn't tell her there were no visible footprints anywhere around the car, no blood inside or out, leading all of them to believe the car had gone over the cliff without anyone in it. If she were thinking clearly, she'd know to ask those questions. He just hoped her mind didn't clear too soon, at least until he could get her back to his place.

From the look of concern on Nash's face, he felt as protective and concerned as Randy. The afternoon of fun and games had shown him just how much she had gotten under his skin, and if he had time for it, he'd question how that had happened in such a short time and what he would do about it. Maybe it was a good thing he couldn't think about it right now.

"Take her back. The state guys will be towing the car. As soon as I've wrapped up here, I'll head back."

Randy took Alena's focus from her sister's crumbled car with a two-finger, gentle nudge under her chin. The look of compassionate concern in his eyes almost broke her composure as her eyes swam with the watery threat of tears. Biting her lip until the pain erased that threat, she said, "Thanks. I know you're doing everything you can. She's not here, so that's a good sign, right?"

"It means there's still hope we'll find her alive." *Slim to none, but that reality will come to her soon enough*, Randy thought. "Will you go back with Nash now?"

Wow, she must really look a basket case if he was asking instead of telling. Why that made her want to smile, she didn't know, but she would take whatever humor she could get right now. "Sure, Sheriff. You know I always take your advice." His quick grin eased her tension until he replied.

"That's my girl."

"Our girl," Nash added.

Oh, good Lord, she thought in disbelief when all her happy places started tingling from those low-voiced praises. She was *so* not going there. Her time with them would be up in a few days and she would be going home where she belonged, regardless of what they did, or didn't find out about Ashley.

"Let's get out of here, English."

Tiredness, both physical and emotional, settled into her bones as they drove back. After her father had died, she'd had to be the strong one in the family, shoulder the burden of caring for both her distraught mother and rebellious sister. Her own grief had been shoved aside to help them cope with theirs, but no matter what she did, how hard she tried, her mother had continued to slip deeper and deeper into depression and alcoholism and Ashley into worse trouble. Alena always felt she'd failed her family, hadn't been strong enough, smart enough, or made the right decisions in how to care for them. What if her decision not to bail Ashley out of jail last spring led to her rash, unsafe behavior when she got out? How could she live with that failure also?

Leaning her head back, she found comfort in Nash's silence and in letting him and Randy shoulder the burden of

Ashley's disappearance for a while. She wanted, needed one night to herself, without having to wonder and worry over where to go or what to do next in trying to get answers.

"Take me to the marina," she instructed Nash when they neared Blue Springs. "I'm fine now and need some space."

"That's the last thing you need, especially since whoever accosted you the other night is still out there. You can spend the night holed up in Randy's loft if you want."

She had never heard him use that implacable tone before, and for some reason that, along with his dictate, set her off. "Like hell I am. Take me to the marina."

"Sorry, luv, no can do."

CHAPTER THIRTEEN

Those simple words of denial uttered without remorse turned her vision red. She fumed in silence in the seat next to him for the ten minutes it took to reach the cabin on the outskirts of town. Night had fallen and the Jeep's headlights were the only light illuminating their way down the graveled drive. A small porch sconce glowed in soft amber when he pulled to a stop in front of the cabin and switched off the brighter glare of headlights. Jumping out, the slam of her door echoed in the otherwise quiet stillness of the forest shrouded lot.

"You've got a lot of nerve," she began before one look at the concern etched on his face sent need slamming into her with the force of a freight train. She thought she wanted solitude to brood, but as he came around the Jeep and pulled her gently into his embrace, her body came up with a better way to cope with the emotions threatening her composure.

As she leaned against that tall, hard body, he rubbed his hands over her shoulders and back in soothing caresses that set her body aflame with desperate longing for oblivion. Arousal grew into hot need that soon drove her into a frenzy of lust almost excruciating in its intensity. Pulling back, she cupped her hands around his head, pulling him down to her with one low-voiced demand. "Fuck me, Nash. Now."

She slammed her mouth onto his before Nash could form a reply, her mouth angry as she ground her lips against his, her tongue desperate as she forced her way past his startled resistance. Gathering his senses, he kissed her back, giving her just a taste of what she thought she wanted but knew she didn't. Not really. She sought escape from the real possibility the outcome of Ashley's disappearance won't be a good one. He gave her a few minutes to lean on him, take from him, then gently gripped her shoulders and pushed her back. They were standing at the foot of the porch steps and he couldn't see her clear enough to read her face, but he felt her anger in her tense body, her need to shove aside the truth for just a little longer in her slight trembling. And it broke his heart to turn her down because he knew she wouldn't understand, at least not right now.

"Come on, I'll pour you a stiff drink and you can take a long hot shower. You'll feel better afterwards. It's been a distressing day."

Gripping his shirt in her fists, she went up on her toes and got in his face. "No, damn you. I don't want a drink or a shower. I want you, I need…" She broke, biting back the rest of that plea. Growing fury and disheartenment drove her on, refusing to allow her to give in. "Now, English. You wanted me out here, insisted on bringing me here." Releasing his shirt, she made quick work of undoing his belt. "Now you can just fucking deal with the consequences, and me."

She had his zipper down and his cock freed before his brain could overrule his body's acceptance of her demands. Her tight grip almost sent his eyes rolling to the back of his head. Making a last-ditch effort to do the right thing, he gripped her hand and pulled her away from him, the cool night air stirring his heated flesh even further.

"Alena, luv, you don't…"

"Don't tell me what I want, what I need."

When she started to go to her knees, his own control and patience snapped like a twig. Jerking her up and against him, he growled, "Stop it," and gave her a small shake that did nothing. She latched onto him again, wrapped one leg around his hips and ground her pelvis against his throbbing erection, her low, taunting laugh his undoing.

"You want me. Fuck me. I promise, if you give it to me hard and fast, I won't regret it. I'll love it." *I need it, I need you, so much I know I'll fall apart completely without this.* It was only by sheer grit she kept from uttering that out loud.

This time it was his turn to slam his mouth down on hers, kiss her with hard possession as he loosened her shorts and shoved them down, no longer able to stand the torment in her voice or the real need vibrating in her body. Releasing her mouth, he spun her around and bent her over the steps. "Brace your hands on the second step," he ordered, swatting her ass, hard.

"Yes!" Alena almost wept from the now familiar pleasure burn of his hard hand connecting with her butt. "More, don't stop, please." Dropping her head between her braced arms, she relished each fiery smack, loved the sound of flesh slapping flesh resounding in the dark, still night. She could hear cars driving on the road, but knew they were far enough back no one could see them. Not that she would've minded. Right now, at this moment, in this place, she didn't care about anything but wallowing in that place of euphoric bliss she knew he could take her.

A soft cry escaped her compressed mouth when he belabored her buttocks with a fast volley of sharp slaps, covering every inch of her globes before tormenting her sit spots then her thighs. Shifting her hips under the painful, heated onslaught, she soon found herself questioning whether she wanted him to stop or needed him to continue. Leaving it up to him, she lifted for the next smacks as he returned to her cheeks, pleading, "Nash, *please.*"

Latching onto her hips, he leaned over her back as he slid into the slick, hot furnace of her pussy. "Had enough, or do you want more?" He pulled back then rammed balls deep back inside her. "This is what you said you wanted, right? To be fucked? Hard and fast, I believe is what you insisted on."

He didn't wait for an answer before lifting up and giving her what she had pushed him into. With deep, jackhammer thrusts, he fucked her just like she wanted him to. The tight clutches of her slick vaginal walls pulled at his cock, her damp release tempting him to let go with his own climax, but he forced back the urge to work her into one more first.

"Again. Come on, luv, you can do better than that."

His words penetrated the fog of pleasure ripping through her, his womb-nudging plunges driving her to the brink within seconds of her first climax abating. If it hadn't been for his tight grip on her hips holding her immobile, his hard fucking would have pushed her forward, flat on her face most likely. Tiny mewls of ecstasy escaped her lips and the pleasure erupted and washed over her again, this time with the feel of his cock jerking in release egging her on.

"What the hell are you thinking?"

Randy's furious voice penetrated the lingering pleasure clouding her senses, and Alena shuddered as Nash withdrew from her still spasming sheath with excruciating slowness. But with his withdrawal and standing to face the blistering anger Randy leveled on Nash, that gripping need took hold of her again. God help her, she didn't know which one she hungered for more, and it had been that way since she first set eyes on them.

"Don't blame him, Sheriff, I forced myself on him. But he petered out on me, so I guess you have to pick up the slack."

"Damn it, Alena." Randy grabbed her hand as she kicked aside her shorts and led her inside. From the glimpse he got of her ass as he drove in, Nash had tried calming her the old-fashioned way. He should've remembered how she responded to spanking and saved his time. As soon as they entered his cabin, she turned on him, jumping into his arms, her legs going around his waist in a tight ankle-lock hold as she latched onto his mouth and sucked the breath from him with her voracious kiss.

With a few steps, he had her pinned against the wall, one hand ripping her halter top down, the other inching under her to clasp one warm buttock and squeeze. Her low moan filled his mouth as he kissed her with as much pent-up frustration and misery over not finding Ashley or a clue to her whereabouts with her car as she expressed. Like Nash, taking her while in such a vulnerable state poked at his conscience, but he succumbed to the constant desire to give her whatever she needed to get through this ordeal. Knowing their girl, he had no doubt by morning she would bounce back to her independent, determined nature that had kept her together thus far.

With a deep breath, he released her mouth and filled his hand with her soft breast as he kneaded the under curve of the buttock he cupped. "You want this, then figure out a way to release my cock *without* killing me."

Alena wanted this so much she had no trouble finding the patience to wedge her hand between them and lower his zipper over his thick erection, her arousal dripping onto his cock head as he rubbed the smooth crown of his mushroom cap over her gaping slit.

"Now, Sheriff, oh, good Lord," she ended on a gasp when he thrust up, filling her with one brutal stroke.

She heard them both chuckle then heard nothing but the roaring of pleasure as he pounded into her over and over, his vigorous fucking abrading her back against the wall as he took her with all the finesse of a rutting bull. Exactly what she'd wanted, needed to get her over this last hurdle. A tight pinch of her nipple along with a light graze over her anus set her off, the explosion coming fast and hard, the wet suction of their mating revealing how aroused she still was. Like his partner, he gifted her with another climax before his cock jerked inside her, his groan of pleasure buried in her neck sending shivers down her arms.

Her wince when he gripped her butt with both hands, lifted her off his erection, and let her slide down him and the wall drew a wicked smile from him.

"Nash really walloped on you, didn't he?"

"Hey, I at least *tried* to hold off," Nash defended.

"Why?" Randy questioned.

Alena laughed weakly at Nash's disgruntled tone coming from where he lounged against a stool at the kitchen counter and Randy's succinct reply. God, these two could disarm her in so many different ways it boggled her mind and offered her something else to worry about along with her sister. As the haze of grief finally lifted, embarrassment over her nudity and her actions unfolded.

Needing to get away, she shuffled out of Randy's reach, keeping her face averted from both of them. "I'm tired. Mind if I turn in?"

"After a warm shower," Randy insisted.

Before she could protest, and she really wanted to, Randy had her scooped up in his arms, Nash following them upstairs. Because she knew it would be futile to argue, and because fatigue wouldn't allow her to do anything else, she let them pamper her through a steaming shower then tuck her into bed with them. Telling herself exhaustion forced her to accept their solicitous care, not need, she fell asleep sandwiched between their naked bodies.

• • • • • • •

Once again she woke to the bright glare of sunshine cutting a swath across the loft bedroom and an empty bed, which was just as well as she recalled her meltdown last night. Rolling over with a groan, she buried her head under the pillow, wondering what the heck had come over her. At the ravine, she had agreed with Randy that Ash could still be alive, maybe just lost or, as usual, being inconsiderate and not thinking to let someone know she was all right. But Nash's refusal to return her to her boat, to give her the space she wanted to assimilate all the facts, and options, had lit a fuse inside her she couldn't extinguish.

Even though she screwed up at the bar and last week at the party, for the past few weeks she had given in to their demands over and over, tried to be an asset, not a hindrance. Was it too much to ask that they give in to her just that once? Apparently so because she was here, wasn't she? The past few days afforded her a glimpse into the overprotective, caring side of both men, as well as the fun-loving side she saw yesterday during the town's activities. She had no problem admitting she got off on their strict, sexually dominant nature, but throw in the other facets and they became a duo that would make forgetting them difficult to do.

Not liking that thought or the memory of how badly she'd ended up needing both of them last night regardless of her desire to be alone, she dragged her achy body out of the comfortable, warm bed. She spotted her shorts and top sitting on a chair, a little dirt-stained but welcome nonetheless. The soreness between her legs and the lingering puffy ache encompassing her butt reminded her they both gave her what she demanded, a vigorous, hard fucking that aided in helping her fall into a deep and dreamless sleep. So, slipping into her clothes, she guessed she did have to be grateful, somewhat, for Nash forcing her to stay here last night.

But that was then and this was now, and she needed to return to the boat and start preparing for her return home on Sunday. Bryan's big bash tomorrow would be the last opportunity, at least for her, to learn anything new about her sister's whereabouts. If they couldn't unearth any new clues, something to go on, she'd have to return home empty-handed with no other option but to hope the police eventually found her.

One way or another. That thought had her stumbling to a stop on her way to the stairs. For the first time, she forced herself to admit she may never see Ashley again, at least not alive. Her heart twisted in painful agony at just the thought. For all their differences, all the trouble she had been over the years, Alena still cared about her. All along, she'd vowed to wash her hands of her self-centered, irresponsible sibling once and for all after this, but right now, she couldn't imagine her life without Ashley in it, so she didn't.

"Positive thinking never hurt," she muttered as she jogged downstairs. Then again, she'd tried thinking positive about Ashley someday taking responsibility for her actions and shaping up to no avail as of yet.

I could get used to this, she envisioned when she spotted the donuts and coffee waiting for her again, a thought that increased the need to get back home where she belonged. Randy swiveled on his stool to eye her with those penetrating black eyes as Nash gave her the same intent, probing look from where he sat on the sofa with the paper in hand. Her heart did that uncomfortable roll in her chest, adding to the desperate urge to run as far and as fast away from Blue Springs and these two as she could. It was definitely time to go home.

Waving her hand toward the plate of donuts, she inquired with a nonchalance she was far from feeling, "I take it you're not too pissed over my meltdown last night."

Randy lowered his black brows in a perplexed frown. "Why would we be mad? You had every right to be upset."

"And I should've seen what you needed. But I did enjoy your eager persistence, luv."

The small smile playing around Nash's mouth almost drew a return grin from her. Almost. Ignoring both men's replies that weren't what she expected and that gave her another warm rush, she snatched a cream-filled, powdered sugar-covered donut. "Mind if I eat this on the run? I have a lot to do if we're going to be at the lake house most of the day tomorrow as I plan on leaving early Sunday. I need to get back home."

From their exchange of knowing looks, they caught the determined strength she forced into her tone. Let them think what they wanted, she knew where she belonged, and it wasn't here despite what her body continued to crave.

Randy pointed to a cabinet above the coffeemaker. "There's a lidded travel mug up there. You'll need something to wash that down."

Surprised but grateful they didn't argue with her, she retrieved the mug and filled it before asking, "Would one of you run me back to the marina?"

Folding the paper and setting it aside, Nash rose and picked up his keys off the small table next to the front door. "I will. Randy needs to get to work. Ready?"

Nodding her head, she remained perplexed and a bit miffed by their easy dismissal of her this morning on the silent ride back to the marina. She felt marginally better when Nash turned to her after pulling to a stop in the marina's lot and asked, "Do you want to drive to Randy's later or have us pick you up?"

"I thought I'd spend the night at the B & B tonight, give you two a break from me." Actually, that idea had just come to her. It would give her the space she needed from them to get her mind back on track with her priorities and the safety she needed since her attacker was still unidentified.

"That's a good idea." Leaning over, he pulled her close for a deep kiss, trying to hide his reluctance to let her go, and his need to insist she stay the night with him and Randy again. He knew she'd be safe at the B & B, but he wouldn't get to watch over her himself, something he found he enjoyed doing.

"Okay then," Alena said when he released her. The confused irritation reflected in her expressive green eyes made him feel better about the decision they agreed on early this morning to not stress her out any more by going along with whatever she wanted to do today, including giving her some space.

"We'll join you for breakfast in the morning. Get some rest today."

She nodded and got out of the Jeep without another

word. Nash watched her walk to her boat, waited until she jumped aboard and waved him off before turning and heading back to town knowing she wouldn't relax any more than he or Randy would today.

• • • • • • •

Cloudy skies rolled in by late afternoon the next day, the threat of rain noticeable in the sultry air as Alena, Nash, and Randy parked in the circular drive at Bryan's lake house. Alena noticed twice as many cars lined the drive as last week and dozens of people mingled around the yard and in and out of the house. Bryan manned the grill again, but because of the weather potential, she assumed, she could see the rest of the food and tables were lined up in the garage at the back of the lot.

With her heart beating a rapid tattoo of excitement, she slid out of the cruiser with Nash's help, determined to get as much out of tonight, and the guys, as possible. If this was going to be the last time she saw them, was with them, she wouldn't let insecurities, embarrassment, or worry hold her back from enjoying whatever they had planned.

"I do like that top."

Nash reached out and ran one finger over her distended nipple, clearly visible along with every small bump of her areola through the thin camisole top she wore with a very short white skirt. After breakfast, the three of them had strolled around town and when they came to the quaint boutique and she saw the camisole on the window mannequin, she knew she had to have it, especially after seeing the guys' eyes light up.

"You're not blushing tonight, Alena. Like what you see?"

Randy picked up her other hand as they strode forward and she didn't look away from the naked woman kneeling between a man's spread legs, sucking his cock or the one lying through a tire swing on her stomach as her lover swung her back and forth on his cock. The position looked uncomfortable, but as a voyeur, she found the scene hot.

"I know what to expect tonight." Her body, never slow to arouse when near the guys, grew warm and tingly in all her happy places.

Stopping at an iced barrel, Nash retrieved two beers and a wine cooler and handed them over before grinning at Randy. "I think I heard a challenge. What do you think, mate?"

Popping the tab, he smirked with the bottle poised at his mouth. "Where's the fun if our girl isn't wondering, and worrying just a tad, about what we'll do?"

Oh, she really didn't like those identical mischievous looks, or, if she went by the warm gush between her legs, she liked them too much. "You promised to feed me first and I'm holding you to it." She followed her statement with a long drink of the cold, fizzy wine that went right to her head.

Not fooled in the least, Nash said, "So we did. Let's go see what smells so good."

They piled her plate with food then took a seat on either side of her at one of the long tables. She sat across from Cora Sue and a man she recognized from last week but didn't know, but couldn't keep up much of a conversation as the guys started tormenting her while they ate by running their hands up her thighs under the table, not stopping at her skirt. Nudging it aside, they slid their fingers inside her thong and stroked the sensitive, bare skin of her labia as if they were petting a cat. She would've purred in delight if she hadn't been frustrated by her growing arousal they seemed in no hurry to see to.

"Why, Alena, you look flushed. You okay?" Cora Sue's wicked grin indicated she knew exactly what was going on under the table, but Alena wasn't above getting payback.

Looking at Cora's companion, she smiled sweetly in return. "What's wrong, Cora? Are you being ignored?"

"Not nice, baby." Randy put his hamburger down,

reached up and yanked down the thin spaghetti strap on her top to expose her breast before grasping her nipple between thumb and forefinger and pinching, as hard as Nash pinched the tender skin of her folds under the table.

"*Ow!*" Damn, she should've remembered payback could be a bitch. "That hurt." She leveled an accusing glare at both of them and ignored Cora's giggles until her companion whipped off her bathing suit top and gave her nipple the same treatment.

"Both of you behave," he ordered in a brusque tone that belied the twinkle in his eyes.

Snorting, Nash muttered, "That'll be the day."

Alena didn't care when Nash lowered her other strap, leaving her top bunched under her breasts, the thin straps around her arms. It was fun bantering this way and added an extra spark to heat up those tingles. She made a good dent in her plate despite their continuous, distracting touches; she just hoped the damp spot she knew would be left on the bench when she rose wouldn't be too noticeable.

She was more than ready to leave the table, and the garage, so they could finish what they started, but Carlee came by carrying a tray of pies that made her mouth water even though she was so full she didn't know where she'd put another bite.

"We'll share one of the cream pies, Carlee."

"Oh, she's a lucky girl, Sheriff." She handed Randy the largest piece and walked off with an exaggerated, jealous sigh.

"I am? Why?"

"Because she knows I like to do this." He scooped a mound of whipped cream off the top with two fingers then passed the plate to Nash, who caught on quick and did the same. "Good idea, chap."

"What are you doing? Don't waste… oh, good Lord!" She clamped her mouth shut when they bent their heads to lick off the whipped topping they had smeared on her breasts and nipples. "Never mind." By the time they finished the pie, several other women were getting the same treatment, soft moans and the sound of slurping, hungry mouths reverberating up and down the table.

"Now look what you've done," she teased when they licked off the last spot of cream. They both looked down at her damp breasts and red, puckered nipples with satisfied grins.

"Damn, we're good." Randy stood and helped her up. "Come on. The fire pit is lit and looks inviting."

They spent the past hour teasing her into heated arousal then, as they stepped over to the circular fire pit surrounded by several seated couples, they gave her no time to grasp their intentions before taking her over. Stopping a foot away from the pit with the woods behind them and the orange-yellow glow of flames in front of them, Randy pulled her back against him, bringing his hands around to cup her breasts.

"She's still overdressed, Nash."

Aware of the avid gazes from the people not engaged themselves, Alena sucked in a deep breath when Nash divested her of her skirt and thong then shoved Randy's hands aside to draw one nipple into his hot mouth with a deep suction. With a low laugh, Randy whispered in her ear, "Guess I need to find something else to do with my hands."

A moan slid past her lips at his slow glide down her waist and Nash's soft bite of her nub, but a swift, startled gasp cut it off short when Randy landed a blistering slap on her bare folds. She whimpered from the next slap, the immediate heat accompanying the pulsing throb causing her tissues to swell and moisten, her body to jerk with lust for these two that never seemed to be assuaged no matter how many times they drove her up. Spreading her legs, she all but begged him for more.

"Good girl."

His soft praise accompanied another swat, then another and another until she jerked her hips forward to meet each descending stroke. By the time he slowed to small taps, she was writhing in his arms, pushing her breast against Nash's marauding mouth in a desperate attempt to get what she needed.

"Please."

"You're so fucking soft here." Randy ignored her plea, cupping the flesh he had abused, her juices dampening his palm. "And so fucking wet."

Releasing her nipple with a long pull followed by a pop, Nash growled, "I need another taste of you."

Nash no sooner knelt before her spread legs, cupped her ass and brought her pussy to his mouth than she exploded in a fanfare of ecstasy, the first touch of his lips on her throbbing labia her undoing. With pleasure sweeping her senses, she barely felt him spread her folds before he drew on her engorged clit with just as strong suctioning pulls as he had her nipples. She lost track of time, of where they were, everyone around her and how many times his diabolical mouth and deep, plunging fingers got her off.

By the time he rose, his hand going to his zipper, her orgasm-befuddled brain started to function again.

"Bend over, baby, and hold onto his waist as you return the favor."

Randy's deep voice and instructions weren't to be denied, and she didn't want to. Trusting them to hold her, she bent, wrapping her arms around Nash's hips and opened her mouth to take him deep. Randy thrust into her still spasming sheath as she pulled back on Nash's cock, his penetration setting off another round of sparks. Thankfully, Nash grabbed her head and took over, fucking her mouth with slow, shallow jabs as Randy fucked her pussy with quick, deep thrusts, the dual assault giving her one more off-the-charts climax before she felt them let go with their own pleasure.

When Randy came to his senses and tucked himself back inside his jeans, he noticed the majority of guests were outside, likely because they'd all be forced inside later if rain developed. He let Nash dress then hold Alena for a moment as he scouted the lot. Bryan was stringing Carlee up at their favorite tree and Kevin, Brad, and Joel were each engaged with someone in what looked to be a happy group on the trampoline on the far side of the yard. It would be now or never if he was going to go against his badge and his friend and snoop for answers.

"I'm going inside. Text me fast if you see anyone heading to the house."

"Be careful, mate."

"Always. Behave, Alena."

The fun she had been having along with the afterglow of sexual pleasure both turned cold as Alena took a seat in the pit next to Nash. She had never been good at waiting, wasn't a patient person, and now proved no exception. She could only hope Randy found something, anything that would give her something to go on.

CHAPTER FOURTEEN

Ten minutes later a light drizzle sent everyone scurrying inside. Nash made sure no one was watching him as he sent a quick text to Randy before taking Alena's arm and following the others in the side door. Both laughter and grumblings could be heard from the guests as they scattered in the great room with a few heading upstairs. He released a relieved breath when he saw Randy coming down the staircase, but the look on his face didn't bode well for their investigation.

They met him at the bottom of the stairs after a quick glance around the room spotted Bryan with a small group gathered in front of the fireplace and Brad and Joel making their way to the kitchen. He saw Kevin come in with his friends, and now assumed he had gone upstairs with some of the others. "Nothing?" he queried in a low voice, squeezing Alena's hand in both warning not reveal anything and comfort for what he knew Randy would say.

"Not a fucking thing. I only had time to rifle through Kevin's room and Bryan's office in a general search. I'm sorry, baby." Randy didn't want to disappoint her, and the forlorn droop to her shoulders and fading light in her eyes tore at him.

"You tried, thanks." Pulling her hand from Nash's, she stepped back from the two of them. "If you'll excuse me, I need a few minutes to myself."

"Where are you going?"

The concern behind Randy's sharp inquiry only added to Alena's misery. "I'm just going to step outside for a minute. I need to clear my head."

"Let's just leave," Nash suggested.

"It's early and we were late to arrive. Let's not send up any red flags if we don't have to." Turning to Alena, Randy noted her taut jaw and knew her stubborn streak was on. "Go on, take a few minutes. We won't stay much longer after you return."

Despair swamped her, dousing the good time she had been having as she slipped out the side door and stood a moment under the overhang, out of the light rain now drizzling down. Knowing tonight would be her last time with the guys and she wouldn't be subjected to any embarrassing moments when seeing any of these people again had enabled her to bask in the attention they were so good at heaping upon her.

Folding her arms across her waist, she hugged herself against the chill the damp spray raised along her arms. So, she would be returning home with no answers and only memories of her short fling with two really hot men to ward off the dismal invasion of cold that came with failure. For weeks, she had coped with Ashley's disappearance by silently ranting against her sister's irresponsible behavior. Now she had to face the real possibility Ash may not have willingly taken off, and that hurt worse than any of the inconsiderate things she had done over the years. Being left in limbo as to what happened would be worse than finding her body. At least then, her and her mother could get closure and move on.

The abrupt slam of a car door reverberating through the otherwise quiet, dark air caught her attention and she peered across the dimly lit yard toward the small turn-around off the circle drive. She recognized Kevin running toward the front entrance of the house, away from a newer model SUV. A sudden thought popped into her mind born of the desperate, aching need to find Ashley that dug its claws in her and refused to let go. What could it hurt to look one more place?

Before she lost her nerve, she scoped a quick scan around the empty lot then dashed over to the SUV. Trying the passenger door, she found it unlocked and took that as a good sign. Bending over the seat, she flipped open the glove compartment, her speedy search turning up nothing but the registration and a packet of condoms. Tossing them back inside, she shut the flap and started to back out when a shiny glint on the floor caught her eye. Running her hand just under the seat, she encountered what felt like a cell phone and pulled it out. Flipping it open, a gasp rushed out of her as she stared down at Ashley's pretty face lit up with her mischievous grin.

Before the full significance of her find had time to settle in, a low curse came from behind her, followed by blinding pain then… nothing.

• • • • • • •

Randy tried not to look conspicuous as he glanced at his watch again. Another ten minutes had gone by, which means Alena had been brooding outside now for twenty minutes, way too long. Breaking into the conversation of the group of five, including him, Nash, and Bryan, he stated, "Excuse me, but Nash and I seem to have misplaced our girl." Leveling a fake smile at Bryan, he added, "I wouldn't want her to get the paddle again."

"I wouldn't mind. She has one of the nicest asses I've seen in a while," Bryan returned with a grin.

"Hey! I heard that." Carlee latched onto his arm and threw him a mock glare belied by the small grin tugging up the corner of her mouth. "Who're you talking about?"

"Alena, and I'll blister her butt myself if she's gotten herself into mischief."

Nash followed Randy to the side door, more worried than pissed like Randy. After her scare on the boat and her public paddling last week, surely she wouldn't have gone snooping on her own again. "She has to be around here somewhere," he said when they stepped outside and didn't see her. "The rain's let up. Maybe she's just walking around."

They circled around back then ended up on the drive where Randy came to an abrupt stop with a curse.

"What?" Nash snapped, working to tamp down the raging panic threatening his composure.

Randy turned his head from the only vacated parking spot on the drive, vividly recalling whose vehicle had been parked there when they arrived. "Kevin's car is gone, and so is Alena."

Neither wasted time as they sprinted back inside, made no effort to hide their desperate search as they raced upstairs and barged into rooms, ignoring outraged complaints as they went, but found no sign of her. "Third floor." Randy led the way as they took that staircase two steps at a time and raced through a fast peek in each room, calling her name in loud voices that drew a crowd upstairs.

Bryan met them at the end of the hall, hands on hips, Carlee and several others standing behind him. "What the hell is going on, Janzen? You know…"

Nash didn't give him time to drill them with a lecture on rules. His usual calm demeanor broke as he imagined their girl in Kevin's clutches, the morgue image of Lisa Ames searing his brain. Fisting his hands in Bryan's shirt, he slammed him against the wall. "Where is he?"

"What the fuck? Who're you talking about? Damn it, Randy, instruct this moron to release me."

"Alena's missing, and Kevin's gone. Where would he go, Bryan?" In that split second, when his friend's face went chalk white, Randy knew their search for Ashley was coming to an end.

Bryan struggled to no avail, his tone desperate as he stuttered, "I don't know. He's not a kid anymore. He doesn't answer to me."

Randy joined Nash in getting in his face, his own temper a hair trigger from forcing him to cross a line any second as Alena's face when she stumbled into his arms last week after being attacked filled his vision. "You know something about Ashley Malloy, about the drugging and attacks on both Daisy Mae and Alena. Don't you two fucking move," he snapped to Joel and Brad, who had been inching back toward the stairs.

Resignation and despair replaced Bryan's belligerence, his face going gray in defeat. "Let me go." At Randy's nod, Nash released him but didn't step back. "That other girl, they got carried away, it was an accident."

"Bryan, *no*." Carlee's shocked whisper and Bryan's admission drew heated grumblings from Joel and Brad before they sealed Kevin's fate with their simultaneous exclamations.

"Hey! I'm not taking the rap for your twisted brother!"

"Me either!"

"An accident doesn't make him twisted," Bryan defended Kevin.

"Fuck this," Nash snarled, withdrawing the photo of Lisa Ames he had been carrying with him for a year now and shoving it in the other man's face. "Does that look like an accident? Take a close look. She was nineteen when she went missing right after being seen leaving a London club last year with Kevin and," he leveled an icy blue glare at Joel and Brad, "you two."

"Who are you?" The deep despair in Bryan's choked whisper had Randy's tone going lethally quiet. If Bryan's silence caused Alena any harm, he'd come after him without his badge first, then slam his ass in jail. "Last week, who told you Alena was up here?"

"Kevin, but…"

"Yeah, that's right. Alena *Malloy* was attacked on her boat two nights later, threatened because she was snooping. Where. Is. He?"

"Bryan, please," Carlee begged him, her eyes swimming with tears when he didn't answer right away and refused to look at her.

"There's a small grove… I'll take you."

"You two are riding along." Nash shoved Brad and Joel none too gently toward the stairs, letting Randy handle Bryan. Fear for Alena's safety propelled them downstairs in a mad dash, Randy tossing out strict orders for the stunned guests to remain at the lake house until he returned before the five of them sprinted to the cruiser and he peeled down the drive as if the hounds of hell were after them.

• • • • • • •

Alena roused to a soft mist dampening her body, wrenching pain in her shoulders and back of her head. Opening her eyes, her heart stuttered then rose to clog her throat with instant fear as she stared into the glittering eyes of a deranged psychopath. An automatic jerk on her wrists tied above her head sent another wave of excruciating pain radiating from her shoulders down her back. Hung suspended off the ground with all her weight pulling on her wrists and shoulders, she grappled with the effort to get her terror under control. A large camping lantern sat on a log, illuminating a soft amber glow around the small, secluded copse. She could hear the splash of the lake shore just beyond the dark expanse of trees, and her gasping breaths of pain-filled fright.

"You're awake. It's about time." Kevin took a step toward her, holding up a knife. A satisfied smile of malicious glee split his lips when she cringed back. "Oh, don't worry. The knife is just for ridding you of your clothes."

She felt the cold steel against her stomach when he slid the blade under her top and sliced up, splaying it open bottom to top in one cut. As he went to work on her skirt, his tone remained almost polite as he asked, "Why have you been so fucking determined to snoop into my affairs, Alena?"

The drizzling mist took that moment to turn into a cold rain, the large drops clearing her head of fear enough for her to demand, "Where is my sister?"

Her skirt and thong fell to the ground as he looked up in surprise before he gave her a bone-chilling, slow grin. Getting in her face, he gripped her hair and pulled her head back as he replied, "In the lake, where you'll be shortly, you stupid cunt."

She would've crumbled under the weight of his cruel disclosure if she weren't tied. His taunting grin and the evil satisfaction lurking in his eyes over her anguished cry enabled her to think past the heart-crushing grief filling her. Calling on her defense training, she waited until he released her hair then head butted his face, hearing the satisfying crunch of bone before she followed with a swift kick to his crotch.

Panting, she actually laughed as he writhed on the ground, one hand cupping his crotch, the other holding his blood-gushing nose. "Randy and Nash will finish you off, you fucking dickhead. That, that was… for… for Ashley." Her bravado crumbled as lamenting regret took hold, followed by a swift return of terror when he rose on shaky legs and she faced a very angry psycho.

She only had time to let out one piercing scream before he closed his hands around her throat, cutting it and her breath off in a tight squeeze.

"This way!"

Bryan crashed into the clearing first, the look of pure, sadistic pleasure on his brother's face as he strangled Alena nearly sending him to his knees. "Kevin, stop, for God's sake, stop!"

Randy and Nash brushed past him, Randy pulling Kevin's hands off her and almost swooning in relief when he heard her cough and gasp for air as he wrestled him to the ground. "Hold on, luv," Nash whispered, his voice shaking with fury and relief as he reached up to free Alena's hands. "We've got you."

She fell into his arms, opened her eyes to see Nash's blue eyes swimming before her then Randy's dark eyes giving her a critical once-over. "Damn it, guys, what took you so long?" she rasped before succumbing to the sweet oblivion waiting for her.

"I'm sorry. I thought it was an accident." Bryan looked with anguished eyes from his brother, who lay cursing on the ground, his hands cuffed behind him, to his long-time friend. "He's my brother."

Randy jerked Kevin to his feet. Bryan's betrayal cut deep, but his tone remained unsympathetic. "And Ashley and Lisa were someone's daughters. You're all under arrest. Let's go."

• • • • • • •

Alena sat on the side of the hospital bed, dressed and ready to go. The night before remained a blur of angry voices, pain, and despair. She remembered being put in an ambulance and Nash arriving at the Portland hospital a short time after her. Other than a few conciliatory words, he had been quiet, giving her the breathing room she needed to come to terms with Ashley's death.

Guilt gnawed at her as she now waited for Nash to return with Randy, who had just pulled into the hospital parking lot with her car. She couldn't help but feel she had failed her little sister, done something wrong, or not done enough to steer her on the right path. Had her refusal to bail her out of jail a few months ago somehow led to her downfall? She tried finding out who paid her bail after filing the missing person's report, but wasn't privy to that information since Ash was of legal age. Now, she suspected Kevin may have been her benefactor, and knowing her sister, she would've latched onto him just to see how much and for how long she could string him along.

Hearing low voices approaching her closed door, she pushed aside thoughts and regrets she couldn't do anything about right now and concentrated on getting home, where she belonged. Glancing at her packed suitcase, she was grateful for Nash's thoughtfulness in picking it up last night and glad she had already been packed and ready to leave this morning.

Following a short rap on the door, both men stepped inside, those intent, probing gazes zeroing in on her. Her body didn't fail to react in its usual manner, with a quick jolt of panty-dampening desire, her heart doing a slow roll that made her even more desperate to get on the road home. Both appeared concerned and tired, but Randy's eyes held the ravages of a long night dealing with the unpleasantness of his job and the betrayal from a friend. She wasn't the only one hurting this morning.

"Well?" she choked out, even though she knew the answer.

Randy released a sigh as he walked over to her and laid a hand on her shoulder. "Divers pulled her out a few hours ago. I don't think there's any doubt it's Ashley even though we have to wait on the coroner's report for official identification. I'm sorry, baby."

She rose slowly, shrugging off his hand and his condolences in order to maintain her outward composure. "Knowing helps, and I'm sorry about Bryan. What happens now?"

Randy stepped back, giving her the space she didn't need to ask for. "Kevin's talking to the DA. He'll be charged with second-degree murder, along with drugging and kidnapping and anything else they can think of to throw at him. Brad and Joel participated in the drugging of you, Daisy Mae, and Lisa Ames in London." Looking at Nash, he saw the anger tightening his jaw, the cold look that came into his eyes and regretted having stood up for Kevin when Nash first arrived. After sitting in on the interrogation, nausea churned every time he remembered the cruel indifference Kevin had shown while admitting to his crimes.

"The three of them partied with Lisa, whom they swear was willing until Kevin wanted to try out autoerotic asphyxiation. They also swore her death was an accident, and," pivoting back to Alena, he told her, "that they suspected Kevin killed Ashley but they had nothing to do with your sister after she left the lake house that night. I don't know if it'll help, but Kevin swore Ashley went along with everything and that he just wanted to 'practice,'" he used his fingers for quotes, "again."

Alena hated to ask, but had to know everything. "But Bryan knew, didn't he?"

Turning from the accusation neither Alena nor Nash could hide, he strode to stare out the window at the dreary, dark day that reflected his mood. "Yes," he finally admitted without looking at them, "he knew. Both Kevin and Ashley drove away in her car that night and a few hours later, knowing his friends wouldn't back him a second time, Kevin called his brother, swore it was an accident and begged for his help. Bryan believed him." He had refused to see or speak to Bryan after turning him over Portland PD this morning.

"Rest assured, Alena, that if the courts are dumb enough to make parole an option for Kevin, I'll be waiting to haul his ass and his friends back to London to stand trial there."

Nash's voice and eyes were harder, colder than she had ever heard or seen, which made her feel better knowing they both stood for Ashley and Lisa. With nothing left to be said or cleared up, she picked up her purse and pulled out a small drive, handing it to Nash as Randy turned from the window.

"It's not much, just a thank you. That's a copy of all the pictures I took the past few weeks. I thought you might like them." Looking at Randy, she gave him a rueful smile. "I know you see those scenes every day, but..." She drifted off, shifting in self-consciousness under his close scrutiny and the way those dark eyes lit with amusement and some other indefinable emotion.

"Thank you, Alena."

"Come on, luv, we'll walk you out."

With nothing left to say, she returned home with a heavy heart and memories of two men she knew she'd never forget.

EPILOGUE

Two days later

Randy clicked the mouse and another photo filled his computer screen, this one of a moose and her calf standing in a stream. Mother had her head turned down at her baby who looked up at her with adoring liquid eyes. It was a priceless moment and stunning photograph, just like the rest of Alena's work they had viewed.

"How long do you think it'll take her to see what we see?" Nash asked, standing behind Randy's chair.

"Knowing her, too fucking long."

"She's headstrong, has a penchant for getting into trouble."

"Yep," Randy agreed, flicking on another stunning scenic photo. Anyone could snap a picture, but few had the knack to wait for that one precious moment in time or the patience to search every angle for just the right one that would change an everyday, ordinary scene into an eye-catching, spectacular vista. Their girl most assuredly had that knack.

"She's fucking courageous."

"Yep." No arguing that.

Heaving a sigh, Nash growled, "I really liked her."

Pushing back from the computer, Randy stood and looked at his friend and now ex-partner. "Well, how long's it going to take you to fill out that application for Maine's Bureau of Investigation, return home and get your affairs in order, then get your ass back here?"

A slow grin spread across Nash's face. "Sent in the ap yesterday, have an interview set up for tomorrow. If it goes well, I'll need a few weeks back home then you're stuck with me even though I'll probably have to get an apartment in Augusta and commute a lot."

"Just as well. You'd probably drive me nuts if you lived here full time. But, for when you are here, and when our girl's not with you or traveling with her photography, I thought we should add a large master bedroom and bath onto the back of the cabin. Not like there's not plenty of room."

Just imagining Alena snuggled between them every night stirred his cock, but Nash couldn't help asking, "You that sure she'll return?"

Shrugging, he slapped him on the back, stating, "If not, we'll go to New York and haul her ass back here. How's that for a plan?"

"Damn good one, mate."

• • • • • • •

Alena spent the first week after her return home missing the guys as she struggled with Ashley's loss and the guilt of having failed her. Both overwhelming emotions left her an open wound she strove to heal. She had the sympathy and support of her friends and coworkers and even sought counseling from the department's psychologist. But none of that seemed to help her get through the nights without tossing and turning as she tried not to imagine if Ash suffered under Kevin's tormenting hands, or her body after they brought it up after lying at the bottom of the lake for over two months.

Making matters worse, her mother went off the deep end completely after she broke the news of Ashley's death, forcing Alena to return her to rehab with little to no hope she would ever get her act together. Losing her daughter had been the last thread holding Evelyn Malloy together.

Partial change came the second week when she could finally bring herself to admit she didn't miss Ashley or the constant trouble she got into, but mourned her young death and what could have been, both between them and in her future had Alena not failed her. She accepted an invite from her friends to have dinner at their favorite sushi bar. Instead of salivating over her favorite salmon sushi roll and enjoying the company of her closest friends, she spent the evening craving Carlee's chicken fried steak and down-to-earth chatter. And missing the guys.

A few days later, she had an appointment with Rico at her salon, but left without a snip when he wanted to undo Cora Sue's handiwork Alena had found so attractive and easy to care for. And she *really* missed the guys.

By the third week, the constant noise of New York and throes of people were starting to get on her nerves. At first, she put her bitchy moods down to grief and stress, but when she started drifting asleep at night picturing herself sandwiched between the guys, the gentle rock of a boat lulling them all to sleep together, she had to concede there was another possible explanation.

At the end of that week, she returned to her studio apartment in tears after photographing the crime scene of a gruesome, triple homicide all afternoon. Cancelling her plans to meet some people at her favorite club, she spent the evening alone looking through her pictures of Blue Springs and missing the guys. Desperate to feel something other than grief and remorse, she spent an hour with her vibrator, recalling every touch, every orgasm the guys drove her to. But all that did was confirm she would never achieve those heights on her own and how much she craved to feel their hard hands and even harder bodies again, hear their low, deep voices that sent shivers down her spine, and see those intent, probing looks that heated her blood and dampened her pussy.

But it wasn't until she visited her mother the next day and found her lucid, her eyes clinging to Alena with both love and regret, and heard her say, "You're not happy here, Alena. I've already lost one daughter because I refused to see what a mother ought to. I had no right to shove your sister's upbringing and problems on you and I have no right to keep you here when you so obviously want to be somewhere else. Go home Alena," that she was free to do what she knew she had to.

Kissing her mother's cheek, she whispered tremulously, "Thank you, Mom. I think I'll do just that, but I'm not going far. I'll be here for you."

Which is how she found herself returning to Blue Springs one month after she thought she'd left this small, backwoods town behind her, returning to claim her guys. The sun had lowered to a bright red-orange ball by the time she turned down Randy's drive, the determination that had her donning the short knit halter dress they bought her and spirited her thus far waning enough to let uncertainty turn her hands clammy. She assumed Nash had returned to London, and her plan was to enlist Randy's support in talking him into coming back. If she could do it then he could do it, she reasoned. But what if she'd read them both wrong? What if they weren't as open to exploring where their relationship could go as she now was?

Pulling next to his official cruiser, seeing the sheriff leaning back on two legs of the wicker porch chair he sat on, tipping his bottled beer up to his mouth and watching that strong, tanned throat work as he swallowed, her body responded with as much fervor as the first time she set eyes on him. Determination pushed back to the forefront and propelled her from the car and up the porch steps. She had a brief moment of pure female satisfaction when his eyes widened in surprise and he spilled beer down his chin, then that toe-curling, intent, probing look entered those obsidian depths and she was lost.

Before she collapsed into a puddle at his feet and started begging, she stepped right up to his front door and grabbed the handle. "I could use one of those." Letting herself in, she saw him rise and follow her before she stopped short when she spotted Nash across the room, standing over a steaming pot on the stove. "You're here?" She winced at the squeak in her astonished tone and both men smiled.

"I am, and I know why I'm here, but why are you, luv?"

Placing her hands on her hips, her gaze snapped back and forth between the two of them as she stated in a much more forceful voice, "Why? Because of you two, I can't sleep, I no longer like sushi, hate crowds and busy, noisy streets, and I fired my hairdresser!" She threw her hands up in disgust with that last admission then started pacing, mostly so she could avoid looking at their identical smirks and knowing glints in their eyes.

"So, since it's your fault I quit my job and leased my apartment, you can just put me up for a few weeks until I can get my feet on the ground doing freelance photography. I've sent out some feelers and have a few small jobs already. And I have savings, but I don't want to go through all of it staying on the boat again and... what're you doing?" She'd pivoted to see Randy pulling a wood paddle out of a kitchen drawer and the two of them advancing on her with small steps and wicked anticipation. An R and an N were carved in the wood, just enough space between the two letters for her to accurately picture those letters sketched white on each reddened cheek.

Her buttocks clenched as she held out her hand to ward them off even though she now wore a grin to match theirs. Taking a step around the sofa, she laughed, saying, "I'm not done talking. Stay back with that thing."

"I don't think so, baby. After we punish you for making us wait so long, we'll show you our plans for the new master suite we're adding on." Randy stepped to the left and Nash to the right, coming at her from both sides.

The thrill sweeping her from head to toe had more to do with hearing how much they wanted her than with the promise of painful pleasure that board represented. Giddy with the first taste of happiness in a long time, she sidled over to the recliner, a few steps further out of their reach before she looked at just Nash. "You never told me what you're doing here."

"Same as you, I'll be starting a new job soon. And waiting for you."

Randy glanced sideways at Nash. "But we're done waiting, right?"

"Right, mate. Let's get our girl."

With a burst of laughter and speed, she made to dash around them, but they were too quick for her. Or maybe she didn't try all that hard. One second she was laughing uncontrollably, and the next she found herself pinned between them, bent over a thick arm, her skirt tossed up and her thong ripped off. The paddle landed with a resounding *whack*, the pain and ensuing pleasure felt like… coming home.

"Damn, we're good." Randy ran his finger over the white outline of the letter R against her red buttock as Nash did the same to the letter N opposite.

Swiveling her face up to him, she taunted, "Yeah? Prove it."

Alena discovered just how fast they could move when she found herself and them stripped bare within seconds, their warm, hard bodies sandwiching hers as the three of them toppled to the rug in a tangled heap of legs and arms. Pleasure devoured her as their hands and mouths traversed everywhere at once. From the very beginning, the two of them had awoken a hunger in her she never knew she had, one that could only be sated by them both. Her mind and body became consumed with the endless wave of orgasms they drove her to until she lost track of everything but the hot, pulsing pleasure.

When her heartbeat had time to slow to a normal rhythm and she could catch her breath, Nash leaned over and whispered in her ear, "Don't worry, luv. If you find yourself getting bored here, we wouldn't mind a baby or two to liven things up."

"Oh, good Lord."

THE END

STORMY NIGHT PUBLICATIONS WOULD LIKE TO THANK YOU FOR YOUR INTEREST IN OUR BOOKS.

If you liked this book (or even if you didn't), we would really appreciate you leaving a review on the site where you purchased it. Reviews provide useful feedback for us and for our authors, and this feedback (both positive comments and constructive criticism) allows us to work even harder to make sure we provide the content our customers want to read.

If you would like to check out more books from Stormy Night Publications, if you want to learn more about our company, or if you would like to join our mailing list, please visit our website at:

www.stormynightpublications.com